FRIGHT NIGHT ORIGINS

TOM HOLLAND

WITH

A JACK ULRICH

CONTENTS

www.encyclopocalypse.com

Dedicated to all the fans who loved and supported Fright Night. I hope you'll enjoy the next chapter of the story.

— TOM HOLLAND

1

THIRST

The black Jeep Cherokee clung to the rain-slicked road as the headlights cut through the darkness ahead. The road wound its way through a stand of old-growth pines as it descended into the valley below.

Moments later, the headlights fell on an ornately carved wooden sign adorned with grapevines that read: "Welcome to Rancho Corvallis, Gateway to Wine Country."

"Too bad you don't drink wine," Billy Cole said with a grin, glancing at his passenger. He turned off the windshield wipers as the rain outside began to subside.

Billy was a big man, six-four and a solid two-fifty. An impressive figure with his swept-back blond hair and hard blue eyes. In his day, he'd been a veritable giant among men, which, of course, was one of the reasons his passenger had chosen him to be his "friend."

"I lost my taste for it long ago," the man said enigmatically.

Billy's passenger was a few inches shorter than him, and his build was slight, almost lithe in comparison. His thick black hair highlighted his perfect features and his pale-hued olive skin.

Arched eyebrows set off his gray eyes that seemed to glint even in the darkness of night.

The passenger had many names over many decades, in fact, over many centuries, and it was always a game between him and Billy what his new name would be. He changed it with every move they made, and they made many. Billy, for his part, tried to stay true to his birth name Wilhelm, but since he had no family name, he picked ones that were easy to remember. Like Cole. His companion, on the other hand, had been known as Gellert cel Catura during his breathing days, so he had to be more creative.

The Cherokee turned onto Valley Way, which passed for the main drag in Rancho Corvallis. The street was rolled up for the night save The Cedar Tavern, a local watering hole, and the old Art Deco Fox theater with its single screen.

The town was a bit on the small side for both men's taste, but it was out of the way and far from intrusive prying eyes. A perfect place to hide.

Billy enjoyed the gentrified feel of the revitalized old town; to see the buildings restored to their former glory filled him with a wave of nostalgia and longing for the simpler time they represented. His companion seemed indifferent. Acknowledged, it had a certain charm to it that people would like. After all, the town serviced a constant stream of tourists who came to visit the wineries and tasting rooms.

"How do you like the new house?" Billy asked. "You haven't said."

"Fine. Dark and old with lots of nooks and crannies, not to mention a full basement. Hard to find out here," his passenger said with a slight smile. "I'm bored with sleeping in a trunk. Not to mention it being a bit uncomfortable."

"Which is why we have something more commodious for you arriving tomorrow," Billy said.

"It's taken long enough to get here," his passenger groused. "At least we have a chest of earth."

Billy nodded. He knew that would make his companion rest better. They had taken it from his home. A small fiefdom from a time long forgotten by everyone except them. He always slept better on earth from his home. His home. A now desolate ruin was once a well-fortified position in a narrow valley above the Olt River in the south of what is now Romania. Now just another decayed vestige of a forgotten war. A fortress that once held back the flood of Ottoman soldiers was now just a tumbled-down collection of rocks near the tiny town of Romniscu.

"Have you picked a name yet?" Billy asked. "I had the lawyer buy the house and add it as an asset to the trust fund. 99 Oak Street. About as mundanely American as you can get."

They had often discussed how land was once held by the strength of steel and will. With the birth of the new world, land ownership was governed by a screed of arbitrary words on a page. Billy could barely abide the softness of this new age. They had watched the rise of this world and they had adapted as best they could.

"Jerry. Jerry Dandrige," his passenger broke the silence.

Billy snorted. Jerry was an obvious, a play on his real name, Gellert. Billy could understand the choice, but he was shocked by the choice of surname.

"Dandrige, really?"

Jerry smiled. His eyes glinted with a hint of sinister glee.

"Dandrige? You're serious about this?"

Aldridge Dandrige, a Protestant Clergyman, had hunted them from Antwerp to Boston and he'd nearly done them both in. They were lucky to come out the other side. It was an odd choice.

Jerry Dandrige smiled at Billy. After all, this was all a poke at him. A shot across the bow about that one time he almost failed at his duty. Billy Cole was not amused.

"Really? You're not serious?" Billy looked at Jerry.

"It just hit me," Jerry paused. "I don't know...I like it."

"Prick."

A smile spread slowly across Jerry's face.

Jerry ran his tongue along his lips. They were thin and elegant, like his entire being.

"I'm getting thirsty," he said.

"You're always thirsty."

"True. Hopefully, we're not too close to our new house."

"About ten minutes away, I'd say."

"Good."

Jerry turned to gaze out the window.

Angelica Suarez was stomping out every step as she fumed. At least the rain had let up. *If Carlos loves his Commodore 64 so much, maybe he should take it to prom*, she thought. Six whole hours of rewinding VHS tapes and telling a stream of mopey teenagers they had no more copies of *The Breakfast Club* really wasn't worth the $2.95 an hour Star Video paid her.

Angelica fumbled in her purse for a cigarette.

"Stop!" Jerry commanded.

Billy hit the brakes. The Cherokee slid to a halt. The young girl on the sidewalk seemed to barely take notice. She was more engaged with her own thoughts.

Angelica finally found a cigarette from the crushed soft pack at the bottom of her purse. Pulling it free, she lifted the cigarette to her lips. With her free hand, she dug around for her lighter.

"You know, those things will kill you," Jerry said, smiling.

Angelica looked up, startled at the sudden interruption. The man standing before her was older, but she couldn't tell by how much. His clothing was immaculate and well-fitted. She could almost see his muscles move underneath the dark fabric as he raised his arm to pull the dangling cigarette from her lips.

"Hey," Angelica said half-heartedly as the stranger tossed the cigarette to the ground.

Jerry smiled.

She caught her own reflection in his deep gray eyes. She seemed to fall forward.

Screw Carlos and his stupid computer, she thought as she felt Jerry's arms pull her toward him.

Angelica Suarez didn't scream as Jerry leaned in and buried his teeth into the soft flesh of her neck. She felt a wave of warmth fill her body, roiling from her feet to her fingertips. It was ecstasy. Her vision blurred and narrowed. Then darkness.

Jerry let the limp body of Angelica Suarez drop to the ground. He looked behind over his shoulder. Billy stood stoically leaning up against the parked Cherokee.

"Nice."

"I told you I was thirsty."

Billy threw himself forward and snatched up the lifeless body of Angelica Suarez with one hand and laid her across his shoulder.

"Not exactly subtle," Billy said.

Jerry looked sheepishly at his companion. He shrugged his shoulders.

Billy glanced around. The streets were empty. He carried the lifeless body of the young woman toward a narrow gap between a building called Gladys Ceramics and another called Eden Carafes. As Billy stepped into the alleyway, he could make out the shape of a dumpster near the back. Lifting the lid, he unceremoniously dumped the lifeless body of Angelica Suarez onto a pile of refuse.

Billy Cole reached into his back pocket and pulled out an old model Barlow folding knife. He flicked the blade open.

"Sorry, little girl."

Billy Cole bent forward and slashed at Angelica's throat with the sharp blade, obliterating the teeth marks Jerry had left on the dead girl.

2

CHARLEY BREWSTER

Charley Brewster sat in the quad at Cushing High School. He had study hall this period but had skipped to spend it outside, looking around, watching the stray truant sneak off campus. Just recently seventeen, Charley was in the first weeks of his junior year. His mother had promised a growth spurt and it had finally arrived, pushing close to six feet tall, making him lanky with a shock of dark hair that never seemed to stay combed. His open honest face made him look even younger than he was. But how he looked was the least of his worries at the moment.

Part of him felt like he would never graduate. Another part of him knew he'd somehow get through it. And then what? College? More school? Or just trying to find a decent job? Neither choice thrilled him, and he hated thinking of himself as just another confused teenager.

The thoughts panicked him. If he did go to college, what would he study? He wasn't particularly good at anything. School wasn't very interesting. Maybe he'd join the Army like his dad or learn a trade.

Charley's thoughts went to an even darker place. He

thought of his dad. Chuck Brewster. Charles Brewster Senior. He'd been an auto mechanic. Learned his trade in the Army and when he got out, he'd spent the rest of his life fixing cars at the local '76 station right there in Rancho Corvallis. He and Charley had picked the beat-up red '66 fastback Mustang that Charley still drove as a project car the two of them could work on to teach Charley about cars. It was intended to serve as bonding time for father and son.

Three years ago, on the way to one of Charley's Pony League baseball games, Chuck noticed a car on fire on the side of the road. He stopped to help a woman and her daughter who were trapped inside. Chuck Brewster had managed to drag them to safety, but the fumes from the burning oil and plastic had done something to his lungs. He ended up in the ICU.

Charley stood vigil, waiting for his father to recover, but when in the end he knew he wasn't going to make it, he had asked him *why. Why had he done it?*

"Always do what's right, Charley," Chuck Brewster said in a rasp. He died three hours later.

That had scarred Charley. He loved his mother, but his father had always been his world.

In the meantime, he wasn't really enjoying high school in Rancho Corvallis, the town he had grown up in where he knew almost everybody. It was near Sonoma in California, wine-growing country, and a lovely place to be. Especially if you liked to drink wine, a vice he hadn't yet acquired. He had a girl he loved, Amy Peterson, his age, in the same class, and they hung out together constantly. He couldn't think of ever marrying her though; he was too worried about going to college. And he couldn't afford to get married until he had a career, a way to make a living, a lesson his mother constantly drilled into his head. But he couldn't make a living if he didn't know what he wanted to be. And he didn't.

He had his mother to worry about, too. His father had died trying to save a mother and her daughter trapped in a wrecked car that had caught fire. It had been three years ago and it had been hard on his mom. Him, too. They had both loved him and saw him as their hero long before he had died saving the two lives of strangers. The car had burned up, poisoning the air and his dad, too. Although tragic, it had given Charley an example to live up to. His father had known right from wrong and done what was right, even though it cost him his life. Charley could never shame him, never. He had to live up to that ideal, but how did that help him decide what he wanted to do with his life?

It didn't, but it did leave him with a sense of responsibility to his mother. Judy, his mom, had scrambled to keep them going. The life insurance had made sure they had a roof over their head, but the funeral bill had wiped out the little she and his dad had managed to save, so she had taken a job at the old Cumberland Winery, working in the tasting room. It wasn't a great job, but it put food on the table and clothes on Charley's back. His mom seemed to like it; she made a lot of new friends and the employee discount on wine didn't hurt.

He had friends, his best one being Ed Thompson, who their classmates had nicknamed "Evil." This drove Ed crazy. He really hated it, but he was always the one who loved horror movies, books, comics, and whatever else he could get his hands on pertaining to wickedness. He had passed that enthusiasm on to Charley, but he wasn't as crazed about it as Evil. He was into all things horror. *Halloween* was one of his favorite movies, but he was equally enthusiastic about *Friday the 13th, Evil Dead, Nightmare on Elm Street*, and above all else, the masterpiece, *Texas Chainsaw Massacre*.

Charley sighed. What was he going to do? He would much rather think about great horror movies than about what he was going to do when he graduated from Christopher L. Cushing High School.

"Hey, Charley," said Evil Ed as he plopped down beside him. "Wasting time again?"

He had a lunch box with the *Poltergeist* image on it, showing the clown poking out from under the bed and grabbing the kid's leg, scaring the hell out of him. It had been their favorite moment from the movie. Evil began rummaging through it and pulled out a chicken leg which he immediately bit down on.

His eating habits were nothing to brag about which didn't help his rep in school. Charley was one of his few friends.

"What's on *Fright Night* tonight?" Charley asked, referring to their favorite late-night TV show.

"*Blood on my Grave*, I think," Evil replied, "but if I were you, I'd be more worried about Trig."

"I'm doing all right in it," Charley said with a frown. He didn't like to be reminded about his struggles with math.

"Yeah, sure," Evil Ed snorted. "That's why you almost fell out of your chair during the last test trying to see my paper."

"I didn't try to cheat."

"No, you *did* cheat," Evil chortled. He loved putting Charley on.

"What's going on with you two?" said a sweet voice, and Charley looked up to see Amy standing there.

He almost flushed with pleasure; she looked so good on this sunny day. She was pretty beyond words, at least as far as he was concerned, with a cheerful face framed by chestnut hair and red full lips that made him want to jump up and kiss her.

"Oh, nothing," Charley said, before adding, "just talking about what might be on *Fright Night* tonight."

"Like hell we were," snorted Evil Ed. He nodded at his friend. "He's failing Trigonometry and if that happens maybe he doesn't graduate. Even if he does graduate, his math scores are gonna be so low, he's never getting into any college."

"Oh, come on," Charley snapped. "I'm not that bad."

"You're worse," Evil said back with a taunting grin. He loved getting Charley upset so much Charley was ready to punch him.

"I'll help you," Amy said to Charley.

"You will?" he said, looking up. He knew this was an offer too good to turn down, especially if it got her to come over to his house.

"Tonight," she nodded. "I'll come over after dinner. Say about seven-thirty? I'm up on all the assignments. Mr. Smith mentioned giving a pop quiz again today. That's as good as saying he's going to give one tomorrow."

"Yeah, sure, tonight," Charley said, rising and cleaning his hands against his pants legs.

It was as though he was about to embrace her, which is what he wanted to do, but the entire school was walking past and watching, so he didn't dare. Everybody already knew he was sweet on her. Evil mocked him mercilessly about it.

"Alright," she said brightly, "seven-thirty tonight." With that, she was gone and on her way to her next class.

Charley looked after her, unable to believe how good she looked from behind. Her clothes were casual school duds that hid her body more than showed it. She was naturally modest, but he didn't have any trouble imagining the curves, especially since they'd been necking madly for months now. Tonight would be another opportunity if she came over to "help" him with his algebra.

"Sit down, Brewster," Evil Ed said, "and pull your tongue back into your mouth. You're panting in front of everybody."

Charley sat down, still looking after Amy as she disappeared into a crowd of students.

"I can't help it," he said. "I'm in love."

"You're in heat, two different things, but you're too young and stupid to know that," his friend replied with a roguish lift of an eyebrow.

"You're still a virgin. How would you know?" Charley shot back. He didn't like anybody, not even his best friend, making fun of him and the girl he loved.

"I watch horror movies," Ed said with a leer. "They're full of sex, violence, and blood. You watch 'em, too. You'd think you'd have picked up a few things by now."

"I don't want to put the world down like you," Charley said. "I want to be hopeful and positive about life. I want to share it with someone like Amy."

"Yeah, sure," Ed said, finishing off his chicken leg, rising, and dropping the bone in a nearby trash can. "We'll see. But if I were you, I wouldn't tell Amy. Probably send her running in the opposite direction." A school bell went off, signaling the next class. "Ah, English and all those great American novels, like *Moby Dick*. I'd rather have it be *Moby Michael Myers*."

He took off, Charley looking after him, idly wondering where they'd all be in ten years. He doubted Evil would ever end up staying in Rancho Corvallis. Too boring for him. He was better suited for Hollywood doing something with horror movies. As for him and Amy? Well, maybe they'd still be here. He didn't know if they'd get more serious, but he was sure they'd be friends for the rest of his life. With that, he grabbed his books and headed for his next class, feeling happy that he'd be seeing Amy that night, even if the evening had to be about her tutoring him on Trig.

3
BODY IN THE TRASH

Deputy Sienna Miller slogged through the thick, rancid mud of the Sonoma County Central Dump. Dozens of mounds of trash dotted the bleak landscape. She looked back over her shoulder to see her training officer, Deputy Mark Wagner waving her forward.

"No reason for us both to get dirty, Miller," Wagner shouted after her before sliding back into the driver's seat of their patrol car.

Sienna Miller had joined the Sheriff's Department at eighteen; she did her three years at the county jail, working with juveniles in Santa Rosa. Now, twenty-two, she was finally out on the streets doing the real job, and what had happened? Her first call was for a body found in a dump. Her three years working in the jail didn't matter. She was right back at the bottom of the totem pole, and it pissed her off.

"Your partner's kinda a prick," Bud White said, looking back at her. He was in the lead as they picked their way through the mounds of trash.

Deputy Miller lifted her head, looking at the portly sanitation worker. Bud White looked like something straight out of

Deliverance, with half his breakfast still clinging on for dear life to his long, straggly beard. Deputy Miller didn't even want to think about the dozens of unidentifiable stains that covered his woolen jumpsuit.

"Body is in quadrant four, just over this mound. Ain't too far now," Bud said, pointing to the forty-foot high pile of trash in front of them.

Thank God it's too cold for flies, Deputy Miller thought as she watched hundreds of seagulls dive into the piles of festering refuse searching for a free meal.

"You ever get used to the smell?" she asked.

"Nope," Bud replied. "Watch yourself going through here."

Bud White navigated a narrow pathway between huge trash mounds. Thanks to the recent rains, the pathway had become a small, muddy stream. Bud paused at the foot of a third trash mound.

"It's near the top, otherwise we might have missed it," Bud offered, pointing toward the top of the trash heap.

"Any idea where the body came from?" Deputy Miller asked.

"Yup," Bud said with a nod. "A commercial dumpster in Rancho Corvallis. We break the dump into quadrants and quadrants into hills. That way, we can keep track of where something came from in case someone dumps something illegally."

"And you're sure it's not a mannequin? I'm going to be pissed if it's a mannequin," Deputy Miller said.

"Seen a lot of mannequins in my time, and I've seen my share of dead bodies; pretty sure I can tell the difference," Bud responded.

The mannequin thing made sense, but the second part made Deputy Miller pause. She guessed if someone dumped a body in Sonoma County, there was a fair chance it would end up in the Central Dump in Petaluma. Maybe Bud *had* seen his share.

"We're going to have to climb up real careful like," Bud said. "Step where I step."

Bud White began to carefully pick his way up the huge pile of trash with Deputy Miller doing her best to follow his path.

"We covered her with a tarp to keep the seagulls off her, but they'd already gotten to her eyes," Bud said looking back over his shoulder.

Deputy Sienna Miller felt her stomach swirl as bile began creeping up her throat. For the first time since she and Deputy Wagner answered the call, she was beginning to understand she was going to come face to face with a dead body.

Bud stopped abruptly and knelt atop the trash heap. In front of him, Deputy Miller could just make out the edges of a blue plastic tarp. She stopped to stand alongside Bud.

"You want me to pull the tarp back?" Bud asked.

"Yeah," Deputy Miller nodded.

Bud lifted the edge of the tarp and Deputy Miller turned, fighting with all her might to keep from throwing up.

"Jesus..." Deputy Miller managed.

"Yeah," Bud White nodded.

The now eyeless face of Angelica Suarez, her throat laid open to the bone, faced upward from under the tarp; brutally murdered and callously discarded.

4

STUDY SESSION

I t was almost seven-thirty when Amy got off her moped in front of Charley's, took off her helmet, and rocked it back on its stand. She didn't tell her dad she was taking it. He didn't like her driving it at night, but she didn't want to ask him for a ride and she didn't want to walk either. She enjoyed riding the scooter and the way it blew her hair back, even when she was wearing a helmet.

She stopped for a moment, taking out a brush to smooth her hair. As she did so, she found herself looking at the huge, empty house next to Charley's. Of course, she'd been seeing it all her life and, in a way, had stopped seeing it. The old house had been the family home of the Cumberland's back when all this land was still part of the original winery. It had been vacant for years now, the previous owners finding it hard to sell. But now she saw the "For Sale" sign in the front, dirty and bedraggled, was now joined by a bright new "Sold" sign right below it.

Her eyes went to the house. It looked in sad shape, a victim of neglect, not to mention age. Most of the houses on Oak Street were two stories, but this one had an attic and an ox eye looking out at the street from the top story. It had a wraparound front porch that sagged and shingles that needed painting. *Whoever bought it had a lot of work to do*, she thought.

She also noticed the lights were glowing on the first floor. Good, but it didn't seem to cheer up the gingerbread pile. There was something off about it, almost evil.

Well, she hoped whoever bought it fixed it up and made it into a nice home. Right now, it seemed like it was about to tip over and crush Charley's much smaller two-story. Banishing the sober thoughts, she walked up to the front door and knocked smartly, hoping he was ready to study instead of watching those stupid horror movies that were on *Fright Night*. It was on at eleven, his favorite time to watch them. Their host, Peter Vincent, was an old horror actor who'd obviously seen better days, much better days. Charley absolutely idolized him.

Charley opened the front door, glancing at his watch.

"Hi, seven-thirty exactly," he said with a smile. "You're nothing if not prompt. Thanks for coming."

She entered, a backpack slung over her shoulder, full of books. Charley closed the door, about to head upstairs with her when they heard his mother call from the living room.

"Who's that, Charley?"

"Amy, Mom," he called back. "She's going to help me with my math homework."

Judy Brewster turned in her chair from where she sat in the living room before the TV. She was a nice-looking, well-shaped woman in her early forties with brunette hair. The volume of the TV across from her had been turned down low. She had been reading a novel that she put down as she looked into the entry where her son and Amy stood.

"Hello, Amy," she said with a smile. She liked the girl and knew her mother well. In fact, the ladies had a weekly game night, with some of the other mothers.

"How's your mom? I keep meaning to call her, but I've been so busy down at the winery."

"She's doing well, Mrs. Brewster," Amy said. "I'll tell her you said hello."

"Please," Judy said, turning back to her novel. It was a crime story, *Death Before Breakfast*, her newest favorite genre.

Amy and Charley started up the stairs. She knew the way to his room without asking. They had known each other since junior high school and had been friends from the start. She had been in his house almost as much as in hers.

"You have to excuse her," Charley said, referring to his mother, as they reached the top and started down the hall to his room. "She's fallen in love with true crime. She just reads one book after another and can't think of anything else."

"My mom is the same way about romance," Amy said, "but at least she knows it's fantasy."

"You don't think all the crime stories are for real?" Charley said as he opened his door, waiting for her to go first.

"If they were, there'd be more people dead than alive."

"Evil Ed would like that," he said with a smile as they entered and he closed the door behind them.

He immediately grabbed her in his arms, kissing her on the lips. She responded and they stood like that for a minute, their tongues entangling, until she finally pushed him away.

"We have to study," she said, "or you'll fail Trig and your mother will shoot you."

"Lay on the bed with me for a few minutes," he said, pulling her toward his single bed shoved in a corner.

She pushed him away. "Study first," she said, dumping her book bag on his desk. "I've got the last five assignments, plus what I think the questions Mr. Smith will ask on the pop quiz tomorrow." She looked up at him. "It's coming. You know it is. In the next day or two."

"Aw, Amy," he said and made another grab at her.

She skillfully evaded him, pulled out the desk chair, and nodded at the other one in the room next to an old barber chair that he had gotten at some auction because he thought it was cool.

"You want to bring up another chair?" she asked and sat primly before the desk.

Charley saw he was getting nowhere with her, at least not this early in the evening, and did as asked, pulling over a straight-backed chair he had clothes tossed over. He dumped them in a corner and sat.

She was right. He had to pass Trig, no matter how much he hated it. If he could only concentrate. All he could think about was Amy and what might happen if he got her to lay in his bed with him. But then, he had been dreaming about that for months and getting nowhere.

"Okay, logarithms," she said, "and complex numbers. Which would you like to work on first?"

"Neither," he said with a sigh, feeling his ardor wilting as he finally faced the reality of learning enough to pass a stupid pop quiz. He *hated* pop quizzes!

5
SPECIAL DELIVERY

The Rancho Corvallis train station had seen better days. Once, it had been the main source of shipping tons of oranges and bottles of wine to San Francisco and beyond. Now, it survived as a once-weekly stop for timber and freight traveling from Portland to points south. Its once-bustling passenger service had gasped its last breath in the late-seventies and the vacant coffee shop and sundries shop sat as a reminder of the death of American rail.

Billy Cole stepped through the doorway of the abandoned terminal. Jerry Dandrige held back, lingering in the doorway.

"This place smells...foul," Jerry offered.

"You can wait in the car. This won't take long," Billy replied.

"No, I want to be sure there are no issues. I don't want to spend another night in that trunk," Jerry said.

Billy continued forward across the trash-strewn floor, headed toward the double doors that opened onto the track side of the station. Jerry carefully followed after him. As the two reached the far doors, a flashlight beam danced across the few remaining intact panes of glass.

"Night watchman?" Jerry asked.

"Our contact, Reg," Billy pointed through the window at a short, burly man in a wool coat and grease-stained jeans. Billy Cole carefully opened the double doors and stepped out onto the platform. Reg Douglas stepped forward to greet him. He paused as Jerry moved into position behind Billy.

"You're late," Reg said.

"We're new here. Still learning how to get around," Jerry offered.

Reg took Jerry in. Not the usual type of person he dealt with, too clean. His clothes were high-end and fashionable. It was then that Reg had the worst idea of his life.

"Box is in offloading, but it's ah...going to cost a little more than I thought to get it released. Train wasn't supposed to stop here tonight, had to use some favors."

Billy stiffened. People never change. He took a step forward, but he felt the gentle hand of Jerry rest on his shoulder.

"Of course, these things can't be avoided," Jerry offered. "How much more are we talking?"

"A thousand," Reg said.

Again, Billy started to bristle, but he felt Jerry's hand clamp firmly on his shoulder. He sank down and stepped backward letting Jerry advance.

"That shouldn't be a problem," Jerry smiled. "Take us to the crate and we can settle up once I am sure it's not been damaged."

"Seems right," Reg said. "It's just over here."

Reg turned and let the beam of his flashlight fall on a single, large wooden crate at the far end of the platform. He began to walk forward. Jerry and Billy fell in behind him. As the three reached the crate, Reg stopped.

"Here it is."

"We need to open it to be sure it's our package," Jerry said.

"Yeah, sure, okay," Reg replied.

From his waistband, Reg produced a small pry bar. He knelt next to the crate and placed his flashlight in the crook of his neck, between his head and shoulder. Working the pry bar into the lid's gap, he began loosening the nails holding the lid in place. After a few strategic levers of the pry bar, the lid popped loose and slid sideways, falling away from the crate.

Reg stood up and grabbed the flashlight with his free hand. He pointed the beam at the contents of the crate. The beam fell across an ornate teak coffin. Reg paused, keeping the beam fixed on the open crate.

"Is that...a coffin?" Reg stammered.

"It is," Jerry replied, a smile forming behind his lips. "You said a thousand. Is that correct?"

"Um...yeah," Reg said.

Reg turned slowly, reluctantly to face Jerry. The blade of a fire ax rushed forward to meet him. Catching him in the throat, it set Reg's head tumbling off into the darkness.

Jerry turned to see Billy Cole ferociously clutching the fire ax, a fine mist of blood painted across the left side of his face. Jerry ran his finger through the blood. He paused to look at it and then licked it from his finger like he was sampling cake batter from a mixing bowl.

"We could have just paid him," Jerry said smiling at Billy.

Billy looked down at the headless corpse of Reg Douglas and started to laugh.

"I thought you were just toying with him," Billy laughed.

Jerry placed his foot under Reg's rib cage and effortlessly kicked him into the air and off the platform.

"Let's get my coffin and head home. He's someone else's problem now."

Billy reared back and tossed the bloody fire ax off into the night sky. It landed a fair distance away in a tangle of brush.

"You got it," Billy replied.

6

COMPLEX NUMBERS

"I can't take this anymore," Charley said as Amy asked him another question about complex numbers that he couldn't answer. He was sitting at his desk, she next to him, books open before them.

"Charley, it's not that difficult," Amy began. "A complex number is expressed as a + bi, where a and b are..."

"Oh, look," Charley interrupted as he saw the time on the clock on his bed stand. "*Fright Night* is just beginning."

He leaned over and clicked on the TV. An old horror movie appeared, the colors bright and deep, mainly red and black. It showed a couple on a huge patio in the back of an even bigger English country house. The male character was young and callow. The female was beautiful, dark-haired, and seductive. It was nighttime, of course.

"Damn," he muttered, "we missed Peter Vincent's introduction."

"Charley, we're not finished yet," Amy complained, but it did no good.

"Let me see what the movie is," Charley said, "then we'll go back to work."

"Aaaaooooohhh....," was heard from the TV, a wolf howling no doubt, a full moon shining down on them.

"*Countess of Blood*," Charley guessed, "may be the film."

Amy gave up and started to quietly put her books back in her school bag. In the meantime, the young insipid juvenile on the TV said, "What was that?" in reaction to the howling wolf.

"What's his name?" Amy asked, meaning the actor. He did look faintly familiar.

"Johnathan, I'd bet," Charley said, totally missing her meaning. "They're always named Jonathan in Hammer films. This is from the fifties, but I'm not sure what year."

Amy sighed and went back to putting the school books away. She knew when it was hopeless.

"Just a child of the night, Jonathan," came the throaty voice of the woman with the juvenile. She was beautiful and seductive in a dark-haired, curvy, high-busted, dangerous way.

"It's chilly out here, Nina," said Jonathan, repressing a shiver.

"Oh, no, it isn't," she said. "It's beautiful. I love the night so."

"I've never seen you so beautiful before, Nina," came the juvenile voice. The actor was staring at her, seemingly more fascinated by her heaving bosom than anything else. "So pale, so luminescent, so..."

"When's he going to figure out she's a vampiress?" Charley asked.

"Probably never," Amy said, glancing at the TV, already bored by the dialogue. It was so predictable.

On the screen, Jonathan suddenly stopped, as if he had forgotten what to say. A long moment passed and then she said, "Yes?"

"Your lips are so red," he said as if surprised and pleased at the same time.

"Are they? Would you like to kiss them?"

They kissed, long and drawn out. Both of them seemed to be enjoying it. It gave Charley an idea. He jumped up and grabbed Amy just as she was about to swing her book bag over her shoulder and leave.

"I wove you," he said, doing his best to mimic the English accent from the movie.

"Oh, Charley," Amy said, no longer quite ready to leave. She liked being in his arms, having him close. They kissed. It wasn't as deep or as long held as the kiss on the TV, but it was deeply felt.

On the TV, the juvenile finally managed to say, "Why are you looking at me so strangely, Nina?"

"Not you, Johnathan. Your neck. Has anyone ever told you it was beautiful?"

Her hand came up to slowly stroke the back of his neck. He was in danger of falling into her eyes but was fighting it, even as he lost.

"No," he answered uncertainly.

"What about you?" Charley said, drawing back and grinning at Amy. "Are you crazy about my neck?"

"No," she answered, "and I don't have fangs either."

"Neither do I," he said, pulling her toward his bed. "Let me show you," and they fell onto the bed.

"Come, lay your head on my breast," the vampiress on the TV screen purred and pulled the trembling juvenile's head down toward her ample breasts.

Just as he finally surrendered, laying his head against those soft fleshy pillows, she reared her head, pulling back her upper lip, revealing...two huge sparkling white fangs.

Neither Charley nor Amy noticed. They were too busy kissing each other, Charley's hand's starting to travel her body, feeling this and that, mainly her thighs and buttocks, and brushing her breasts.

On the screen, just as the dark-haired buxom vampiress was about to sink her fangs into Jonathan's unprotected jugular, a tall, saturnine man stepped out of the darkness, wearing a rather daffy houndstooth, plaid Victorian suit, and a long brownish cape. He carried a wooden box over his shoulder, hung from a leather strap. This was Peter Vincent with his vampire killing kit.

He put it down, flipped open the top, and pulled out a wooden stake and mallet. Standing tall, he reared back as he loudly proclaimed, "Stop, you creature of the night!"

On the bed, Charley broke the clinch and looked toward the TV. "Oh, look," he said, "Peter Vincent is appearing just in time to save the day. Or should I say night?"

He busily watched as Amy, now a little frustrated herself, glanced at the screen. The dark gorgeous vampiress leaped to her feet on the screen, letting the hapless Jonathan fall to the stones below. She faced Peter with a hiss, her fangs sparkling in the moonlight.

"Who are you who interrupts my nightly feeding?" she said, her speech slurred by the fake fangs protruding above her lower lip.

The man drew himself up to his full height and thundered at her: "I am Peter Vincent, Vampire Killer!"

"Go, Peter, go," Charley said from the bed, cheering him on.

Amy pulled his head down, kissing him deeply, trying to take his attention off the screen. It wasn't hard. He began to kiss her again, his hands traveling under her blouse, up toward her breasts.

On the TV, Peter Vincent launched himself at the vampiress, stake and hammer held up. But Charley and Amy didn't notice. They were now rolling on the bed, one on top of the other, both in the throes of their passion.

7

AMOUR

Charley Brewster and Amy were still wrapped together on his bed, Charley panting heavily, though every now and then stealing a look at the TV. She was mainly distracted with keeping his overly active hands at bay. They had just slipped under her blouse and worked their way to the back where they fumbled to undo her bra.

"Charley," she said, trying to warn him to stop, but he was not discouraged. He finally slipped the catch, freeing her youthful breasts.

"Charley," came her voice again, sharper now as his hands traveled around to her front and slipped their way up.

Charley didn't stop, no more than Peter Vincent did on the TV screen. He threw Nina to the ground and leaned over her, pounding the stake into her heart. He didn't notice (and only a keen observer of the movie would) that the stake was turned the wrong way around. He was slamming the blunt end into her heart, or, at least, it seemed that way as blood erupted into his face, causing him to wipe it away even as he kept pounding the stake.

But it wasn't noticed by either Charley or Amy as he finally reached the softness of her breasts, cupping them both.

"Charley," she erupted, almost yelling in his ear, and threw him halfway off the bed.

He rolled on his back with a loud sigh, looking at the screen. The movie had ended and been replaced by the interior of a local TV studio, a tacky graveyard the centerpiece. Peter Vincent, much older now, was rising out of a papier-mâché coffin and filling the screen as the credits of the terrible movie crawled across the bottom.

"Charley, Peter Vincent's on," Amy said, catching a glimpse and hoping for a respite.

It didn't work. "Forget Peter Vincent," he said as he rolled over, half on top of her, and started trying to get his hands under her blouse once more.

"But you love him," Amy said, pushing his hands down.

"But I wove you more," Charley said, with his dopey vampire accent as he struggled with her.

On the TV screen, the host of *Fright Night* intoned in his best theatrical voice, "This is Peter Vincent, bringing you *Fright Night Theater*. Tonight's journey into horror was *Blood Castle*, one of my favorites. And for a very good reason." He smiled right into the camera. "I star in it."

"No!" Amy said very sharply this time, pushing his hands violently away.

"Jesus, Amy," Charley said, climbing to his feet, no longer interested in *Fright Night* or its host, Peter Vincent. He was still caught between frustration and teenage lust. "Give me a break! We've been going together almost a year and all I ever hear is 'Charley, stop it'." But then he saw how upset she was and softened. "I'm sorry, Amy."

She softened, too. "Me, too. I'm just scared that's all," she said, caught between doubt and guilt.

Should she do it or not? She was sure of his love for her and she felt the same, but she still felt doubts. She was a virgin and ashamed to admit it. No, proud of it. Only, she would never tell anyone. The girls today would only laugh at her, like something out of *Carrie*.

She finally decided with a silent nod to herself and pulled him to her with a passionate kiss. When she pulled away from him, she said, "Let's get into bed." Charley stared at her, his mouth dropping, hardly able to believe his luck. Was this to be that moment? He hadn't told her (hell, he hadn't told anyone), but he was still a virgin, too.

"You mean it?" he said. She reaffirmed her decision by pulling him in for another kiss.

Just as he was about to say something, he caught a glimpse of movement out the window in the yard below, between his house and the old crumbling Victorian. With his interest snagged, he looked more closely, trying to see better only to realize it was two men carrying something.

One of them looked huge. The other, cloaked in a gray over-coat that went almost to his ankles, was almost as tall. They must have bought the house next door. Charley couldn't remember how long it had been vacant. Seemed like years since anyone lived there. He'd gotten used to passing by the different realty signs that adorned the lawn, replaced only as time or the weather had worn them down.

His mom had mentioned that someone bought the house, but he hadn't really paid much attention. He'd seen stuff arriving, tools and lumber to fix it up, but he hadn't seen the new owners. Was this them? And what were they carrying? He peered harder through the darkness and finally figured it out. *But it couldn't be*, he thought.

They were carrying a, a what? A coffin?! Charley's eyebrows shot up. Could it really be a coffin?

He moved to the edge of the window, staring down through the darkness. It *was* a coffin, a long shining mahogany casket with shiny brass fixtures that glinted in the moonlight.

The two men stopped before double storm doors to the basement. The big guy in the lead leaned down and threw them open one-handed while the other continued effortlessly to hold his side of the coffin. With that, they began to descend the steps into the basement.

"Charley, I'm ready," Amy said in a small hesitant voice from the bed, distracting him.

Charley looked at her. She had her blouse off, although she was holding it in front of her, modestly covering her breasts, free at last from her bra. But he was no longer interested.

"Amy," he said, looking back out the window, "you're not going to believe this. There are two guys out in the yard and I think they're carrying a coffin."

Amy's eyes went to the TV screen. A trailer for next week's *Fright Night*, some stupid movie called *Blood in the Fog*, was playing and showing the exact same scene in a muddy, mist-strewn bog.

"Sure," she said, becoming angry. How could he be talking about a stupid horror movie when she was offering herself to him? "And they're on the moors, right?"

"Amy, I'm, serious," he said, putting the binoculars he'd grabbed off his desk to his eyes.

"So am I," she snapped. "Do you want to make love or not?"

"Amy, quick! Come here. You've gotta see this," he said, as sex was completely forgotten. Down below, the two figures with the oblong box had almost disappeared into the basement.

In reply, all he heard was the bedroom door slamming. He whirled to find Amy gone. Tossing the binoculars on the bed, he dived after her.

8

LATE NIGHT MISCHIEF

The Jeep Cherokee pulled to a stop in the back of the old Victorian.

Jerry was still laughing to himself in the passenger seat. Billy looked over at him as he put the car in park.

"What's so funny?" Billy asked.

"I was just marveling at how easily you separated poor Reg from his head with that ax," Jerry offered.

"I guess it's like riding a bike, some things just come back to you easily," Billy replied.

Jerry and Billy exited the Jeep and made their way around to the back. Billy opened the tailgate. The Jeep was parked between their house and a small copse of woods and shrubbery that shielded them from the smallish two-story house next door. There were lights in both stories of that house, but Billy felt certain their activities would draw little attention. Modern people were so distracted by televisions and creature comforts that they had little sense of the world just outside their door.

Billy reached into the back and stripped the black plastic tarp away, revealing the ornate mahogany coffin inside. Hand-carved by a master woodworker nearly five hundred years ago, the elegant brass fixtures had been added in the late eighteen hundreds to further accentuate its beauty and to make it increasingly difficult to disturb its occupant.

He used the cap lifts to crack the lid, peering down at the casket liner of ruby-red silk damask.

"Good," he said, "not disturbed by the trip at all."

Jerry was very fond of this particular coffin. It was the twin of the one he'd buried his long-dead wife in and it felt comforting to him. With the addition of a little soil from his homeland, it was perfect for a long, undisturbed slumber.

"Shall we?" he asked Billy with a nod.

Billy grabbed the front end and pulled the coffin out of the back of the Jeep, Jerry taking the other end effortlessly, using a single hand to lift the heavy coffin. To show his ease, he kept his free hand tucked in his trench coat pocket.

Billy smiled.

They started toward the cellar door on the side of the old Victorian and across from the lit second-story window of the two-story next door.

9
MATH AND OTHER DISTRACTIONS

Charley pounded down the stairs after Amy, catching her in the entry before the front door. He was talking as he came to a halt in front of her.

"Okay, okay, maybe it wasn't a coffin," he said, "but I did see two guys carrying something into that house..."

"I don't understand you," Amy said, tears welling up. "First you want to make love, and then you don't..."

A voice from the living room stopped them cold. "Amy, Charley, what's wrong?"

They clamped their mouths shut, turning to look through the archway into the living room. Judy Brewster, Charley's mom, sat there, watching the ten o'clock news on the TV, an open book on her lap. This one was about the Hillside Strangler, two guys who killed ten women in the late seventies. Reading it made her shiver.

Charley knew what the book was, one of her true crime novels. They all had titles with "murder" in them, like *Unsolved Murders*, *Serial Murderers*, and *Cold Case Murders*. As long as they had something to do with killing, she was reading it.

He had thought it began with his father's horrible death,

but then he had realized it was more than a year later when she had finally started to recover from grieving. Perhaps true crime took her mind off the way he had died, but Charley didn't understand the connection. Otherwise, she was perfectly normal, if there was such a thing in a town as boring as Rancho Corvallis.

"Um, nothing, Mom," Charley managed.

"Get in here you two," his mother said.

Amy recovered at hearing Mrs. Brewster call to them, quickly pulling herself together. She tucked her blouse in, buttoned it to the top, and stepped into the living room. Charley followed, the two of them trying to act normal (whatever that was) so Charley's mother wouldn't start to question what they were doing upstairs (if she could take her eyes off the book which she was avidly reading).

"Are you kids having a lover's spat?" Judy Brewster asked, her attention split between the news on the screen and the open novel in her lap.

Charley forced a smile. "No, Mom, nothing like that," he lied.

"Well, there's nothing wrong with it." She tapped the book. "It's says right here that the divorce rate is seventy-six percent higher among couples who don't argue before marriage. This couple didn't argue, which is why the wife poisoned her husband."

"Mom," Charley said, horrified by the thought. Sex, yes. Marriage, not so much. At least not yet when he couldn't even afford to rent all the movies he wanted at Blockbuster. As for murdering one's spouse, he didn't even want to think about it. "We're in high school. We're only juniors."

"Oh, yes, that's right," Judy said, her eyes straying back to her book which was her real interest. "Well, it never hurts to plan ahead."

"Will you remind your mother that we are playing poker at

her house this weekend? I'm bringing the cheese puffs; she's making the dessert."

"Yes, Mrs. Brewster," Amy said, in control of herself again and calming down. She looked at Charley. Her face softened and her heart opened. She did love him, didn't she? "Well, good-night, Charley."

"Yeah, goodnight," Charley said, already distracted again, moving toward the window that looked out at the side of the old crumbling Victorian next door.

"Goodnight, Mrs. Brewster," Amy said, hoping Charley might walk her to the door so they could talk in private.

"Night, Amy. Thanks for helping Charley with his home-work," Mrs. Brewster said.

"Anytime," Amy said. Since Charley was still staring out the window, Amy made one more attempt to gain his attention.

"See you tomorrow, Charley?" Amy managed as he walked away, not looking back as he peered out the window. That was it. She slammed the front door as she exited the house. It was so loud even Judy involved in her book had to notice.

"Charley," Judy said, looking up, "that wasn't very nice, not walking Amy to the door."

"Mom, there are people next door," Charley said, hardly hearing her. There were lights glowing on the first floor now and someone was moving around. The basement lights were off. Was the coffin still down there? Had that box been a coffin at all?

"Oh, I guess the new owner's moving in," his mother answered.

"What new owner?" Charley asked.

"Didn't I tell you? Bob Hoskin, the Realtor, said he finally got rid of the place."

"Who'd he sell it to?"

"I don't know. Some fellow who fixes up houses for a living.

Supposed to be very attractive though. I just hope whoever he is, he knows what he's getting into with that house. It's going to take a lot of work." She paused a moment, trying to find her place in the novel.

But Charley didn't hear her anymore. He was staring at the lit windows on the first floor and wondering who the new neighbors were. And why they'd carried a coffin (he was sure that's what he'd seen, no matter how ridiculous it seemed) into the basement.

Lost in his own thoughts, he didn't notice the TV. Neither did Judy, buried in her book. Too bad, because there was a newsreader, blonde and attractive, reading in a serious way. "And now for tonight's local news. The body of a man has been found near the train station on 3rd street. Apparently, the body was decapitated, and the police have ruled it a homicide. Police have not released the man's identity pending the notification of his next of kin..."

10

PREPPING

Jerry watched as a shirtless Billy Cole bent, hefting the ornate coffin into place upon a narrow slab of recently dried concrete. His back and side still bore numerous battle scars he'd collected before becoming Jerry's blood servant.

"Is there a way to make it look, I don't know, less obvious?" Jerry asked.

"Give me a second. I've nearly got the mechanism in place," Billy said as he stepped back and worked on an old armoire that was held halfway up in the air by ropes.

Jerry nodded.

The basement was cluttered with rows of debris and discarded furniture mostly covered in white sheets. It helped give the illusion that Jerry and Billy actually cared about their state.

The basement was dark except for a few bare light bulbs dangling down the middle. Half-windows were built in at ground level to provide some air if the owners had ever cared to let fresh air inside. Air was the last thing on the minds of Jerry and Billy. Billy had already painted most of the panes black, to keep prying eyes and, more importantly, sunlight out. The entire space had been secured against daylight getting in, which, of course, was necessary for Jerry's safety.

Billy fiddled with something on the backside of the armoire. When he finished, he pulled a small lever he'd installed alongside the stone wall of the basement. The armoire slowly lowered, pulled down by counter-weights that ran through the center of the hollow body of the false piece of furniture. The armoire was held steady by a length of track that connected it to the wall. The falling armoire hid the coffin on the raised concrete dais in what was now a hidden room. Billy threw the small lever up and the armoire slowly rose, revealing the coffin again.

"You'll have to stoop a bit. Low ceilings," Billy said with a nod.

"Very good," Jerry murmured approvingly.

No one would ever find this hidden space, not without looking hard and long, which would provide whatever time he needed to awaken and kill them even if it was daylight outside. Vampires were weaker during the daylight hours, but they were far from helpless. To disturb a vampire while he was sleeping was a risky proposition and Jerry was more than willing to kill any would-be slayers if the need arose.

At the back of the hidden space was the real wall and a window, covered by a blackout curtain, tacked into the frame. Jerry ducked underneath the hanging armoire and walked up to it, giving it a knock with the back of his finger. He could hear the tap of glass behind.

"Awful easy to rip down, isn't it?" he said, referring to the curtain.

"Yes, but there's a pile of wood behind it. A big pile," Billy said. "Take someone a lot of work to clear it away and it won't cast suspicion if someone is poking around back there."

Jerry nodded. He trusted Billy. After all, he'd kept him safe for more than five hundred years, enough time to get to know each other very well indeed.

Beside the space made for his coffin was a short table. On it set a chest, ancient and ornate. The chest was carved with Cyrillic lettering and adorned with intricate geometric patterns.

Jerry carefully undid its latches and opened it, looking down at the deep dark rich earth that filled it.

"Ah," he said, running it through his fingers, "my bed. It feels so cool and comforting."

He dusted the dirt off his hands back into the chest and closed it, carefully latching it once more. He didn't like to lose even a few grains. He looked up at Billy.

"A little patch of home."

Billy looked up and smiled. "Hopefully, it will take the edge off."

Billy was still working on the false front of the armoire that covered the hidden space.

"Almost done here," he said. "I want this to work smoothly."

Jerry stepped outside and, with that, Billy triggered the catch once more. The armoire slid down, leaving the two of them staring at the armoire which hid the room and its ornate coffin on the other side.

"Very good," Jerry said with a smile. "Shall we go upstairs and start to make that look livable?" With that, the two turned toward the stairway to the main floor above.

11

THE RARE HOMICIDE

L t. Lennox turned the powder blue Capri onto the cracked asphalt of the train station's parking lot. He slowed as Sgt. Gia Alvarez waved him toward a line of parked cars near the front of the station.

"I came up here to get away from this," Lt. Lennox muttered to himself as he slipped on a pair of dark glasses to protect his eyes from the early morning glare of the sun.

Art Lennox had spent twenty years with the LAPD, the last ten working Robbery-Homicide, right in the middle of Los Angeles' serial killer infestation. The normal homicide rate in the city at the time had been too much for the police to handle; toss in a bunch of whack jobs and Art Lennox knew he had to get out.

On paper, Rancho Corvallis seemed perfect; a safe, affluent small-town smack in the middle of wine country. Sure, it was boring, but Lt. Lennox was ready to give boring a shot. He parked the Capri between two cruisers. He shut off the car and took a deep breath.

Tap, Tap, Tap. The unmistakable sound of a nightstick against glass startled him. He looked up quickly to see Sgt. Gonzalez grinning at him through the driver's side window.

Sgt. Emilio Gonzalez was a powerfully built man of average height. He had a nose that looked like it had been broken several times but had never healed correctly; his left ear was slightly cauliflowered. Rumor was he'd been a boxer set to go pro as a middleweight when his number came up in the draft. He'd served as an Army medic and then studied forensics back east. He now headed up Rancho Corvallis PD's crime scene investigation unit.

"Jesus Gonzalez! You trying to give me a heart attack?" Lennox said as he cranked down the window.

"Sorry, lieutenant. Just wanted to catch you before you tried to go in through the station," he said. "The boys are working the inside. They found two sets of shoe prints in the dust, so they are photographing them."

"Any fingerprints?" Lennox asked as he exited Capri.

"Some partials on the front and back door. Hard to say if they'll be enough to get a match," Gonzalez said.

"Who called it in?" Lennox asked.

"A line crew checking the tracks ran across the body early this morning. When they radioed in, their supervisor called the station," Gonzalez said. "Uniforms took their statements, but they didn't seem to know anything useful, except the guy's name."

"Really?" Lennox was intrigued.

"Reg Douglas, a train mechanic who works the line between Portland and Los Angeles," Gonzalez said. "Reg was a habitual scumbag; domestic violence, public drunkenness, disorderly conduct, and possession of stolen merchandise."

"Public service killing?" Lennox asked.

Gonzalez nodded.

The two men headed around the side of the train station toward the platform. As they rounded the corner, Lennox could clearly make out a pool of dried blood as well as what appeared to be arterial spray directed toward the edge of the platform. The spray pattern appeared to be fanned out from the area of the blood pool but appeared to be partially interrupted as if an object, that was now gone, had occupied that space.

"Looks like the killers might have taken something with them when they left. If we find it, it might still have blood on it," Lennox said.

"Probably not going to help. It was a packing crate. They broke it to pieces and tossed them in that dumpster," Gonzales said, pointing to a dumpster on the other side of the platform, "We bagged them up and I had Liu and Bautista transport everything in the dumpster down to headquarters."

"I bet they love you," Lennox said.

"I felt pretty bad about it because Bautista did locate the potential murder weapon," Gonzales smiled.

"What was it?" Lennox asked.

"Fire ax taken from a glass case near the back door of the train station. It was tossed over the tracks into a patch of bushes on the other side."

Gonzales carefully stepped around the blood evidence and headed toward the edge of the platform. Lennox followed close behind him, careful to step where he stepped. As they reached the edge of the platform, the two men looked down. Kneeling next to the body was Dr. Lee Greenleaf, the local medical examiner. Greenleaf was thin and ancient-looking, completely bald with prominent liver spots on the top of his head. He was well past his retirement date, but he hated fishing and he'd never picked up golf, so he figured he'd just keep on doing what he was doing until they forced him out.

"What you got for us, doc?" Lennox asked.

"Male, white, in his forties, now comes in two pieces," Greenleaf said pointing at the head sitting a few feet to the right of the body. "Strange thing is, judging by tissue retraction and the lack of tearing at the wound site, my initial interpretation is our victim was standing when he was struck by a single powerful blow."

Lennox and Gonzales looked quizzically at Greenleaf.

"It was a level swing bisecting the spinal cord between the C5 and C6 vertebrae," Greenleaf said, almost giddy. "I haven't had a lot of experience with clean decapitations; heads just don't come off like they do in all those slasher films the kids are watching these days."

"Blood splatter pattern says he was on the ground when his heart was still pumping," Gonzales countered.

"Yes, the heart will still beat after brain death, Emilio, as long as the muscles still have oxygen," Greenleaf said.

Sgt. Gonzales hated it when Dr. Greenleaf used his first name. It felt like he was back in grade school.

"So, we're looking for Kull the Conqueror?" Lennox asked.

"Maybe a crazed lumberjack?" Gonzalez added.

"Scoff all you like. I'm just reporting the facts," Dr. Greenleaf retorted.

"Sorry, doc, it's just tough to wrap my head around it. Let us know if the autopsy turns up anything else," Lennox said.

"Of course," Greenleaf replied.

Lennox and Gonzalez turned back toward the train station and carefully bypassed the blood evidence. As they approached the side of the train station, they saw the looming figure of Chief Gil Madden barreling toward them.

"What the hell is going on?" Madden boomed.

Gil Madden was a large man, the size of an NFL linebacker; his high and tight haircut was just starting to gray. His haircut, faded bulldog tattoo, and generally caustic demeanor were mementos from his time in the Marine Corps. He pulled an unfiltered Lucky Strike from behind his ear and lit it in a single motion by striking a blue tip match across his thumbnail.

"Hey, chief, what are you doing here?" Gonzalez asked.

"A body drops in my town, and you think I'm going to sit on my ass waiting for a report?" Madden said. "Tell me what we've got."

Lennox recapped what they'd learned so far. Madden listened intently, letting Lennox finish the whole rundown before he asked any questions.

"So, we're probably looking for two killers that had some business with the victim. What are we thinking? Drugs?" Chief Madden asked.

"Nothing in Reg's background that links him to drugs, but maybe he was looking to up his game," Gonzalez said.

"Lennox, have DeShawn run down Reg's known associates and have Dent talk to his co-workers. See if anyone can get us a line on what he was up to. And find out why the hell the train stopped here last night," Madden ordered.

"What do you mean?" Lennox asked.

"Train wasn't scheduled to stop here last night. It only stops on Wednesday mornings. Been that way since '79," Madden said. "But it did last night. Find out why and maybe we find our murderer."

12

SCHOOL DAZE

Kids were flooding out of the classrooms as the sound of the bell began the race to their next class. Charley emerged from one of them, holding a test paper and looking none too happy about it.

Amy had been totally right. The teacher hadn't even waited a day to spring the pop quiz. Now, he was wishing he'd spent more time studying and not grappling with her on his bed, not to mention watching *Fright Night*. Then, there were the guys with the coffin last night. What was that all about? They were still working in the house next door when he'd finally fallen asleep. Night owls, them not him.

Evil joined him, falling into step beside him. He cut him a glance, seeing his scowl.

"What's wrong?" he asked.

"This," Charley said, lifting his paper. "The bastard. Why didn't he tell us he was going to spring a pop quiz?

"That's the point to a pop quiz, Brewster," Evil Ed hooted, "to surprise you."

"Thanks, teach," Charley groused, shoving the paper into his notebook.

Evil Ed cut him a glance. "You hear about the murder last night?"

"No, what murder?" Charley said, surprised.

"They found a headless guy at the train station," Evil said with a delighted grin.

Charley looked at the grinning Ed and unconsciously took a step away from him. Ed was a little too excited about a headless body for Charley's comfort.

"So, who was the guy?" Charley asked.

"I don't know. Some hobo, maybe," Evil said.

"A hobo?" Charley said with a frown. "Are hobos still a thing?"

"I don't know," Evil said, delight flooding his voice again. "What does it matter? Someone cut his head off."

"I'm just asking," Charley said,

"Rancho Corvallis just got a little more interesting," Evil said. "Maybe we finally got our very own ax murderer."

"You're so sick, Evil," Charley said, pushing him away.

Just at that moment, he looked up to see Amy walking by, her head held high, and looking in every direction but his. She'd tried to help him last night. If only he'd paid more attention.

"Hey, Amy, I'm sorry about..." Charley said, trying to get her attention.

No such luck, she kept right on going, disappearing into the crowd. Evil Ed cackled.

"What's wrong?" he said. "She finally find out what you're really like?"

"Buzz off, Evil," Charley said.

"Oh, call me anything you want," Evil Ed said with a grin. "Only you're the one failing Trig, not me."

With another high-pitched laugh, he walked off, leaving Charley staring miserably after Amy. Maybe he was in more trouble than he thought. If he was, he sure understood. He'd been a total jerk last night. How was he ever going to make up with her?

13
JUDY BREWSTER

Charley pulled his '66 red fastback Mustang into the drive of his house and got out, carrying his schoolbooks, and headed for the front door.

The Mustang was the love of his life and he was constantly fixing it up, being careful to get production parts from the junkyard. No after-market for him. He'd just finished filling in the rust spots with Bondo and was trying to earn the money to give it a new paint job.

He had been working after school at Benton's Hardware, but they'd had to let him go. It seemed like everyone was pressed for cash right now, most of all him. If he could pass Trig, he'd find another job. Until then, he was married to his school books, no matter how frustrating he found it. Especially after failing the pop quiz today.

He bent over to pick up the newspaper on his way, rising up just as a cab pulled up to the curb. An absolutely stunning young woman exited. She was tall and svelte. She wore a tight-fitting robin's egg blue dress that highlighted her cloud-brushed eyes. It was all Charley could do to not stare and gawk.

She looked around, her gaze finally landing on him. She looked at a piece of paper in her hand.

"Is this 99 Oak Street?" she asked.

Charley almost choked trying to find his voice. She was gorgeous, sexy, with model good looks; completely out of place in backwater Rancho Corvallis and she was talking to him.

"No, um...no, that's next door," he finally managed with a nod.

She shot him a smile and gave him a little wave. Charley felt the rush of heat to his cheeks. The woman turned and headed toward the forlorn Victorian next door. He followed her with his eyes as she climbed the listing front porch and knocked on the door. It opened and she disappeared inside. He didn't catch a glimpse of who had answered the door, but it had to be one of the guys he saw carrying the coffin into the basement last night.

Charley finally remembered to breathe; the air came out in a sharp whistle. He stared at the house next door. Moments later, a light came on in an upstairs window, bright enough that he even saw it in the daytime. Charley turned toward his front door. He entered and headed down the hallway to the kitchen. His mother was preparing dinner, some kind of casserole as usual. At least it didn't look like tuna.

Let's be honest, Judy Brewster was no cook. Charley could remember that had been the only source of contention in the Brewster household when his father had been alive. In fact, it had become sort of a running joke. His mother would buy a new cookbook and torture him and his father with her miserable attempts at new recipes. Charley and his father had been over the moon when Domino's finally opened a franchise in Rancho Corvallis. It meant that salvation from their dinner was only thirty minutes and a phone call away.

Charley handed his mom the paper. She paused to study it for a moment.

"Can you believe it? A murder right here in Rancho Corvallis," Judy said.

"Yeah, Evil said the guy got his head cut off or something," Charley replied.

"Charley, I really wish you wouldn't call him Evil. His name is Ed. You have no idea what kind of trauma you might be causing him," Judy said.

"Aw, come on Mom," Charley replied.

"I mean it," Judy said. "Here, take your plate; it's chicken casserole."

Judy Brewster dished a sloppy heap of elbow macaroni, canned chicken, and peas onto Charley's plate; he accepted it reluctantly.

"I'm going to eat this upstairs; I have to study for my Trig class," Charley said.

"Okay, well, have fun," Judy said. She was engrossed in the newspaper coverage of that rarest of things in these parts, an actual homicide.

Judy Brewster was a true crime junkie. From her days in college reading Truman Capote's *In Cold Blood* and Vincent Bugliosi's *Helter Skelter,* nothing made her happier than reading about the dark and dirty details of a crime. Sure, she loved a good whodunit, but nothing got her going like an actual tale of real-life criminals.

Charley stopped by the kitchen sink, to push a couple of spoonfuls of his casserole casually into the garbage disposal while staring out the window at the old Victorian house as his mother scanned the paper.

"Have you seen the new guy next door yet?" he asked.

"No," she answered absently, "but I did hear he's got a live-in carpenter. My luck, he's probably gay."

"No, I don't think so," Charley said with a chuckle, thinking of the hot-looking girl he'd just seen go into the house.

"Why? What do you know that I don't?" she asked, giving him a look. She'd heard the amusement in his voice.

"Aw, nothing," he said. "I've gotta go study. I'll see you later."

He cut a beeline for the door, his mother looking after him as he disappeared out the door.

"Study? You?" she said, which was really a dig to make him hit the books.

She wasn't happy with Charley's grades. That's why she'd made him quit track and baseball. They'd argued a lot about that. He'd wanted to do what he thought his father would have wanted, but she'd felt he wasn't focused enough on his grades.

She'd loved Charley's father, but she wanted Charley to be more than Chuck Brewster had been. She wanted him to have the chance to do something other than work with his hands for the rest of his life. Judy wanted Charley to go to college and have the type of experience she'd had. She certainly didn't want him to follow in his father's footsteps; the Army, the war. Those things had broken Chuck. She didn't want Charley to ever go through that.

Judy returned to the newspaper. Some poor girl had been found in the dump in Petaluma. Her eyes had been eaten by seagulls.

How horrid, she thought.

Why would seagulls do that? Seagulls always seemed so peaceful.

14

RECAP AT THE MORGUE

Dr. Greenleaf looked up from the headless body of Reg Douglas as Lt. Lennox and Chief Madden entered. Trailing behind them was Det. Paul Dent. Dent was tall and lanky with electric blue eyes and whitish-blond hair. He loped when he walked, unlike Lennox and Madden who seemed to walk with intent and purpose. Paul Dent was affable, a trait that served him well during interrogations. People seemed to naturally open up to him. Lennox doubted he'd get much out of the dead body on Dr. Greenleaf's table.

"Gentlemen," Dr. Greenleaf greeted the officers.

"Morning, Lee," Madden replied.

"Just finished. Haven't had time to type anything up," Dr. Greenleaf said.

"Then give us the broad strokes; we're on the clock here," Madden said.

"Sure, Gil," Dr. Greenleaf said, turning back toward the body of Reg Douglas.

Dr. Greenleaf pointed toward the corpse's neck. "Single, precise cut to the neck with a sharpened object. It tore the soft tissue and severed the spinal cord between the C5 and C6 vertebrae. The body shows no signs of defensive wounds on the hands or arms."

"So, he didn't see it coming?" Lennox asked.

"I'd assume not, or he wasn't capable of defending himself. He may have been impaired. I've ordered toxicology, but it may take some time to get the results." The doctor paused. "I've got to say, though, we're talking a one in a million shot here."

"What do you mean?" Lennox asked.

"All the indications show our victim was standing when he was attacked. The tissue shows signs of uneven separation, meaning it was torn rather than cut. The attacker made a single strike that removed the head from the rest of the body using a relatively dull edge. The killer must have tremendous physical strength."

"Great, we got Conan the Barbarian running around Rancho Corvallis lopping heads off hobos," Chief Madden said.

"Anything else you can tell us, doc?" Madden asked.

"Found some metal fragments embedded in the C6 vertebrae. Sent them to the lab in Sacramento. Might tell us more about the murder weapon," Greenleaf offered.

The officers nodded. Dr. Greenleaf pulled the sheet over the body of Reg Douglas. The three cops turned and started for the door.

"You want to look at the other body?" Dr. Greenleaf asked.

The men paused.

"What other body?" Madden asked.

"Sheriff's department pulled her out of the dump in Petaluma. The deputies that brought her in said she was one of ours. Said she came from a commercial dumpster here in town," Greenleaf offered.

Madden looked at Lennox and then at Dent. Both men shrugged.

"You've got to be kidding me. They can't pick up a phone?" Madden fumed.

"Dr. Greenleaf walked over to the wall of cabinets used to store the dead and opened the metal door. With a little effort, he slid the tray containing Angelica Suarez's body from its compartment. He pulled the sheet back to reveal her eyeless corpse.

"Female, late teens, early twenties. Caucasian, possibly Hispanic. Three deep lacerations to her throat. Preliminary cause of death appears to be exsanguination," Dr. Greenleaf said.

Lennox leaned over the body and looked closely at the wounds on her neck.

"Anything that links her death to our dead man?" Lennox asked.

"One had his head cut off and it looks like someone tried real hard to remove hers. Also, she doesn't show any signs of defensive wounds either," Dr. Greenleaf said.

"What about her eyes?" Dent asked cupping his hand over his mouth.

"The birds got them," Dr. Greenleaf said.

"Dent, call the sheriff's department and get me their report on this. If they give you any grief, I want you to drive down there and make yourself real irritating until they hand it over," Madden ordered. "Also, did we hear anything back from Sacramento on that partial print?"

"Not enough there for a good match. They're going to keep running it, but they don't seem too hopeful," Dent replied.

"We know anything about the dead guy?" Madden asked.

"Dent ran him down. Reginald Allan Douglas, thirty-two of Yermo, California. Couple of misdemeanors, receiving and possession of stolen goods, kiting checks, that sort of thing.

He's been mostly clean the past couple of years since he started working as a mechanic for the railroad," Lennox said.

"Thing is, though, the train wasn't supposed to stop here that night," Dent interjected. "Seems the engineer reported a drop in oil pressure and Douglas recommended they stop here so he could troubleshoot the problem."

"You think maybe Douglas interrupted something? Wrong place, wrong time?" Chief Madden asked.

"Could be. Maybe he saw something that got him killed," Dent offered.

"Could also be he made it so the train had to stop; he was the mechanic after all. Who better?" Lennox said.

"Seems like you boys have a couple of theories and fuck all for answers. Guess you got some work ahead of you," Chief Madden said. "Better call Gonzalez down here and have him fingerprint that poor girl. Maybe we'll get lucky and get an ID on her."

Madden turned and headed toward the morgue's exit.

15
TRIG INTERRUPTED

Darkness had fallen while Charley was hard at work at his desk. The gooseneck lamp lit his Trigonometry book, making it easy to read, even if everything on the pages was still gibberish to him.

Over his shoulder, a light snapped on behind the shade in the window next door, but he didn't lift his head to see it. If he had, he would have had a direct view of the room next door, or at least the window, given that the shade blocked what was going on inside that room.

Suddenly, a woman screamed, high-pitched and terrified, ripping the night's stillness. Charley whirled, sending his math book crashing to the floor. He stared out the window at the lit window in the house next door. It came from there, didn't it? It sure sounded like it.

A woman, a young woman, had screamed like she had just seen the most terrifying thing in the whole world. Then, silence, as though something had stopped her scream. Something abrupt and sudden. He didn't have to ask what. His imagination supplied all kinds of answers, none of them good.

Charley stared at the window, trying to repress a shiver that shot up his back. Something was happening over there. Something terrible. To whom? That beautiful girl he'd seen going into the house earlier that day? Could it be her?

But what had happened to her? All thoughts of studying Trig were suddenly gone, probably for the rest of the night. Little did he know, they were gone for the rest of his life. He had started putting things together: two guys carrying a coffin into the house, a murder the day before that Evil was going on about.

It had to be connected but how? There was a dead guy at the rail yard and strange new neighbors seen carrying a coffin into a house where a girl had just screamed. What the hell was going on in Rancho Corvallis? What the hell was going on in the house next door?

Charley leaned back in his chair, determined to give the whole mess a good think. Within moments, he was asleep, and the facts of the world swirled together with the fantasies of the dreaming world.

16

THREE'S A SERIAL KILLER

"Tell, me it's not another one," Lennox said, more to the heavens than to the officers gathered around the body of the young woman in a stand of reeds. She wore a blue dress bunched around her ankles, exposing her naked body. It looked like it had been pretty before it had been smeared with mud.

They were just on the edge of the Cumberland Historical Site, near the Old Mill Bridge.

Sgt. Gonzales looked up from the nude body of the latest victim. "Three's a serial killer, right, Art?" he said wiping his hands on his plastic slicker.

"Yeah, but we're not sure it's the same guy," Lennox managed.

"I'm going to go out on a limb here," Gonzalez offered.

"Let's hope you're wrong," Lennox replied.

"Yeah, sure," Gonzales said, kneeling back down.

"So, what are we looking at?" Lennox asked.

"Dead, White, Naked, and Headless," Gonzales said. "Maybe, early twenties. Tough to say without the head."

"So, this time the killer kept the head?" Lennox asked.

"See, you think it's the same guy," Gonzalez said.

Lennox ignored him.

Officers kept the curious away, though there weren't that many. The area was remote, frequented mostly by dog walkers and joggers. The body had been discovered less than thirty minutes ago and the press hadn't gotten a whiff of it yet. That was a small blessing.

Lt. Lennox turned to the chief. Gonzales had been close when the call had gone out so he'd been first on the scene. A park ranger opening the old mill for tourists had noticed something odd under the bridge that served as part of the walking path through the area.

"This one's a body dump. She was killed somewhere else," Gonzalez said turning back toward Lennox and Madden.

"Well, that's something," Chief Madden grunted. "Anything else?"

"Not much," Gonzalez said. "Ass clown cut her head off, just like our train station victim. Only this time it looks like he kept it."

"Shit," the chief said as he knelt closer. Lennox stood behind him. A noticeable tremor erupted in Lennox's left hand. He gripped it hard with his right, trying to stop it from shaking. His heart beat faster; his throat went dry. Sweat began to bead on his forehead.

"You okay, Art?" Chief Madden asked looking back at his detective.

Art Lennox fumbled in his pocket for his emergency pack of Chesterfield's. He shoved one into his mouth and in a smooth motion, he lit the business end. Taking a long drag, he finally managed.

"I'm okay."

The chief peered at the body.

"We know anything about her?"

"Nothing to go on. No purse, no ID. We fingerprinted her, and I had Batista run the card back to the station and fax it to Sacramento," Gonzalez said. "For now, she's a Jane Doe."

"We think it's the same guy who did the train yard killing and the Jane Doe from the dump?" Madden asked.

Lt. Lennox stepped forward and took a long drag off the Chesterfield. His hands still trembled.

"Wish it wasn't, but it almost has to be. Victimology aside, this is a small town and two bodies have been decapitated and the third was nearly so. You've had, what, three homicides in ten years all related to ongoing domestics?"

Chief Madden nodded.

"Now we've got three in as many days. We've got someone who likes killing."

"Fuck me," Chief Madden offered.

Dr. Greenleaf made his way toward the assembled officers. They parted as he approached. He knelt.

"Jesus," he muttered.

Greenleaf pulled a magnifying glass from his kit and studied the victim's neck.

"Different weapon. Serrated edge, like a saw," he said.

"Well, that's something," Chief Madden offered.

"I suppose. Doesn't tell us much, just that the killer maybe had more time with this victim," Greenleaf said. "This is odd," he added.

"What?" Lennox asked.

"There's a break in the pattern. The tissue is mostly jaggedly torn, but there are two smooth semi-circles in the flesh about an inch and a half apart."

"What does that mean?" Lennox asked.

"No idea, but it's definitely noteworthy," Greenleaf added. "I'll know more when I get her back to the morgue. Any luck finding her head?"

"Haven't found it yet," Gonzales said, "but we're still looking." He nodded at several officers moving along the riverside, toward the old bridge.

Lennox, Madden, and Gonzalez moved away allowing Dr. Greenleaf's assistants to move in and begin prepping the body for transport.

Officer Jenny Liu was manning the tapeline that held back the spectators. As the three of them approached, they noticed Amanda Ross from *The Sacramento Bee* standing behind the caution tape. She approached them.

"Chief Madden, you've got two bodies in as many days. Is Rancho Corvallis in the grips of a murder spree?"

Madden stiffened. He hated the press. Doom peddling parasites, the lot of them, but he forced himself to smile.

"Amanda, we've got two unrelated incidents at this point. No reason to think this is a spree or that they are even connected," he said through clenched teeth.

"But aren't both victims headless?" she asked.

Gil Madden vowed to find the shit heel squealer who had let that cat out of the bag. Breathing hard through his nostrils, he tried to summon some composure.

"Amanda, we're looking at facts, not giving ourselves over to wild conjecture. We have no concrete evidence tying this homicide to the one that occurred at the rail yard," Madden explained.

A man stepped forward. Madden clocked him immediately. David Eisenberg, a Ken Doll in a suit, forty-something, and the local anchorman of the KTLU News.

"Chief Madden, do these bodies have anything to do with the eyeless girl found in the Petaluma dump?"

Even a blind dog sometimes finds a bone.

"What?" Madden managed.

"Do you think it's connected?" Eisenberg asked.

Gil Madden just stared. Art Lennox stepped forward.

"We're still awaiting further information from Sonoma County Sheriff's officials about that poor girl. Pending official notification from the sheriff's department, we are treating them all as separate incidents."

"That's all we have at the moment," Lennox added.

Madden, Lennox, and Gonzalez headed toward where their cars were parked.

"Motherfuckers," Madden muttered.

"It's gonna get worse. If some stringer from LA or SF picks this up, we'll have major news outlets up our asses," Lennox said.

"So what?" Gonzalez said.

"So, the pressure to solve this is going to get a lot worse," Lennox said.

"Get this sorted and quick," Madden said before climbing into his squad car and speeding away. His driving let his men know how pissed he was, not that they'd had any doubt before he got behind the wheel.

17
AT HOME WITH AMY

Amy Peterson sat on her bed with her backpack on her lap. A giant poster of Duran Duran's album *Seven and the Ragged Tiger* hung above her headboard. She flipped through a copy of *Teen Beat*; it had a Chad Lowe on the cover, but she was more interested in the article about the wild life of Duran Duran. As she tried to force herself to be interested, her mind kept drifting to the events of the other night when she'd finally decided to give herself to Charley only to be ignored when he'd become distracted.

It hadn't been a decision she'd made lightly. Sure, a lot of her friends had gone all the way with their boyfriends, but Amy didn't want to be the star of her very own after school special about teen pregnancy. She had great grades, and plenty of extra-curricular activities; when the time came, she'd have her pick of colleges. She had a plan for her life. She wasn't sure Charley did. She was pretty sure she loved him, but sometimes she couldn't see how things were ever going to work out for them. Amy fantasized that they would graduate and go to the same college; they could even get an apartment.

She tossed the *Teen Beat* across the room. Maybe it was her fault, she thought. Maybe she'd played hard to get for too long and he had lost interest. He said he loved her, but maybe he was fed up with waiting, and now that she was ready, he was falling out of love. Amy tried to fight off the thoughts. She hopped off her bed.

Right about now, Charley would be heading to the mall, probably to Johnny's Burgers to get a shake and fries just in case his mom made something inedible for dinner. She was going to go down there. Then what? She wasn't sure.

Amy looked in the mirror. Taped to one corner was a strip of photos from a photo booth of her and Charley at the county fair last year. They were smiling and goofing around. They were happy.

Amy knew what she needed to do, she was going to go to Johnny's Burgers and let Charley off the hook. Maybe offer to help him with his Trigonometry again. And then, if things got heated, this time she was going to be ready for it.

·

18

JOHNNY'S BURGERS

Charley sat alone at Johnny's Burger's, the after-school hangout. It was on the second floor of the Sheridan Mall and shared a wall with Astrocade, a video arcade filled with coin-operated distractions. It had white walls and strategically placed neon signs; mainly, it had noise. New Romantic music and the latest British New Wave blared from the jukebox.

Charley sat alone at a booth trying desperately to understand sine and cosine.

Charley tried his best to tune out the *buzz, bing,* and *zap* of the video games next door while the inane blare of daytime soaps rang from the TV suspended on the wall of the burger joint.

The scream he'd heard the night before had taken its toll on him. He hadn't been able to get back to sleep last night. He had turned off all the lights and crawled into bed, only to keep getting up and looking at the window in the house next door, but he'd never been able to see anything in the darkness.

Finally, at four in the morning, he'd checked his watch, but the light was still out. So, all he was doing was staring into the blackness of the room. As he cursed not being able to get back to sleep, he fell into a mind-numbing slumber. When he'd awoken that morning, the first thing he did was check the window of the house next door. The shade was still pulled down and there was nothing to be heard but silence.

That hadn't stopped him from thinking about the scream all day. Now, in the soda shop, he couldn't keep his eyes open, much less study his accursed Trigonometry. Suddenly, Amy slipped into the booth opposite him, looking cuter than the proverbial button.

She was even smiling at him as she said, "Hi."

Charley looked up at her startled, and because he was never fast on his feet, especially since he'd hardly slept last night, barely managed to reply with a, "Hi," of his own. He swallowed and kept going. "Look, I'm really sorry about the other night..."

"It was my fault, not yours," she said, cutting him off.

He stared at her, not able to believe his luck. He was going to have a chance to make up with her.

"It was?" he said, still dumbfounded, but this time he reached across the table and took her hands. "Look, Amy, I love you. And I never want to fight with you again, okay?"

Amy broke into a big smile, "I'm so glad we're getting this straightened out," she said and she was. She'd had a miserable last couple of nights, too, upset by their fight, and wishing she hadn't let herself get so irritated with him. "I've been miserable. You don't know what it's been like..."

Over her shoulder, Charley suddenly saw that the TV had gone to the local news, and a photo of the girl he saw going into the house the day before was on the screen. How could he not recognize her with the blonde hair and those blue eyes? The only thing missing was that blue dress that made her eyes stand out.

He stopped listening to Amy. His gaze was fixed to the screen and she trailed off as she realized she had lost him.

She stared at him, her gaze hardening. "Charley, are you listening to me?" she said, but he wasn't. Instead, he abruptly rose and left her sitting there, staring after him.

He came to a stop under the TV, looking up at it as the newscaster's voice was heard under the picture of the girl. "Cheryl Lane, a known sex worker, was found murdered this morning..."

Evil Ed appeared beside him, staring up at the screen along with him. "Know what I heard last night on the police band?" he said with a giggle.

"What?" Charley asked, so distracted he hardly heard him.

"That's the second murder in two days," Evil said with a nod at the screen. He giggled again, louder this time, his voice filled with glee. "And get this. Both of them had their heads cut off. Can you believe it?"

"You're sick," Charley said, looking at him for the first time. He wondered if he should tell him he'd seen the latest victim and then decided he should. "I saw her yesterday going into the house next door."

"What?" Evil said, stopped for the moment. "What are you talking about?"

"I heard a scream in the house next door last night," Charley said, getting more and more convinced of what had happened as he put the pieces together.

"What?" Evil said, hardly able to believe what his friend was telling him. "You telling me it was the girl who was killed?"

"It was the girl we just saw on TV," Charley said with a nod, more certain of himself than ever. "She was murdered in the house next door. She had to be. I'm telling you, I heard a scream from the room next door last night."

"Hey, Charley," Evil Ed said with a nervous grin, no longer so sure of himself, obviously hoping that what Charley was telling him wasn't true. "You're putting me on, right?"

"I am not putting you on," Charley began, only to hear a voice behind him.

"Charley," Amy said.

Charley stopped talking and turned to see Amy. *Oh my gosh*, he thought. He'd forgotten all about her. Before he could say anything, she mashed a chili cheeseburger into his face, grinding it in before she whirled and stomped out the door, leaving him standing there, dripping with onion rings, mashed bun, partially eaten ground round, mustard, and ketchup. All the kids looked at him and laughed uproariously.

Evil Ed was the worst of all, giggling wildly and pointing at him as he hooted, "Oh, you're so cool, Brewster, I can't stand it!"

19
BILLY COLE

The Mustang pulled into the drive and Charley exited the driver's side. He glanced up toward the house next door as he walked toward the back door. The Victorian house loomed over him and he didn't like the feeling. He didn't even know the full name of the men who had moved into it. Billy-something was one of them according to his mother, but he didn't know the name of the other guy.

All he knew for certain was he'd seen the girl go into that house, heard a scream from the second-floor room, the one with the shade pulled down, and then she'd shown up dead. And it all started when those two guys carried a coffin into the basement.

He came to a stop, and quickly darted across the side yard at the half-windows built into the bottom of the Victorian house. They were meant to provide light and air into the basement, but now all of them looked shuttered or blacked out somehow. How could that be? He put down his books and headed for the closest half-window. He frowned when he got close; the glass looked painted black.

He wondered about the back of the house. Were there

windows back there that would give him a glimpse into the basement? He walked around to the back and looked for more windows, but all he saw was a pile of wood, like the owners had bought some for the fireplace. He leaned over the newly-placed wood and saw a window. A piece of plywood was in front of it. This window was bigger than the half-windows to the side, but it was just as securely blacked out.

Did the owners not want anyone looking into the basement? Charley wondered what they might be up to down there. He'd only seen them once and that was the night he and Amy had fought. The night he thought he saw them carrying a coffin into the basement. What did they need a coffin for and what did they do to that girl? Had they killed her? He wasn't really sure, but something was going on. What? Damn it, what???

There were double storm doors into the basement around the side, where he'd seen them carrying the coffin. He moved back to the side, slowly passing the blacked out half-windows. Maybe the storm doors were unlocked. Maybe he could open one of them and peek into the basement.

In the basement, Billy Cole dragged the paint brush along the glass of the half-window, so the black paint blotted out the light. Through the tiny gap left to be covered, he saw a slender young boy cautiously approaching the house.

Well fuck, Billy thought to himself. *The kid next door has gotten it into his head to play Hardy Boys and come over and see what's what.*

Billy was going to have to nip this in the bud. Hard.

Outside, Charley came to a stop above the wooden doors, built on a slant to the ground. Did he dare? They didn't look like they were locked. They were unlocked a couple of nights ago. Maybe they still were.

Well, there was only one way to find out. He gave a quick glance around. Then, he stooped down, grabbing the handles when...Billy Cole suddenly appeared on the edge of the porch, leaning over, looking out at him.

"Hey, kid, whatta you doing?" he snarled.

Charley jerked back, letting the doors slam shut with a bang that made his heart jump and looked up at the towering Billy Cole. He was leering at Charley as if he'd like to leap off the porch and break every bone in his body.

"Nothing," Charley said, backing away.

Billy's smile broadened. He was enjoying himself.

"Oh yeah? Well, just make sure that it stays that way, kid," he said, the threat clear. His cold stare into Charley's eyes made the boy speechless. He was suddenly drenched in a cold sweat as he gave a weak nod of understanding.

Then, Charley whirled and ran for the back of his house, leaving Billy looking after him. When he heard the back door slam shut, he grinned, sensing the boy's obvious fear of him. A job well done. Then, he disappeared back into the old Victorian house.

20

THE HUNT

Jerry Dandrige was hungry, so he'd eschewed Billy's advice, and made his way to the Cedar Tavern. Jerry sat at the end of the bar, close to the front door. He cast his gaze across the room. The crowd was rough and consisted of mostly working-class men already deep in their cups. This meant he'd be exotic, strange, or something new.

At the end of the bar sat Tina. She reminded him of his first love so long ago, Maria, and the love that he had lost. It was all part of the curse, the price he had paid for avenging her death the first time. The price for repaying a betrayal that had destroyed his home and left his people at the mercy of a tyrant.

He had been a loyal son and a loyal servant to his God and King; he did all that was asked of him without question. His blind allegiance had cost him everything, but it was his grief and anger at his loss that would cost him his soul.

It was in January of 1476 that a message arrived from King Mathias of Hungary. It was a request for both financial and military aid to force the Ottoman forces out of Bosnia. Unable to refuse the call to arms, he gathered his small but well-seasoned army and headed toward the conflict, leaving behind a small garrison to defend his family and lands.

The Bosnian campaign was brutal and bloody, made more so by the participation of Vlad the Second, The Impaler, who once again affirmed his namesake by ordering thousands of Turkish troops to be impaled on wooden stakes by slaughtering Bosnian civilians with impunity. Vlad's scorched earth warfare sickened the man known then as Gellert cel Catura, and Vlad knew it. They had met with the other commanders to discuss strategy before war was begun and it had not gone well. Vlad wanted to kill everyone whereas Gellert had argued for negotiation once their superior strength had been established. Vlad, bloodthirsty as always, would have none of it, so Gellert had stood down. It was not his place to question Vlad who King Mathias had recently restored to the title of Voivod of Wallachia.

But Vlad knew of Gellert's disdain for him and his methods. He also knew that Gellert had amassed a small fortune in the past few years, something Vlad himself was sorely lacking. So, as the campaign in Bosnia neared its end, Vlad dispatched a portion of his forces to return to Wallachia and take Gellert's land and wealth. Gellert was unaware of this treachery as he and his war-weary forces slowly made their way back home.

The horrible sight that awaited him upon his arrival would shatter his world forever. The road to his home above the river was lined by the impaled corpses of soldiers and civilians who had given him their fealty. It had panicked Gellert for he knew his beloved was inside that castle. As he approached, he saw the bodies of his household servants hanging from the battered walls. Inside, he found his wife, Maria, and her handmaidens, drenched in their blood; they had taken their own lives rather than be ravaged by the invaders.

Gellert broke at the sight of his beloved. It destroyed him like nothing else had ever done. He locked himself in his study, refusing food or drink, and there he grieved, beating his breast, and rending his clothes, until finally he began to think of revenge. In his days as a student, he'd known of the dark texts, the books that spoke of secret congress with powerful creatures, of pacts, and bargains. Those books had fascinated him in his youth, and he'd acquired a few at great peril. It was these books he turned to now in the hopes of finding a means for revenge.

For days on end, he performed the rituals found on in their pages, but nothing happened. Exhausted, suffering for thirst and hunger, he was ready to welcome death and join his beloved Maria.

"Just take me. Let me have peace, then," he said, collapsing on the stone floor of his study.

"Seems a shame to give up now," a voice behind him spoke.

Gellert turned, the candles tossing frenzied shadows across the edges of the room. Emerging from one of those shadows was a tall man in fine dark clothes, his face obscured by the hood of his cloak.

"Are you the devil?" Gellert managed.

The figure laughed, the sound booming and echoing in the small stone room.

"I'm afraid it would take more than your weeping and gnashing to get the attention of the Prince of Lies," The Dark Man said. "No, I am simply here as a guide. You seek a pathway to revenge, and I know of such a path."

"I'll give you anything, money, fealty, the souls of my enemies," Gellert offered.

"These aren't things you own or that you, yourself, value," The Dark Man smiled and Gellert felt a cold chill on his skin. "There is only one thing that matters to you." The Dark Man pointed to a tattered portrait of Maria now made whole with the wave of his hand. For a moment, the portrait seemed alive. Maria's smile and her eyes appeared so realistic. It was as though she looked out upon Gellert from behind the canvas.

"But she is gone, cruelly taken from me," Gellert cried.

"I don't speak of your dear Maria. I am talking about the *love* you shared. Would you give up that love to have your vengeance? Would you live out the rest of your days never again knowing the joy and contentment her love brought you?"

"She is gone, taken from me, and it is that loss that drives my hatred," Gellert shouted.

"Then you agree to never again know love? In return, I will give you the means to hunt and destroy your enemies, including Vlad Tepes, the Impaler. You will be a scourge set free."

"I will do whatever it takes to see my enemies driven into the ground," Gellert agreed.

The Dark Man closed the distance between him and Gellert in a blink of an eye. Gellert looked up from his knees as The Dark Man extended his hand. In it was a vial containing a thick, dark, reddish liquid. The Dark Man removed the vial's stopper.

"This is the sacrament by which we bind our agreement. Drink of it and have your revenge."

Without hesitation, Gellert took the vial and drank its contents. Pain racked his body, forcing him prone. His face contorted and his hands clawed at the stone floor.

"Birth is painful, but the pain will pass," The Dark Man said as he withdrew a parchment from his cloak.

"Your new life comes with great power, but it also comes with its own perils." The Dark Man tossed the parchment on the floor near Gellert. "Heed the words I have written down."

Gellert picked up the parchment and looked up to find The Dark Man was gone.

Gellert in his grief hadn't understood what he had bargained away. He'd been given great power, longevity, and the means to crush his enemies, but after he'd taken his revenge, he would be alone. Always alone. The Dark Man's deal had been even crueler than that because the soul is immortal. As the years wore on, and his enemies rotted in their graves, Maria's soul would return to him, in different bodies, but with the same promise of the love they had once shared. His punishment was that each time, she would be ripped from his life.

His vengeance had been brief, but his torment would be eternal.

Jerry's thoughts returned to the present and to a young brunette named Tina across the bar. She'd been unfortunate enough to have caught his eye and now was firmly entranced by his powers. As lovely as she was, Jerry knew the soul in her was not that of his long-lost Maria. The brief elation he had felt when he'd first laid eyes on her gave way to simple hunger.

He silently crooked a finger toward the door where Billy Cole, waited outside in the Jeep. He left, and as all the women he desired did through endless time, she silently followed.

21

THE STAKEOUT

Charley had the house next door staked out, which is to say he sat in his old barber's chair in his bedroom while peering out the window. It was pitch black outside and all the lights in his room were off except for the flickering of the muted TV. It was Peter Vincent, of course, on *Fright Night*, another one of his old films with his younger self playing the vampire hunter. Charley held his binoculars in his lap, staring across the way at the dark window in the house next door, waiting for something to happen.

He yawned, doing his best to ignore how tired he felt. The tension was unbearable, knowing that a possible killer lived next door and that no one would believe him without proof. He promised himself he would not fall asleep. He would stay up all night if need be in case something happened next door. Just as he reassured himself how determined he was, his eyelids began to flicker and finally slammed closed. His head slumped forward on his chest. His promise to stay awake was forgotten as he slipped into his dreams, none of which he would remember when he awoke. He didn't know then that when that moment came, he would wish he was back in his dreams and not reality.

Oh, yes, he would.

22

MEMORIES

Jerry stood in his room, looking at Tina, the young woman he'd taken home from the local bar. She was at the window, a perfect statue, not moving, and hardly breathing. His window was open to the night, hardly seeing the window in the house across the way. It didn't matter anyway. The window was dark. Nobody was home or, if so, they were fast asleep. Either way, they were no bother to him and the young woman who'd come home so willingly with him and Billy.

Tina, that was her name. She was very pretty, faintly reminiscent of his first love, except that she didn't move. She was frozen by his silent mental command, to await his coming embrace, an embrace that would give her an ecstasy that she couldn't imagine and would have no time to savor, for it would be the last thing she would ever feel.

So be it.

She looked faintly like the oil painting of his beloved that he kept on the wall. His gaze shifted to it, glowing in the moonlight. It had been 1908, just before The Great War. She was his first love reborn, the sixth time he had found her since he had been cursed, only to lose her like he had each time before. He couldn't help himself, standing there, thinking about her; the love of his long, never-ending existence.

It was late in the summer of 1466 when Gellert had first laid eyes on her. His father had been summoned like many nobles to Pest to attend a meeting to discuss the ongoing tensions with the Ottoman Turks and had brought Gellert along with the hopes of finding him a suitable marriage. Gellert had been forced to endure being paraded about like a prize stud horse. So, he took to riding his horse late into the afternoon to avoid the tedium of court life.

He had ridden his stallion to the edge of the slow-moving river and dismounted, letting the animal drink as he gazed at it, seeking some kind of peace. It was then he had looked up and seen a lady on a mare doing the same as him, dismounting to stare at the river, seeking some kind of solace he could only guess at.

She saw his figure in the waning daylight and gave a startled gasp. He bowed, trying to show her he meant no harm. "Madame," he said. "Gellert, son of Janos Bashara."

"Maria of Lipany. I am relations to the King of Bohemia, be they distant relations," she answered, her gaze bravely meeting his.

He thought she was the most beautiful woman he had ever seen. The two of them stood on the banks, the soft whisper of the passing river providing a sensual music all its own.

"We are both out at an odd hour. The sun is nearly down," he said. "And here we are, alone with our thoughts. I wish that I could allay your anxieties but then we're both just meeting and are unknown to each other."

He took a step closer to see her better. She had a finely cut face with a thin nose highlighting her high cheekbones. Her

face, the way she stood, her head held high, the confident stillness of her body, and everything else about her spoke of her
refinement and grace.

"I have heard of you," she said. "They say you were studying
to be a priest, but were recently called back by your father when
your eldest brother, Istvan, took ill."

"Yes, but he has taken a turn for the better in recent
months" he said.

"Thank God's merciful blessings," she said, seemingly in
earnest.

Gellert found this charming, endearing.

"So, have you come to court like the others, to talk war with
the Turks?" she asked.

"Sadly, I believe my role here is as fodder for the marriage
bed. It seems my father does not have enough land and seeks to
sell me into an advantageous exchange," Gellert said.

Maria giggled.

"And here I thought only women knew their lot in life was to
be bartered away," Maria said.

Gellert blushed and looked sheepishly at the ground.

"Only months ago, I'd been promised to the church and the
cloistered life of books and masses," he offered. "I had never
envisioned another outcome..."

His voice drifted off as she watched him, seemingly as
drawn to him as he was to her. It might have been the magic of
the moment, but she could feel the force.

"And now?" she asked.

"I find the idea becoming more appealing with each
moment I stand in your presence," he said.

As he spoke, Gellert realized he moved closer to Maria. He
was now just a foot or two away from her. He wanted to reach
out and touch her, to hold her.

"We have just met," she said sensibly. "Surely you don't credit me with such a grand change of heart?"

"In this chance meeting, a whole world of possibilities has begun churning in my head," Gellert said as he bent forward and took her soft hands in his.

"Basking in your radiance, I begin to understand the poet's words in a way I never have before," Gellert said gently releasing Maria's hands.

Maria studied him. "You have a gentleness about you, but there is also a boldness I find so refreshing."

She stepped forward and kissed him gently on the lips and so their love was sealed. In the weeks that followed, Gellert lobbied his father hard to pursue an arrangement with Maria's family. Janos Basarab was more than happy at the prospect of exchanging his youngest son for the potential of new lands in Bohemia and favor with its kind.

Within a few weeks, they were betrothed and married shortly after. As a wedding gift, Gellert's father granted him control over his southern holdings near the river Olt, taking the new lands he'd acquired from the marriage contract as his own. Undaunted, the newlyweds set out to make a home amid the high, rocky peaks of the new fief of Wallachia. But then, so much had gone wrong.

Jerry jerked his head back as though slapped, trying to drive the horrid thoughts from his mind and not succeeding. He shifted his gaze to the girl he had taken from the bar and seized on her, willing himself to forget the past and root himself in the present. She still stood by the window, frozen until he mentally released her. Looking at her made him realize how pressing was his thirst. He had to drink. Now.

He pressed the button on the tape recorder he had in a shelf and low sensuous music, a driving beat hidden low beneath the song of the violins, began. He moved toward her. She would be his now, and being his would perhaps drive the memory of Maria out of his mind. If not, it would at least satisfy the dark craving that drove him.

23
THROUGH THE WINDOW

The TV was flickering white snow in the dark room, the channel long ago having signed off for the night. Soft, sensual music snaked through Charley's open window, slowly dragging him back to wakefulness. Groggily, he opened his eyes to find himself staring into the lit window of the bedroom next door. He sat up with a start.

There was no shade drawn now. He could see clearly into the room. A teenage girl stood there, slowly unbuttoning her blouse. Charley rubbed his eyes, hardly able to believe what he was seeing. As he watched, open mouthed, she slowly dropped her blouse to the floor and stood there, bare breasted.

Charley gulped, fumbling for his binoculars. He got them to his eyes just as a man, tall and elegant, stepped out of the shadows behind the girl. Charley didn't know his name, but he watched as he glided across the room toward her with incredible grace. To Charley, the whole thing had a dreamlike quality that made it even more difficult to believe it was actually happening.

But it was. He was seeing it with his own eyes right then and there. The man was maybe forty, almost beautiful with pale alabaster skin and thick luxurious, jet black hair. He stopped behind the girl, sweeping her hair back with one hand, exposing her vulnerable throat, even as he grabbed her shoulder with the other, steadying her.

He slowly leaned down as though to kiss her. Charley watched through his binoculars, unable to tear his eyes away. The man's upper lip began to pull back, revealing fangs, long, razor sharp, and sparkling pearly white in the moonlight flooding in through the open window. The girl didn't move, staring straight ahead, as though hypnotized.

Suddenly, the man stopped, the fangs poised an inch above her vulnerable throat. He slowly turned his head and stared out the window and across the yard, directly through Charley's window, as though seeing him clearly in the darkness of his room.

He could see him watching, Charley was sure of it. He slipped out of the barber's chair and took a step back into the deeper darkness of his room. His hand instinctively went up to his own throat. Then the most amazing thing happened.

The man reached out and grabbed the pull chain on the shade. Charley's eyes widened. The man's fingernails, no, not fingernails, claws, inches long at least, wrapped themselves around the pull chain and slowly drew it down, cutting off Charley's view of the room.

Charley stood there, the binoculars slipping from his hand. They fell to the floor with a thump he never heard as he whirled, dashing out of his room, across the hall into his mother's room. She was sound asleep, but that didn't stop him from shaking her awake.

"Mom, you've got to get up. I can't believe what's happening next door."

Judy turned over, taking off her sleeping mask. She'd taken

to wearing it to make the change from the day to night shift and back. It helped her sleep, or at least she thought it did.

"What? What are you talking about?" she asked sleepily.

"He had fangs. The man who bought the house next door had fangs!"

"Oh, that's lovely, Charley," she said with a yawn. "I have to get up at seven tomorrow."

She started to turn over. He was about stop her when he heard a car door slam outside in the back yard. He jumped to the window, peering out into the back of the house next door just in time to see the huge man who'd scared the hell out of him the day before walking away from a shiny new black Cherokee Jeep.

Charley whirled and dashed out of the room, leaving his mother lifting her head, looking after him. "Charley!" she called, but he was gone.

With an unhappy look, she finally realized she had no choice but to get up. She sat up and reached for her robe. Now, where were her slippers? She was always losing them.

Charley raced down the stairs, taking them two at time, and whipped around the newel post, headed for the kitchen. A moment later, he slipped through the back door and into the bushes that separated his house from the one next door. There, he crouched down, watching the black Jeep. The back hatch was open, as if waiting to be loaded, the yard empty in the moonlight.

Suddenly, the back to the Victorian house banged open and the big guy came out. He was carrying a large bundle in a double plastic trash bag over his broad shoulder. Charley's mouth fell open as he realized it could easily be a dead woman's body. More specifically, it could be the body of the woman he'd seen upstairs about to be bitten moments earlier by the handsome guy behind her.

He'd had fangs. What the hell was he involved with? The big

guy dumped a hefty-looking, body-length garbage bag in the back of the Jeep and slammed the hatch shut, crossing toward the driver's door. There was suddenly a terrific whoosh through the air over Charley's head and he instinctively ducked. There was the sound of beating wings and the bushes bent around him. The moonlight momentarily blacked out as if something big had just flown overhead. Something *very* big, like a bat. A bat? Oh, my God, he was losing his mind. Then there was a thump as though something, or someone, had just landed. The silence returned.

Charley lifted his head, peering through the bushes just in time to see a shape, more like a shadow of a man, step out of the darkness near the back of the Jeep. It was the same guy he'd seen upstairs, and he didn't even know his name. The guy who wanted to fix up houses, and his carpenter roommate. There was no way in hell he believed either of these guys were about restoring houses.

The shadowy man glided toward the Jeep, flowing across the ground in a silent elegant gait. He raised something in his hand and spoke to the other man.

"You forgot something," he said in a purr that was both threatening and powerful at the same time.

It was the voice of a man, no, a creature, used to commanding. He tossed the purse to the bigger man, but it didn't just fly through the air. It *sped* through the air, as if magically tossed so fast it blurred. Charley's eye's widened as the big guy caught it one-handed, and he blinked rapidly, not able to believe what he was seeing.

Then he became aware the elegant man had pulled an apple from a pocket and opened his mouth to take a bite, a big bite. The apple gave way to a loud *crunch* as the force of his teeth sank deeply into it. *Was this his dessert or was he just cleaning his teeth after draining his victim dry?* Charley wondered.

Just then, the back door to Charley's house banged open, sending a shaft of light into the back yard. His mom, Judy, stood there in her robe, looking out into the darkness.

"Charley!" she said, calling loudly to him.

The tall elegant man stopped before he took another bite of the apple, searching the bushes with his eyes. The darkness didn't seem to bother him at all, as if he saw as clearly in the night as Charley did in the day. Charley's eyes widened as he saw the man's gaze fix on him in the darkness. He raised the apple a bit and tossed it. It landed and rolled to a halt right in front of Charley's now terrified eyes. It had a huge portion missing, as if this might be a preview of what might happen to him — or his neck — if the guy got ahold of him.

When the man took a step in his direction, Charley leaped to his feet, giving himself away, and raced back to his mother.

"What are you doing?" she asked as he bundled her through the door, slamming it behind him. Jerry Dandrige, who had just tossed the apple, smiled as if satisfied with his aim. Billy Cole took a step forward, as if to follow Charley and his mother, but Jerry raised a hand, stopping him. He nodded at the vehicle and he and Billy climbed inside. They drove down the drive and into the street with their burden in the back, on their way to dispose of the evidence.

24

CHARLEY CONFIDES IN JUDY

Charley sat at the kitchen table, his head in his hands. They had come inside less than an hour ago and he'd been trying to convince his mother of what he had seen ever since. He was utterly failing. He racked his brain, trying to figure out how to convince her and couldn't come up with a way, not one she'd believe anyway.

She put a cup of steaming hot cocoa she'd just made in front of him. "Hmmm...this microwave never melts the marshmallows right. Drink that," she said, handing him a cup and trying to calm him down.

He looked up at her, thinking he was about to go mad.

"Mom, I don't need hot cocoa right now. I didn't have a nightmare. They did kill a girl over there."

He was almost shouting, but he couldn't stop himself. He had to convince her. If he was right, her life was in danger. His certainly was now. The killers had seen him hiding in the bushes, watching them put that body in their Jeep.

She reached out a hand for his forehead, afraid he might be running a temperature. "How late did you stay up studying?"

"Mom," he said, shoving her hand away. "I'm not sick. The guy did have fangs and a bat did fly over my head and a second later, he stepped out of the shadows. Now, don't you see what that means?"

"Jerry Dandrige," she suddenly said, stopping him.

"What?" he looked up.

"That's his name. The Realtor told me. Said he was a real nice guy. His friend is Billy Cole, a licensed contractor apparently."

"They're not nice guys and that big guy with him is not a licensed contractor."

"Really?" she said, licking the chocolate powder she'd used to make the cocoa off her fingers. "Then what are they?"

"The guy you call Jerry Dandrige is a vampire. The guy with him must be under his power."

"What?" she stared at him in shocked disbelief.

"You heard me, damn it," he insisted. "A vampire!"

Oh, my gosh, she thought. *I really have been working too hard at the wine tasting room.* She'd been feeling that way ever since she'd started taking the late shift that kept her there until eleven at night, but the tourist season was approaching and business was picking up. Now, she definitely felt guilty for leaving him alone so many nights.

"It's all those horror movies you're watching, isn't it?" she said.

"No, it's not the horror movies. That's Evil Ed's mania, not mine. I saw a girl over there though, out my window. It looks right into the house next door."

"What did you see in the window?"

"I've told you ten times," he said, almost bursting with frustration. "A girl. And he bit her. With his fangs."

"Charley," she said, taking a seat opposite him across the

table. "It's cause I've been working so many nights, isn't it? All you do is watch that corny Peter Vincent on TV..."

"It isn't Peter Vincent. This Jerry Dandrige had claws."

"Claws?" her eyes widened at the thought.

"I saw them when he pulled down the shade," Charley said. "Then, just when you came out calling to me, I saw them dump a body in the back of their Jeep. I'm sure it was the girl I saw upstairs."

"Charley, please," she said, "you have to calm down."

He bit down on his lower lip. He saw this was getting him nowhere and, worse, it was upsetting her. He didn't want to do that. She was his mother.

"Okay," he said, putting his hands on the table and bracing himself. "I'm calming down."

"Good," she said with a smile.

"He's still a vampire."

"A what?" she said, staring at him in disbelief.

"A *vampire*!"

"Charley..." she said in protest.

"Forget it. I'm going to bed." With that, he shoved back from the table and rose, looking down at her. He softened. "I love you, Mom. Don't worry. I definitely have seen too many horror movies." *Or not enough*, he thought. "I'm going to bed."

He left, Judy looking after him. She swallowed and rose, putting the dishes away. She was definitely going to talk to Mr. Caputo, her boss at the Grapevine Tasting Room. He had to get someone else. She didn't want to work until eleven at night anymore. Not when Charley was like this, imagining vampires next door.

That stopped her. It was like *The Stranger Beside Me*, that book by Ann Rule. Ann had worked with Ted Bundy at a Suicide Prevention Hotline. She'd never suspected he was a killer; he had always been so charming. Maybe Charley had seen something strange. She shook her head. No, it couldn't be. Charley was just overreacting.

Vampires weren't real and there were plenty of horrible things in the world without having to invent new ones. And with that thought, she headed upstairs back to her bed.

She was exhausted and had to work tomorrow.

25
MORE DISBELIEF

"What?" Amy said again, unable to believe her ears.

It was the following morning and Charley was sitting at the same kitchen table, Amy across from him now. Thank goodness it was Saturday. He had called her and begged her to come over. He had something important to share with her. However, it was like the conversation with his mother the night before had never stopped, just the person he was trying to convince of what had happened was different.

"You heard me," he said, feeling increasingly hopeless. "My next-door neighbor is a vampire and the guy with him is his servant. Like Renfield in *Dracula*."

Amy stared at him, a smile slowly spreading across her face, as if she had finally figured it out. "Charley," she said, "is this some sort of a trick to get me back?"

"What?" Now it was his turn to stare at her incredulously. Then, he realized what he had to do. He had no choice. "Forget it. I'm going to the police."

He rose from the table. She rose with him. He made a move for the door and she stepped into his way. She was looking at him like she was taking him seriously for the first time, and was convinced he was absolutely stone cold crazy.

"Charley, you can't go to the police, not with something like this. They'll lock you up."

He whirled and was out the back door of the kitchen before she could stop him. She stared after him, not knowing what to do. He was gone, and with him, his mania, for that's what it had to be. His fandom of horror movies had finally gotten ahold of him and driven him mad.

The question was, what was she going to do about it? She loved him. She couldn't let him make a fool of himself, destroy himself. If he kept talking like this, it would get all over school. Everybody in Rancho Corvallis would hear about the crazy Charley Brewster. It would turn him into a laughingstock. The boy who cried vampires? She had to stop him, cure him. *But how?* she wondered, becoming increasingly desperate and not knowing what to do.

26

OK, WE HAVE A SERIAL KILLER

Chief Madden pulled up in in his squad car and got out. They were in an overgrown stand of trees near the rear parking lot of the Sheridan Mall. Sgt. Gonzales and Lt. Lennox were already there, along with Dr. Greenleaf and his crew from the coroner's office.

The press corps was out in full force. There were two local reporters he recognized. One was Eisenberg, from the local TV station. The other one, Amanda Ross, worked for *The Sacramento Bee*. She mostly wrote about tourism and the local wineries, but she was probably looking to get off writing that fluff in order to move onto more serious news. A couple of others he didn't know jostled around behind the yellow police tape trying to get a better view of the scene.

The mere fact that they had more of them show up meant Madden was going to have to start dealing with them officially. He was going to have to admit Rancho Corvallis had a serial killer on its hands. The reporters shouted a few questions as Madden ducked under the yellow tape. They would have followed him, but the other officers there held them back. Thank God.

"Okay, so what is it this time?" the chief asked Lennox, eyeing the body the coroner was working over. The headless body of another young woman was left unceremoniously leaning against a small tree. She was naked and her clothes were nowhere to be seen.

"Another woman," Lt. Lennox said. "Another body dump. Nothing that gives us any clues as to where he's doing the killings."

"Damn," the chief said, rubbing his forehead. He felt a headache coming on. "Okay, so we have a serial killer."

"Sure looks that way, but his modus operandi is all over the place so far," Lennox said. "Only thing linking them is the severed heads, and now it looks like he's started keeping them as trophies."

"Did he leave any evidence this time?"

"Nope, or none that we've found so far," Det. Lennox said, sympathizing with the chief. "He's been real careful since the train station. Hate to say it, but he's getting better with practice."

He was just as upset and frustrated as his chief. He was also watching the local reporters, straining to get through the police line to start throwing questions at them. Four murders. One in a quiet town had been enough to set them off. Now, there were three more and they had nothing to tell them.

Dr. Greenleaf came over. He looked discouraged. "Nothing," he said, assuming that Lennox had already told the chief, "but I did see something this time."

He held up a Polaroid picture, passing it to them. Both men studied it. It looked to be a closeup of the dead girl's throat.

"What is it?" asked the chief.

"There," Dr. Greenleaf said, pointing at two red pinpricks down toward the body's clavicle.

"Needle marks?" said Det. Lennox.

"Maybe. Could be the killer is injecting them with a sedative to make them easier to handle. I took that snapshot when we first arrived and the body was still fresh. They were definitely made before the poor girl died."

"Doesn't really tell us shit," the chief said. "We need to know if they had drugs in their system."

"Sorry Gil, but toxicology has to be run by the state lab in Sacramento. I've sent tissue samples, but those tests take time."

Sgt. Gonzales came over, nodding at Det. Lennox. "The station just got a call from a teenager on Oak Street. A Charley Brewster. Said he sounded frantic. He wanted a policeman in front of the house next door. Said he'd be waiting."

"Did he say what it was about?" Det. Lennox asked, wondering why he was being bothered about a call out that any beat cop could handle.

"Just that maybe he'd seen a girl killed in the house next door last night," Sgt. Gonzales answered, his eyes going to the body. The coroner's people were thankfully finally bagging it, about to take it back to Good Samaritan, the local hospital where Dr. Greenleaf had his office.

"So, I'm elected," grunted Lt. Lennox.

"Thought you'd want to know, especially under the circumstances," the sergeant answered and moved away.

"Got a call. Might be something. I should go check it out," Lt. Lennox said turning to Madden.

Madden hardly nodded, distracted by his conversation with the doctor.

Lennox headed for the Capri. He had a faint glimmer of hope that this Brewster kid would have some real information, but Art Lennox had been doing this a long time. Once the news gets ahold of these things, the weirdos start coming out of the woodwork.

27

LT. LENNOX ON THE CASE

Art Lennox pulled the Capri to a stop in front of a red fastback Mustang. It was from sometime in the late sixties, but he liked the design. Probably too much car for a kid; he saw a lot of speeding tickets in Charley Brewster's future. It needed some bodywork, but he supposed when the kid got the money, he'd do it. It looked like it had been prepped with epoxy.

He got out to meet the kid who hopped out of his car. He was tall and lanky, Art figured no more than eighteen. He had a flop of dark hair that made him look like he needed a haircut. He was also pumped up with excitement.

"Lieutenant Lennox," he said. "You called the station house?"

"Yeah, Charley Brewster," the kid said, introducing himself. "Did you find another dead girl?"

"It's all over the news. You wouldn't have called me if you hadn't heard," the cop said. *Did the kid know something?* he wondered. *He sure hoped so.* "Why did you call?"

"Cause I saw a girl in that house last night," Charley nodded at what he was now thinking of as "The Dandrige house." "I live right next door." He gave a glance to the much smaller two-story right next to it.

"What about this girl?" Lennox asked, wondering if the kid would ever calm down. He was definitely excited. "What'd you see?"

"The guy who owns the house, he and his roommate, they just moved in. He was undressing this girl last night."

"How do you know?" Art asked, thinking, *Shit! The kid's a Peeping Tom.*

"The window is directly opposite mine. I saw the two of them, one of the guys who lives there, and this girl," Charley said. He thought it was better if he kept his suspicions of the true nature of Jerry Dandrige to himself. "She looked drugged or something."

"You're sure about this? If the guy was with his girlfriend, he isn't going to be too happy with you having me roust him."

"She wasn't his girlfriend. Something was wrong with her. She was under his control. It wasn't natural."

Art Lennox studied the kid. Under normal circumstances, he would have blown him off, but not now, not after three murders, the last of which he'd just come from. "All right," he said. "Let's go talk to him."

He started for the house, Charley hot on his heels.

"Remember, there's two of them," Charley said. "His room-mate is a big guy, scary if you ask me."

They made it up the sagging front steps and stopped before the solid front door. There were slices of windows to either side. Ragged shears hung there that didn't let one see clearly inside. Only shapes could be seen if something moved inside.

Creepy enough, the detective thought. Maybe the kid *did* see something.

Lt. Lennox gave the door a sharp knock. It reverberated throughout the house. Det. Lennox and Charley could hear it, but they heard nothing more. It was as if the big house was deserted. Then they heard footsteps, heavy footsteps of a large man, approaching. Billy Cole appeared on the other side of the lights to either side of the door, peering at them though the flimsy white shears.

Charley, of course, recognized him immediately. The brute had scared him badly the day before when he had dared approach the storm doors into the basement. Charley was glad to have the officer with him this time.

Charley hoped he could be brave now as the door opened and Billy Cole stood there. "Hi, can I help you?" he asked in the friendliest, disarming of ways.

Whoops, Charley thought. *This isn't going to be easy*.

"Mr. Dandrige?" Lt. Lennox asked. It was the name Charley had given the dispatcher and he remembered.

"No," the big man said, "I'm his roommate, Billy Cole."

Art Lennox flashed his badge. "Lt. Lennox, Homicide. Mind if we come in?"

"No, not at all. Come on in," Billy said and stepped back, the policeman walking inside, followed by Charley.

They found themselves in a huge two-story great room. A broad, once magnificent staircase with a landing halfway up, led to a second-floor balcony at the top of which a huge multi-colored stained-glass window stared down. There were doors to the right and a hallway to the left. The big room had wainscoting and wood paneling that, at one time, must have been magnificent although not so much anymore.

The floor was a mess of cardboard boxes and heavy dark Victorian furniture, a number of them still under white dust covers. Clocks lined one wall, a dozen or more, none of them working, and all set at 6 p.m. There was one other thing Charley immediately noticed: no mirrors. He didn't have to ask himself why. He knew, the question was if he could convince the Lieutenant.

"This is quite a place you have here," Det. Lennox said.

"Yeah, we're restoring it," Billy said.

"Where is Mr. Dandrige?" Det. Lennox asked.

"He's away on business. Is there anything I can help you with?" Billy asked pleasantly, turning to them. "As you can see, we're still in the process of moving in."

"There was a murder last night," Det. Lennox said in a businesslike way. "Charley lives next door and thinks he saw the victim in this house."

Billy looked at them, visibly shocked. "That's impossible. I was here with Jerry all last night. There was nobody else in the house."

"That's a lie," Charley said quickly. He nodded at the much bigger man. "I saw him carry her body out in a plastic bag. He dumped it in the back of his car. It was a Jeep."

"What do you say to that, Mr. Cole?" Lt. Lennox said, watching the other man carefully for his reaction.

"The kid's obviously crazy, officer," Billy said, seemingly relieved to finally know what was going on. "I did take some bags out last night, but they were full of trash. Here, let me show you."

"Look, the bag I saw had a body in it, not trash," Charley said.

"You, uh, actually see the body, Charley?" Billy asked.

"Well, no, but..." Charley began.

"Okay," Billy said. "Look, uh, let me take you out back. I'll show you the bags I put in the garbage."

He took a step for a hallway that no doubt led to the back of the house and the kitchen. "Okay, let's see them," Lt. Lennox said, about to follow him.

It was more than Charley could take. He could feel his credibility with the cop slipping away. He had to do something.

"Look, I can prove he's lying," Charley blurted out. "Let's look in the basement instead."

Det. Lennox and Billy Cole both stopped, turning back to him. "What's down there, Charley?" Lennox asked.

Billy stared at Charley, his eyes drilling into him. A small smile was playing around his lips, taunting Charley, as if daring him to say more. "Yes, Charley. What's down there?" he asked, pushing the teenager.

Charley met the big man's gaze and found his tongue stuck to the top of his mouth. The seconds were ticking past. He had to say something, but couldn't find the words.

Billy smiled at the cop. "Well, obviously, the boy's made a mistake, officer. You know how kids…"

"A coffin," Charley said, bursting out with it. "That's what's down there, a coffin. I saw them carry it in."

Let. Lennox looked at him, dumbfounded. "What?"

"Yes, and you'll find Jerry Dandrige in it," Charley said in a rush, seeing no reason to stop at this point, "sleeping the sleep of the undead."

At this, Billy Cole and Art Lennox had a laugh at Charley's expense.

"Well, for Heaven's sake, what are you talking about?" Lt. Lennox asked him, totally mystified.

"He's a vampire," Charley said, now totally panicked he was losing the cop. "I saw him in that room last night. He had fangs and he bit her on the neck."

Billy Cole burst into laughter and made a sign of the cross with his fingers, holding them up, as if to ward off Charley. "Uh oh," he said.

"For Heaven's sake," Det. Lennox said, now thoroughly disgusted. The kid was making a fool of him. He grabbed

Charley by an arm, hustling him toward the front door. "C'mon."

"But...what are you talking about?" Charley managed to get out, but the policeman cut him off. "Wait. We can't just leave like this!"

"I've got a coffin for you," Lennox said.

Billy got to the front door in time to open it for the cop as Lennox passed, holding Charley by the arm.

"Sorry about this, Mr. Cole," the policeman said.

"Anytime," Billy Cole said with a big smile, totally enjoying himself as Det. Lennox rushed Charley out the door.

Billy closed it behind them, watching as Lennox hustled Charley down the walk to their two cars. Billy's smile was bigger than ever.

Outside, Charley was still arguing as Lennox dragged him toward his squad car. "But I tell you, Jerry Dandrige *is* a vampire."

"Sure, and I'm Dirty Harry," Lennox snapped, almost throwing Charley up against the side of his squad car he was so mad. "Do you realize how serious this is? We have a serial murderer on the loose. We don't need to mess with a kid getting his jollies off."

With that, he shoved Charley aside and climbed behind the wheel, looking out his window at the teen. "Now, let me tell you something, kid. If I ever catch your ass down at the station house again, I'm throwing it in jail forever!"

With that he fired the engine and took off down the street, leaving Charley staring after him, his red Mustang sitting forlorn and alone at the curb behind him. He suddenly heard the creak of a door opening above him and whirled, looking up at the second-floor porch. Billy Cole stood there, staring down at him. A toothpick hung lazily from his mouth and there was something very disturbing in his eyes, like murder. Charley's murder.

Charley slowly backed up to his red Mustang until he bumped to a stop against the car. The man was staring at him, still smiling, but about what? He glanced up at the sky above. The sun was sinking. *Oh, shit, dusk is coming*, Charley realized. He glanced at his watch. A little past four, dark by six or six-thirty, not that far away. And what then? He was alone in his house with a vampire and his helper next door who knew he knew about them, and he had nobody to protect him, nobody to help him.

Except maybe Evil Ed. He was the real mad horror fan. He'd know what to do, or at least Charley was praying that he would. He leaped into his Mustang and roared down the street, Billy Cole staring after him the entire time, that smile never slipping away.

28

EVIL ED

Charley pulled his car to a halt in front of the small two-story with a screech and hopped out. He raced up the walk and through the front door without bothering to knock. Why would he? He'd been going to this house since he'd been in grade school. His best friend, Evil Ed Thompson, lived there.

"Evil," he called out as he pounded up the stairs.

He knew he needed help. Dusk was on the way and he had no defenses against the monster he knew lived next door. Worse, he had exhausted himself of possible allies in his fight to stay alive. His mother didn't believe him about Jerry Dandrige, no surprise there. He could even understand it. His own girlfriend didn't believe him. This was harder for him. Because they loved each other, she should at least be concerned for his safety. Then again, he knew his claim about his next-door neighbor was so crazed that even he could understand her disbelief. The lack of support from the police, even with all the murders in town now, had been a major letdown.

But he wasn't sure how you kept a vampire at bay much less kill one. Oh, he knew what the movies said, but were they true?

Who knew? Only someone who had really fought one and Charley didn't know anybody like that. He doubted anybody did. He'd never believed in creatures of the night, not really, until now. Now, he *really* believed, especially after what he'd seen last night.

However, there was hope. He was sure Evil would know. Charley liked horror films. He liked the surge of fear when a moment worked, and when they were terrible because they made being afraid of the darkness seem silly, but he was nowhere near as knowledgeable as Evil was about the rules governing vampires. His friend was a walking *Encyclopedia of Horror* and that's exactly what he needed now. And fast.

"Evil," he said as he burst through the door into his friend's room.

Ed sat at his desk, busily hand painting a monster model of a ghoul as Charley skidded to a halt by his side, breathing hard. The room was a veritable museum of horror, movie posters of the classical Universal monsters decorated the walls: Wolf Man, Frankenstein, The Invisible Man, the Mummy, Dracula, Gill Man, and, of course, Abbott and Costello meeting damn near all of them. The shelves were full of monster masks and models and anything by Stephen King, Edgar Allen Poe, and H.P. Lovecraft. The floor was littered with EC horror comics.

Evil glanced up at Charley, paint brush in hand, unhappy to be disturbed. "And to what do I owe this dubious pleasure?" he said with a lift of an eyebrow.

"The vampire knows that I know about him," Charley said, trying to catch his breath. "Or at least he will when he awakes."

"What are you talking about?" Evil asked.

He looked at his friend like he'd finally flipped out, which didn't surprise him at all. Evil was sure that Charley was much too balanced to be sane. He just hid his craziness better than he did his own.

"I have a vampire living next door to me and he's going to kill me if I don't protect myself," Charley said, sure his best friend would believe him.

After all, he'd been hoping since the fourth grade that monsters were real. He'd even been the one who'd turned him on to Peter Vincent.

Instead, Evil's eyes widened and he giggled. He managed to say, "What?"

"C'mon, Evil, I haven't got time to explain," Charley said, his desperation growing. "Just tell me what to do to protect myself."

"Very funny, Brewster," Evil said, deciding that Charley was putting him on, and turned back to his painting.

"Evil, please, I'm not kidding," Charley said, the fear inside him surging. A glance at the window told him dusk was almost here. "Tell me what to do," he begged.

"Don't call me Evil anymore. Why should I help you anyway?" Evil said, painting the arm of his model vampire. It was Dracula and he loved it.

He hated people calling him Evil. It was because everybody in school knew about his fascination with horror and monsters and thought it was funny. They'd been bullying him with that name since he was in junior high and all he did was hate it more and more every day (but at the same time he found it funny and liked the way it set him apart from all the other dummies he had to go to class with who had boring names like Dave and Jake and Bill. Ugh).

"Look, I've got eight bucks," Charley said, digging in his pocket for cash. "You help me and it's yours." He pulled a handful of crinkled bills from his pocket and held it out.

Evil could always use another horror model. He'd seen a troll he liked from *Darby O'Gill and the Little People*, so he grabbed it.

"Well, far be it from me to turn down a fool's money. Now,

where and when do you expect this vampire to attack?" he asked with a giggle of disbelief he was making money so easily.

"In my bedroom, tonight," Charley answered seriously.

Evil Ed put down his paint brush and picked up a dime store cross from his desk. He handed it to Charley, more serious now. After all, he was dispensing knowledge that he was very proud of.

"Start with this, but you must have total faith in it for it to work. Then, get some wolfbane..."

"What?" Charley asked. He'd heard of wolfbane from some old werewolf movie. He couldn't remember the title and he didn't know what the stuff was or where to find it.

"Forget it," Evil said, seeing the confusion on his friend's face. "Get some garlic, links of the stuff you can wear around your neck and hang from your window. If he comes for you, that'll be the way. Then, of course, there's holy water. But you gotta get a priest to say a blessing over it first."

He went back to painting his model as Charley stared at him. *He'd paid eight bucks for this?* he thought to himself.

"That's it?" he said.

"I'm afraid so. Of course, they can change into wolves and bats at will, so I don't know what you can do about that. Wolfbane is supposed to stop it, at least according to some authorities. But your best protection right now, Charles, is that a vampire cannot enter your house without being invited by the rightful owner first."

"Are you sure about that?" Charley said, beginning to feel a little better. Not much, but a little.

No way was he ever inviting Jerry Dandrige into his house. His mother either. She was working so hard she was hardly ever home.

"Positive," Evil said, flashing him a big smile.

If there was one thing he was confident about, it was his

knowledge of vampires. He'd read every book about them and bought every Grimoire, their magic Book of Spells, that he could find. Most of them were nonsense, but he'd gleaned enough from them he was clear about the points they agreed on. Being invited into the house before they could enter was one of them.

"Relax, Charley," he added. "You're safe."

"Thank you," Charley said, truly grateful. At least he knew how to vampire-proof his room. That was a start. He glanced at a window. Dusk was falling. "Oh, no, I'm almost outta time. See you later. I hope." With that, he whirled and dashed out of the room, Evil staring after him. He pointed his finger like a gun and slowly pretended to shoot himself in the head. "Trig, it gets 'em every time," he murmured and turned back to the model he was painting.

29

A VERY SPECIAL GUEST

Bang, bang, bang went the hammer as Charley finished driving the nail deep into the wooden frame. He stepped back, studying his handiwork. Yup, the window was nailed shut and there were strands of garlic hung around it like Christmas tree lights. No way was a vampire coming through that window. The cross Evil Ed gave him sat on his desk, shoved up against the window. Yup, he could easily reach it if he had to. Everything looked perfect, and just in time. Darkness had just fallen outside.

"Charley," he heard his mother calling, her voice echoing up the stairway from the floor below. "Could you come down here a minute, please? There's someone I'd like you to meet."

Feeling good about himself and his protection, Charley turned and walked out of his room. He came down the stairs, taking them two at a time, almost hopping with joy. He'd vampire-proofed his house. He entered the living room to find his mother turning to him with a smile, a drink in her hand. The drink was alcoholic by the look of the ice rattling around in the glass.

"Yeah, Mom?" he said.

"Charley, this is our next-door neighbor," she said with a smile, nodding at a tall wing-backed chair, the best in the room, "Jerry Dandrige."

Charley froze, looking at the chair. He couldn't see the man sitting in it beyond his legs and one hand raised, holding on to the side of the chair, his long elegant fingers tapping on it. One of them held a dark silver ring.

"Hello, Charley," the occupant said, leaning forward to expose his smiling face.

There was something disturbing about it, as though such good looks could only be to hide an inner putrefaction. It was as though his blinding beauty, the perfect features, the swept-back raven hair, and now the smile full of sparkling white teeth were just a cover for some sweet sickly internal rot, hiding just beneath the perfect white skin.

He rose, his smile widening as he took in the terror in Charley's eyes. He held out his hand, waiting for Charley to take it. It amused him, watching the teen's terrified reaction, at least to Charley it seemed that way. Judy watched her son for his reaction, oblivious to the subtext between the two.

"Well, Charley, don't be rude," his mother said, put off by her son's hesitation. "Shake hands."

Charley slowly took Jerry's hand, shaking it as one would the hand of a recently disinterred corpse. Judy smiled, pleased with her son, but not his next question.

"What's he doing here?" Charley asked, his loathing not far beneath the surface.

Judy smiled, missing it entirely. "I invited him over for a drink."

"You what?" Charley said, his mouth dropping open in horror.

"I invited him over," she said, a bit taken aback by her son's reaction, but still missing its depth and terror. "Why?"

But Charley didn't reply. His eyes were locked with those of Jerry, who only smiled, a picture of easy charm, totally comfortable in their house. He spoke in a voice that flowed like honey, dripping charm and nascent sensuality. It was oozing from his every pore.

"What's the matter, Charley?" he purred. "Afraid I'd never come over without being invited first? You're right. You're quite right. Of course, now that I've been made welcome, I'll probably drop by quite a bit."

His voice changed, dropping an octave, filled with his double meaning, his gray eyes suddenly flaring and burning into Charley.

"In fact, anytime I feel like it." He glanced at Judy. "With your mother's kind permission, of course."

Judy smiled back at him, totally enraptured. "Oh, Jerry, anytime. It's so nice that someone interesting has finally moved into the neighborhood. It's so dull around here. I mean, how many nights can you play Trivial Pursuit?" Now her smile changed, becoming more inviting in answer to his seduction. "Right, Jerry?"

"Right, Judy," he said, but his gaze was on Charley, measuring the teen's reaction.

The vampire looked like he was on the verge of laughing in the teen's face at any moment.

Charley began to back across the room, his terror rising, knowing that now he had no defense to this monster, not if he wanted to invade the house. He suddenly hit an end table, almost knocking a vase off into the floor.

Judy looked at her son. He was ghost white.

"Charley, are you all right?" she asked.

"Yeah, Mom, I'm fine," the teen gulped, as he continued to retreat for the stairs. "I've just gotta get back to my Trig, that's all."

"Nice to meet you, Charley," Jerry said, his voice suddenly dripping with double entendre. *"See you...soon."* And, unseen by Judy, he winked at the teen.

That was all Charley needed. He whirled and bolted up the stairs, disappearing out of sight. Judy turned to Jerry, still oblivious in the face of Jerry's charm.

"You know, our town really isn't as boring as I make it sound," she said with a coquettish smile, almost inviting him to take advantage of her right there and totally unaware of it. "For instance, there's a dance at the church on the first Friday of every month."

"Really?" Jerry said, finally turning his attention to her.

"Really," she replied with a come-hither smile.

He ignored it, smiling his own secret smile at how well it had gone. He took a sip of his drink, totally satisfied with himself. The boy would be no problem now, not if he had any brains. He had gotten the threat. He couldn't be so stupid as to challenge him, and if he was, well, Jerry Dandrige would take care of that, too.

But he really hoped it wouldn't come to that. After all, they'd only just arrived. It would be a shame to have to pack everything up and move to yet another town. Killing his neighbors might bring too much unwanted attention. He'd lived a long time and he'd tried to be careful to conceal his nature. Humans might be weak and easily manipulated but they made up for this with sheer numbers and they could move about freely in the daytime, the time he was most vulnerable. If enough of them knew his true nature, he'd be in great danger. Fortunately for him, humans had all but convinced themselves his kind didn't exist. Most of them anyway...

30
CHARLEY'S ROOM

The Dandrige and Brewster houses sat quietly on Oak Street, wrapped in the darkness of the soft night air. There was hardly a sound to be heard. Everyone was in bed, fast asleep with no lights on except for an errant porch. It was an ordinary enough image, two houses sitting there on a small-town street, but there was something disturbing about it.

If one were to study it long enough, it might occur to the viewer that the much larger Dandrige house almost looked like it was about to pounce on its much smaller next-door neighbor.

Not that anybody inside the Brewster house was aware of this, not Judy Brewster anyway. She was sound asleep in her bedroom, wearing her much-favored sleeping mask, which she thought helped stop her frown lines. A soft breeze wafted through the curtains of her partially open window.

The second-floor hall? Dark and quiet, swept with shadows of the moon through the window at the far end. As for Charley, he was asleep but not in his bed. No, he had dozed off again in his antique barber chair. It had turned out to be soft enough for him to sleep most comfortably. Of course, he meant to remain awake and ready, just in case Jerry Dandrige, who now had full access to his house because of his mother's naive invite, but Charley had not been successful. The excitement, fear, and adrenaline of the day's events had exhausted him and he had fallen sound asleep.

Suddenly, the huge shadow of what might be a flying creature, a bat perhaps, was seen through his window. If only he were awake to see it, but he wasn't. The beating of thick wings was heard, but once again they did not waken him. A second later, something was heard landing on the roof above with a heavy thud.

That woke him. He sat bolt upright in his chair, fully awake in a flash, listening hard. His hand held the dime store cross that Evil Ed had given him. He had fallen asleep with it. He stared up at the ceiling, listening and waiting, but there was nothing to be heard. Perhaps it was a dream. Perhaps not.

Then he heard it, what sounded like soft footsteps walking across the roof above him. Heading where? The closest window in the house to him, one unprotected by nails and links of garlic strung everywhere, was at the end of the hall outside. Holding the cross tightly, Charley rose and walked to his bedroom door.

He unlocked it and stuck his head out, looking toward his mother's bedroom and the window to the outside and then down the hall toward the stairway. Nothing to be seen, nothing to be heard, no more footsteps on the roof, no more beating of wings. Silence and darkness.

Then he heard it, a scratching from downstairs, like fingernails squeaking on glass. He tiptoed to the landing, staring down at the shadow encrusted portico below. The noise was louder now. It was coming from down there. Clutching his cross tightly, he began to descend the stairs.

But he missed what was really happening. Jerry Dandrige stood above the sleeping Judy Brewster, her eyes covered by the sleeping mask. The window was open behind the vampire. He turned, heading for the door. As he did so, he passed her bureau mirror. If Judy had been awake and watching, she would have been shocked. He did not cast a reflection. He slipped out into the hall, softly closing her door behind him. Then, he grabbed the handle firmly and gave it a quick jerk. A soft *crunch* was heard as he dislodged it from its hinges, wedging it tight against its frame. Satisfied, he turned for Charley's door and began to softly whistle. The tune? Why, "Strangers in the Night." What else?

He slipped into Charley's room, closing the door quietly behind him.

In the meantime, Charley had come to a halt at the bottom of the stairs, staring through the archway into the living room. There, he saw the source of the scratching. A tree branch, caressed by the wind, was slowly moving back and forth across the glass of the window. Relieved, Charley slipped the cross into his pants pocket and turned, walking back up the stairs. He came down the hall, past his mother's door, hardly giving it a glance as he disappeared into his own room.

Inside, he shut the door softly behind him, locking it, and sat in his desk chair, turning on the TV, only to rise again nervously and walk to the window. He stared out across the side yard at the window into Jerry Dandrige's house. Dark and silent. That should have made him feel better, but it didn't. His hand reached into his pocket, feeling the cross. That gave him some relief, but not enough.

He was so involved in his own thoughts that he never heard the closet door behind him sliding open and the horror he was so worried about stepping out. Jerry Dandrige, in all his silent, elegant glory began advancing on Charley until he came to a halt directly behind him. He waited as Charley slowly sensed the presence, his eyes widening with horror as he realized the vampire was standing right behind him. He whirled and the teen opened his mouth to scream, but Jerry grabbed him by the throat before he could and clamped down. The vampire smiled, inches from his face.

"Now we wouldn't want to wake your mother, would we, Charley?" His smile widened, revealing his fangs. "Then I'd have to kill her, too. Right?"

Charley only stared at him, helpless in his steel grip, unable to speak, unable to even nod. Then Jerry picked him up and threw him casually across the room. Charley smashed into the closet doors, busting them, and ended up in a heap at the bottom among his clothes, boxes falling on him from the top shelf.

Jerry sauntered across the room and reached out, grabbing him by the throat again, and lifted him one-handed into the air.

"Do you realize how much trouble you've caused me?" he hissed; his good nature gone. "Spying on me, almost disturbing my sleep this afternoon, telling policemen about me —"

He slammed him into a wall so hard that plaster dust rained down on Charley. He held him several feet off the floor as his legs dangled. Jerry leaned in, pressing his face close to Charley.

"You deserve to die, boy —"

He slowly began to choke Charley, cutting off his breath, turning his face purple, making his tongue begin to protrude. Then, he suddenly stopped, staring at the teen's face.

"Of course, I could give you something I don't have — a choice," he said, referring to something which Charley did not understand. "Forget about me, Charley. Forget about me and I'll forget about you. What do you say, Charley?"

For an answer, Charley's hand reached into his pocket for the cross Evil had given him and whipped it up to thrust in Jerry's face. No way. Jerry's hand snapped out with blinding speed, grabbing Charley by the wrist and holding it as far from him as he could, slowly beginning to squeeze Charley's wrist.

"It's not that easy, Charley," Jerry said. "I have to see it and, if you noticed, I'm not looking at it. I'm looking at you."

Charley's face writhed in agony as his wrist was squeezed, the bones beginning to crack, and the cross slipped from his numb fingers. Jerry stared at Charley, no forgiveness in his face, just fury. Charley stared back in terror; he could do nothing else.

"Fool," Jerry said in disappointment.

"If you kill me," Charley gasped, "Everybody will be suspicious. My mother, the police..."

"Not if it looks like an accident," Jerry said with total confidence.

Still holding him by the throat, Jerry released his wrist and yanked the desk away from the window. He tore the lock out of the window with the flip of a finger, and threw it full open, easily tearing the nails from the frame. *Pop, pop, pop* they went. As for the links of garlic, it was as though they weren't there to him.

"A fall for instance," he said with a grin. "I believe it's the most common of household misfortunes."

He started to slowly, inexorably push Charley out the window. The teen craned his neck, glancing over his shoulder. The hard ground was a good thirty feet below. A white picket fence with sharp points directly beneath promised to impale him. He turned back to the vampire, fighting for a handhold, grabbing the frame with one hand, trying to keep himself from being pushed back first out the window.

His flailing hand caught a framed photo of Amy on his desk. It went flying out the window. He looked down as it fell, spearing itself on one of the spiked fence posts, shattering and stabbing her through her beautiful, kind, smiling face.

Charley knew he was next, the vampire's strength making him seem puny. His fingers began to slip from the window frame, his other hand desperately scrabbled blindly for something, anything on his desk that might help him.

He seized a wooden pencil that he lifted high in the air and slammed the point down into Jerry's hand that held him by the throat. It punched through and came out of his palm. With an unearthly scream, Jerry whirled away from Charley, grabbing the pencil protruding from the back of his hand. Smoke rose from where the wood had pierced his dead skin (how can it be alive when he is not?). He ripped it out with one swift motion and flung it across the room. He slowly raised his head, staring at Charley. His face was shockingly no longer human. Oh, no, not human at all.

It was deathly gray with skin wrinkled and ancient, a mouth full of deadly fangs, thick hair slicked back into a widow's peak, and eyes flickering a piercing red. His jaws dripped with thick saliva as if he could taste Charley before he even attacked.

Suddenly, Judy could be heard rattling her bedroom door in its frame, trying to get it open. She was calling out, "Charley! Charley!"

She must have heard the noise of their fight, and the roar of Jerry's pain. Judy's struggle to get her door open became louder all the time.

Jerry's head whipped back and forth between the door in the hall and Judy's struggle and his initial target, Charley, as he tried to make up his mind if he had time to kill the teen and still escape. He certainly wanted to. With every turn of his head, the horrible vampire's visage lessened and he became more and more human looking.

It was all happening so fast; Charley could not process it. His mind was revolting, freezing up. The thing had changed into a monster in front of him and was now reverting back as he reasserted self-control. What kind of thing could do that? A thing so powerful he could not even imagine.

Suddenly, his mom's door across the hall started to give way with a groan. Hissing with frustrated fury, the vampire whirled and dashed out into the hall.

Charley finally managed to throw off his shock and plunged after him into the hall where he skidded to a halt. The window at the far end had been flung open. He leaped to it, sticking his head out, staring up at the night. Suddenly, on the roof above him, there was a now familiar flapping of powerful wings beating their way into the air. *Where was he going?* Charley wondered. He didn't know as the wings faded into silence.

Charley pulled his head back in and closed the window. He turned to find Judy stumbling out of her room, having gotten the door open at last.

"Charley, what is going on?" she said, her eye mask hanging around her throat.

Charley thought fast, not wanting her involved and certainly not wanting her in any danger. "Nothing, I just had a nightmare," he said quickly.

She was instantly concerned. "You know, I had one last night. I was reading *Kill Again and Again* and I opened my eyes and thought I saw someone in my room. I almost screamed before I realized it was my clothes tossed across my chair. It's all those crime novels I read..."

Suddenly, they both heard a dull screech, as if metal were being bent, then nothing. Judy stopped, turning toward the closed window as Charley peered through the glass at his backyard. He saw the shadowy form of Jerry Dandrige slipping out of their garage and crossing toward his own house.

"Now what is it?" his mother asked.

She took a step toward the window, only to have Charley grab her, gently guiding her back toward her bedroom. "Nothing, nothing, just, uh, raccoons in the garbage again. Why don't you go back to sleep?"

"But, sweetie, what about your nightmare? Do you want a Valium?" she asked.

She went through stages where she was on this and that as she sought sleep, depending on what shift she was working. It was like she'd been hearing the Stones song about Mother's Little Helper and had taken it to heart.

"No, I'm fine now, honest," Charley said, hating any and all pills. He was terribly aware of addiction, given what he had seen happening to some of his friends at school.

"Well, I do need my sleep," she said a yawn. "I start the night shift tomorrow. Three o'clock in the morning is so bad for my complexion..." she continued as she pulled her bedroom door closed.

"Night, Mom," he said.

With that, he pushed her through the door into her bedroom, closing it behind her. He looked at it. Off-kilter. He'd have to fix it tomorrow, but he didn't have time now. He turned for his own room. He still had his own problems, like the vampire next door.

31
THE PHONE CALL

Charley locked his door behind him and flipped on the TV for company, hardly looking at it as he paced his room, lost in thought.

The bedroom next door was dark with no shade pulled, but no light on either. It was *Fright Night* again on the TV screen, featuring another horror film. It was the last thing he wanted to see when he had a real horror living next door. He was just about to lean over and shut it off when his phone rang as loud as a gunshot; it made him jump.

He looked at it like it was about to bite, as it rang again, louder it seemed this time, in an insistent, *pick me up or I'm gonna bite you* kind of way. He grabbed it, pressing it to his ear, but said nothing. If Jerry wanted to speak to him, he'd let him begin the conversation.

Suddenly, he heard the vampire's sibilant whisper. "I know you're there, Charley. I can see you."

Charley slowly turned, staring out his window. The room across the way was lit now and Jerry Dandrige stood there, the phone to his ear, staring directly at Charley. Yes, indeed, he did see him.

In fact, Jerry stood there, reveling in the boy's obvious terror. Billy knelt before him, wrapping his hand with a bandage that was already stained with blood, the excess dripping into a stone pedestal that reached up to within a foot of his long elegant fingers.

Drip, drip, drip went his blood, every drop of which Billy would drink when the bandaging was done and Jerry had given him permission. It would only strengthen their bond. That and the promise to make him fully a creature of the night, something that Jerry would never do, but Billy lived in endless hope. He'd been that way for hundreds of years now, always faithfully serving him, able to go out in the daylight, and always guarding over him while he slept in his coffin, safely hidden in the basement right now.

It was a fatal twist that Charley Brewster had seen them carrying it in there several nights ago, right after he'd quenched his thirst from his first murder in this sleepy little town. He probably shouldn't have done it, but his existence was made of things he never should have done. It had started this drama that had brought him to the confrontation tonight.

"What's the matter, Charley? Scared? You started this, Charley, and I'm gonna finish it. I just destroyed your car, Charley," Jerry said, his voice heavy with threat. "But that's nothing compared to what I'm going to do to you tomorrow night."

Jerry hung up and slowly reached out, drawing the shade so he didn't have to see that disgusting juice bag next door that had actually had the temerity to attack him, and worse, hurt him.

Wood piercing his body burned like hell (and he should know what hell burned like, having been there every moment since he'd surrendered his soul to that very devil that ruled over Hades). It was an agony, an injury for which he would never forgive the boy. He stood there, plotting various scenes of revenge, one more painful and humiliating than the other.

Across the side yard, Charley stared out his window at the pulled shade. He slowly hung up his phone, sinking onto his bed, thinking hard about what he was going to do to save himself, and coming up with no answers. He felt hopeless. No one believed him, and it didn't seem like they ever would.

He was alone, facing a monster now driven by vengeance. He didn't want to think of what Jerry would do to him or anybody he cared about. They were all in danger and none of them suspected anything was wrong, except that he was dangerously delusional.

It made him sick, horrified, and so scared he was shaking. Then, he realized his TV was playing, the volume on low but still audible. Peter Vincent was speaking.

"Good evening, horror fans," Peter said on the screen with a modest smile. "I hope you're enjoying *I, A Vampire, Part 2*. It's one of my best." He coughed, clearing his throat, seemingly looking right out of the screen at Charley. "Did you know, there are a lot of people who do not believe in vampires?"

Charley straightened, his gaze suddenly riveted to the screen as Peter continued. "Ah, but I do. Because I *know* they exist. I have fought them in all their guises: man, wolves, bats. And I have always *won*! That is why they call me The Great Vampire Killer."

He took a dramatic pause, straightening up to make himself look bigger and more impressive; his chest puffed up. "Now, watch me do it."

The horror flick came back up on the screen with a much younger Peter stalking Dracula through a drafty castle, a stake and mallet in hand. Charley watched the movie with renewed, if not fervent, interest.

"Get him, Peter," he whispered to himself as he watched, his eyes glued to the screen.

"Get him! Get the damn vampire!"

32
RAGE

Jerry Dandrige was in a foul mood. That little shit, Charley Brewster had shoved a piece of wood through his hand. Jerry turned away from Billy, his patience gone. The boy had pulled his shade so there was no satisfaction in torturing him anymore. With a guttural snarl, he pulled free of Billy's ministration and leaped to his open window, and threw himself out, turning into a bat even as he fell, his strong wings lifting him up and out across the street. The thirst wasn't what drove him. Instead, what consumed him now was rage.

As he soared above the darkened houses, he scanned the streets and alleyways. He wanted to wield his power without the restraint he had shown on Charley; he wanted to feel someone come apart in his bare hands.

He swooped down a quiet street of houses; in the distance, he could see two heat traces moving underneath the canopy of trees. Dropping lower, he could clearly make out a young woman walking her dog.

Jen Tyne had heard about all the craziness happening in Rancho Corvallis, but she felt safe in the company of her Black

Labrador, Clover. Clover was sixty pounds of solid muscle; anyone messing with her would come away regretting it.

Jerry passed over the woman and swooped down over her a little above tree level, his wings held out and down for the lift that gliding demanded. That way, neither she nor her dog would hear the beating of his wings and become alarmed. He wanted his hunt to end here.

He landed behind a tree farther down the street from the woman, standing there as he made the transition. The bat form of him lengthened, getting taller even as the wings drew in and became arms and the clawed feet became legs. Finally, his narrow bat head with its elongated nose and bulging eyes became more recognizably human.

In fact, before he was through, he had turned into the human ideal of handsomeness. He stepped out into the path of the approaching woman and her dog. Jen noticed him and her forward walk faltered. Clover let out a low growl, but then Jerry moved into the moonlight so she could see his face more clearly, his attractiveness proving a fatal lure for Jen. As for Clover, she eased back against Jen's leg trying to protect her owner.

Jen stepped around Clover and walked toward him now, coming up with a smile. "You startled me," she said, "especially with the murders going on in town."

"Murders?" he said, wondering how the news was portraying what he and Billy were doing. "How horrible. I wasn't aware someone had been killed here. I've only recently moved into the old Victorian over on Oak. We haven't even had a chance to set up our television set."

"Oh, my, no TV? I don't know what I would do without my stories," Jen said. Clover stepped backward trying to distance herself from Jerry. Jen pulled her leash tight.

Jerry looked past Jen; he could see the Jeep Cherokee turn

onto the street. Billy pulled the Jeep to a stop on the far side of the street. Good, old Wilhelm, always looking after him.

Jerry knew it was time to act. Clover shifted again trying to put herself between Jerry and Jen. Clover snarled.

"Clover!" Jen corrected her, trying to calm her down.

Clover knew what Jerry was even if Jen was clueless.

She reined back on the leash, pulling the animal away. "I'm sorry," she said.

Jerry's eyes shifted; they flashed yellow. A wave of fear passed over Clover; she bolted trying to drag Jen with her. Jen was frozen, her eyes locked with Jerry's. She dropped the leash. Jerry moved in, seized her by the shoulders, and pulled her close. Jerry let go of all pretenses of humanity and let the beast inside him rise to the surface. His face began to shift, his mouth filled with fangs, and his jaw lengthened.

Jen wanted to scream but managed only a whimper, as Jerry's mouth tore into her windpipe, ripping it from her neck. Jerry reared his back and let Jen's blood wash over his face. The warmth on his cold skin felt invigorating. He clamped down on Jen's shoulder, pushing his teeth as deep into her flesh as they would go. He drank deeply.

Jen Tyne didn't feel the usual ecstasy Jerry's embrace granted to his victims; instead, she felt only terror and pain. Jen was thankful for the cold embrace of unconsciousness. Jerry let her lifeless body fall to the ground.

Billy pulled up in the Jeep and got out. "You feel better now?" he asked.

"No," Jerry said, his features returning to human form. "Should have killed Charley and his mother. I think that would have made me feel better."

Clover whined, drawing Billy's attention.

"What about her dog?" Billy asked.

"She won't be a problem; she knows an apex predator when

she sees one," Jerry said.

Jerry turned and shot Clover another look. The dog snarled once more, but turned and bolted down the street, realizing it would be next on the dinner menu if it didn't make itself scarce. Clover disappeared into the darkness.

Smart dog, Jerry thought and knelt next to Jen's mangled body on the sidewalk. His thirst was getting the better of him. He used to be able to feed tiny amounts from his victims without having to kill them, simply mesmerizing them into forgetting the feeding. But the longer he existed, the more blood he seems to need to survive. The thirst was never satiated.

Jerry rose from the body, alive just a few moments before, but not anymore.

"She's gone," he said, "but I am losing control. The thirst is becoming too much. All this feeding has already brought unwanted attention. It's just a matter of time before the police start making our lives difficult."

"Not to mention it might draw the attention of some of our old enemies," Billy said. He had warned Jerry to restrain himself, but he hadn't listened. He hardly ever did. It was why they had to move so much. "You want me to dump the body somewhere?"

"You better drive it far out of town, and dump it some place remote."

Billy nodded and lifted the limp body of Jen Tyne and tossed it in the back of the Jeep. They both got inside and drove back toward Oak Street.

Inside the vehicle, Jerry stretched.

"That wasn't as satisfying as I had hoped. I should have just killed Charley," Jerry said.

He held up the hand that had been pierced by the pencil. The wound was now completely healed, but he still scowled at the memory.

"What are you going to do with him?" Billy asked, mildly curious, and sure it was going to be especially horrible. He wanted to savor it.

"I'm still planning," Jerry said with a fanged smile, "but something even more terrible than whatever you're thinking."

On that note, Billy turned into the driveway of the old Victorian, and stopped to let Jerry out.

"I'll be back before dawn," Billy said as Jerry exited the Jeep.

"I think I am going to turn in early. I'll leave my clothes out so you can wash the blood out," Jerry said smiling.

Jerry entered the quiet house and made his way down to the basement. He stripped the bloody clothes from his body and let them drop to the floor. Even from the depths of the basement, Jerry could hear the engine of the Jeep churn up as Billy pulled away.

He concentrated, listening for sounds of movement from the house next door. He could hear Charley, pacing around in his bedroom. Still unable to sleep. Good. Jerry knew he was alone in his room, wrapped in terror, and worrying about what Jerry might do next. It was well he should.

When Jerry pulled the lever, the armoire rose silently into the air, revealing his sleeping place on its concrete pallet. He slipped inside, pulling the lever once more. The armoire slipped down and he was safe again. Walking to the coffin, he opened it with one hand and stared down at his home earth. It was so beckoning.

He slipped inside and laid down, feeling the comfort. Then, he reached up with one hand and pulled the lid down with a solid click. Ah, true sleep at last. He'd been generous, even kind. Charley had had the audacity to refuse his charity. He would have to kill Charley, and perhaps his mother as well. He let the idea of Charley's final moments fill his mind. It was a nice dream for him to fall asleep to.

33
PETER VINCENT, VAMPIRE KILLER

Peter Vincent walked out of the brick TV studio in his street clothes, moping toward his car. He was in his fifties, not as tall as he looked on TV but still tall enough with sandy hair, dyed to cover the gray. He was by nature very theatrical, but at this particular moment, he was also very depressed. Very, very depressed.

Charley jumped out from where he'd been waiting between two cars in the parking lot and hurried over.

"Mr. Vincent, sir," he called, trying to be respectful and at the same time feeling awed by actually seeing his hero in the flesh.

Peter ignored him, continuing to walk toward his car, an old-fashioned 1962 Studebaker Lark, that seemed to be kept in prime condition. Charley, a car fan, thought it was cool and fitting for his hero even as he fell in, walking beside him.

"Could I talk to you for a minute?" he asked.

Peter ignored him, continuing toward his car.

He had his vampire kit slung over his shoulder and carried a small suitcase. Charley had no idea why, but he was glad he had his vampire killer stuff with him, especially considering what he was going to ask him.

"Please, Mr. Vincent," he persisted, "It's very, very important."

Peter finally halted, resigned to the fact the boy was not going to stop bothering him. He pulled a fountain pen from his coat pocket, holding it up.

Peter sighed and said, "What do you want me to sign?"

"Pardon me?" Charley said, confused.

"Well, you do want my autograph, don't you?" Peter said, already losing patience with the teen.

This was not the time to bother him, but then fans never understood that he had problems of his own.

"No, sir," Charley said, still intimidated by Peter. "I was curious about what you said last night on TV. You know, about believing in vampires."

"What about it?" Peter said curtly. His patience really was gone.

"Were you serious?"

"Oh, absolutely," Peter said. "Unfortunately, none of your generation seems to be."

"What do you mean?" Charley asked. He could feel his idol's frustration and was immediately concerned for him.

"I have just been fired because nobody wants to see vampire killers anymore," Peter said, venting his frustration, "or vampires either. Apparently, all they want are demented madmen running around in ski masks, hacking up young virgins. Now, if you'll excuse me."

He flicked his fingers at Charley, motioning him to step aside, which he did. Peter immediately began toward his car once more. Charley quickly fell in beside him.

"*I* believe in vampires," he said, trying to reassure his idol.

"That's nice," Peter said, touched by the boy's obvious

attempt to cheer him up. "If only there had been a few more of you, perhaps my ratings would have been higher."

"In fact, I have one living next door to me. Would you help me kill him?" Charley asked with totally naive sincerity.

That stopped Peter cold. He jerked to a halt, turning and staring at the boy. "Pardon me?" he said, sure he had not heard correctly. Or at least hoping he hadn't.

"Well, you know the murder of that girl that happened a few days ago?"

"Yes," Peter said, looking at him doubtfully.

"The guy who lives next door to me did it. He's a vampire."

There was a moment as Peter digested that and then he became angry. "If this is your idea of a joke, I am not amused."

He took a step for his car and Charley impulsively grabbed him. He needed help. He couldn't let Peter blow him off. "Mr. Vincent, I am not joking. I am deadly serious."

Peter stared at him and saw he was totally sincere, which meant the teen was crazy, certifiably insane. What else could he think? It made him decidedly nervous.

Carefully, never certain of how crazy some fans might be, Peter said, "Well, if you will excuse me..."

He stepped around Charley and made a quick beeline for his car.

"Mr. Vincent," Charley said, hurrying after him, "you have to believe me. I'm telling the truth —"

Peter stopped at the back of his car and quickly fished out his keys. The boy was making him really nervous now. Nothing like a mad fan to make him wish he wasn't a movie star, especially a *horror* movie star.

Charley stopped by his side as the older man opened the trunk and dumped his small suitcase and vampire killing kit inside.

"C'mon, you just said you believe in vampires..." Charley

began.

"I lied," Peter snapped, emphatically slamming his trunk lid shut. "Now, if you will leave me alone."

He quickly passed around to the driver's side door, opening it to get in only to have Charley push it shut. He stared at Peter, desperately doing his best to convince him he was telling the truth.

"Now, you have to listen to me. The vampire tried to kill me last night and trashed my car when he didn't succeed. Now, he's gonna be back after me tonight, Mr. Vincent. If I don't get help he's going to kill me —"

Peter shoved him aside, hopped into his car, and quickly locked the door behind him, obviously terrified of Charley. As he started the engine of the old Studebaker, Charley beat on the window.

"Mr. Vincent, please just listen to me for a second. Mr. Vincent, please. Wait, Mr. Vincent. Please, wait!"

But Peter definitely didn't and backed up, speeding out of the parking lot, doing his best to put as much distance as possible between him and Charley as fast as he could. Charley ran after him, yelling at the top of his voice.

"Mr. Vincent, please..."

But Peter was gone, leaving Charley alone and looking after him hopelessly. He finally realized it was useless. Nobody believed him and nobody was going to. He had no other choice but to face the crushing reality; he was going to have to go home and face Jerry Dandrige all by himself. But how was he going to do that? He knew from the night before he was helpless against Jerry Dandrige's strength and guile. He also knew the vampire wanted vengeance. And he not only had to save himself but protect his mother and his friends, too, if the vampire went after them.

He had to figure something out. He *had* to.

34
DEAD DOG WALKER

L t. Art Lennox could feel Chief Madden approaching behind him, his thundering steps and the waves of angst pouring off him were almost palpable. Madden lit a cigarette as he stopped just behind Lennox.

"Dammit Art! That's five!" Madden said.

"I know, chief, I know," Art sighed.

The two men stood at the top of a bank of a drainage ditch on the edge of a lightly wooded area close to the site of a new housing development. Laying in a few inches of stagnant water was the headless body of Jen Tyne. She'd been reported missing late last night when she took her dog out for a walk and the dog returned home without her.

"We've doubled patrols at night, we're drowning in over-time, and still we've got bodies turning up," Madden said.

Sgt. Gonzalez appeared on the opposite bank of the ditch, along with Officer Bautista.

"We're going to pull her out of the water and get her up on the bank so Doc Greenleaf can get a better look at her," Gonzalez said.

Madden nodded.

Gonzalez and Bautista made their way carefully down the slope of the ditch. Upon reaching the bottom, Gonzalez unfurled a black body bag and laid it alongside Jen's body. The two men carefully picked up her body, turned her onto her back, and laid her on the bag. They grabbed the edges of the bag and gingerly made their way up the slope of the ditch.

"Anything obviously different about this one?" Madden asked.

Sgt. Gonzalez knelt and examined Jen's body.

"Looks like a bite mark on her shoulder; maybe her dog took a chunk out of her," he offered. "Everything else looks consistent with the others."

"Wait," Gonzalez suddenly said. "She's got bruising on her shoulders. Looks like someone grabbed her and held her by the upper arms."

"Here comes Greenleaf. Maybe he can shine some light on those bruises," Lennox offered.

Gonzalez and Bautista turned to see the aged medical examiner walking across the dusty vacant lot toward the gathered officers.

"Gentlemen, I suppose we have another one," Greenleaf asked.

"Looks that way, Lee," Madden replied.

Dr. Greenleaf carefully lowered himself to get a better look at Jen Tyne's body. He removed a pair of latex gloves from his kit and stretched them over his bony hands. Greenleaf pressed his fingers into the area of the neck wound pulling back the flesh.

"Not the same clean cuts as the other bodies. It almost appears as if an animal may have taken a bite out of the neck tissue. A closer examination will tell me more."

"You think we might be looking at a copycat?" Madden asked.

Dr. Greenleaf shook his head.

"It's too early to say Gil," Greenleaf replied. "There's peri-mortem bruising on her arms, and what appears to be a ligature mark on her right wrist."

"Maybe she just fought back," Lennox offered. "The others hadn't shown any defensive wounds, but maybe she'd been able to resist."

"Hey!" Chief Madden shouted pointing at something behind the men on the other side of the ditch.

Greenleaf, Gonzales, and Bautista turned quickly. Jimmy Howison, a reporter for *The San Francisco Chronicle*, had managed to evade the police cordon. Jimmy raised his camera and clicked off a few pictures as Bautista and Gonzalez moved toward him.

"Have some respect you damn vulture!" Dr. Greenleaf shouted at Howison.

"I'm just trying to report the truth," Howison said.

"Report it from the other side of the yellow tape with the rest of the parasites," Madden yelled.

Bautista and Gonzalez seized Jimmy by the arms and lifted him off the ground.

"What about freedom of the press?" Jimmy asked. "You can't just push me around."

"This makes five bodies in less than a week. Don't you think it's time to call in the FBI or the State Police?" Jimmy asked.

"No comment," Madden shouted.

Lennox turned to Madden. "I hate that guy; he used to work for *The Herald Examiner*. He was constantly shoving his way into investigations and breaking rules. We had a party in Robbery Homicide when *The Examiner* kicked him loose."

"Looks like they just pawned him off on the brothers at *The Chronicle*," Madden said

"Poor bastards," Lennox said.

The two men chuckled.

Gonzalez gave Howison a final shove sending him back behind the yellow tape with the other reporters as a few members of the press took photos of the incident.

Lt. Lennox stared at the line of reporters and watched as Howison disappeared into the crowd. If Howison was here, it wouldn't be long before the rest of the major papers started sending in their heavy hitters. This was going to turn into a circus. Lennox examined the ditch. The killer or killers must have tossed the body from the vacant lot. There were not any shoe prints or tracks leading down to the body, which lent credence to the idea they were dealing with multiple killers.

He suddenly jerked to a halt. *Wait a second*, thought Lennox. There were two guys living in the house next to Charley Brewster. Even if the kid was a nut, he might have been on to something. Two guys, new in town. Cole and Dandrige. Lennox wondered when they'd bought the house and how long they'd been there. It seemed damn coincidental. Art Lennox hated coincidences.

He took out his notepad, and scribbled a reminder to find out what he could about when the house was sold and see if he could track down when they moved in. Also, he'd send inquiries out to Sacramento and San Francisco to see if either had a file on the men. Hell, it might be worth it to make a call back to Los Angeles to check on them.

Maybe the Brewster kid *had* seen something, but his hormone addled brain had just misinterpreted it. The kid had said the girl looked drugged or something, in a daze. Maybe that explained the lack of defensive wounds on three of the victims. They might have screwed up with this last one and she was able to fight back.

"Hey, Dr. Greenleaf," Lennox said. "Any word on the toxicology results from the other victims?"

"It's only been a few days," the coroner answered without looking up from his examination of the body.

"Hey, chief," he said to Madden. "I'm taking off to do a little research. Need to make some phone calls, maybe hit up the hall of records."

"I don't know what the hell you're going to find there, but as long as you're working..." Chief Madden said, watching CSI work and looking really unhappy, like a man who knew they were finding nothing.

That made Det. Lennox more desperate to follow every lead, even if the only one he had come from a delusional teenager spouting vampire nonsense.

35
FEAR AND MORE FEAR

Amy rode up in her moped, coming to a stop in front of Charley's house. She hadn't seen him in school that day and was worried, especially after their conversation about vampires. She wasn't the only person. Evil Ed was on the walk almost at the front door. He turned back as she got off her moped.

"Hi," he said as she came up. "Why are you here? I thought you dumped him."

"I thought you weren't talking to him anymore," she said.

He grinned, his spiky hair standing straight up. Nobody in school combed their hair like that, but he did whatever no one else did. It's one of the things that made him "Evil."

"Why would I do that?" he asked.

"Charley said he asked you for help about the vampire next door." She nodded at the Dandrige house looming over them, even in the noon sunlight.

"He asked for advice. Very different thing. You haven't answered my question."

"None of your business," she shot back and stepped in front of him, going into the house.

"Ah, so you *do* like him," he yelled after her and followed.

They hurried up the steps, Amy in the lead, calling, "Anybody home?"

No one answered, so Amy and Evil Ed burst through the door into Charley's room and skidded to a halt. The room had been transformed from a normal happy kid's room into an armament camp for a vampire assault. The window had been nailed shut again, and strands of garlic, a dozen at least, hung from the curtain rods. Crosses and crucifixes were everywhere, in every imaginable shape and size. Candles were lit throughout the room, giving it a soft glow and putting a nice sandalwood aroma into the air.

Charley sat in the middle of the floor, whittling a stake from a slat of grape fence, one of a dozen piled beside him, already done. A hammer sat on the bed, close at hand.

Amy and Evil Ed stared around, amazed despite themselves.

"What's all this for?" Evil asked.

"Self-defense, not that I think I'll need it," Charley said, his jaw set. "He'll be dead before nightfall."

"Who will be?" Amy asked, exchanging a worried glance with Evil.

"Dandrige. I'm waiting for the guy he lives with to leave and then I'm gonna go next door, find his coffin, and pound this through his heart."

He held up the stake he was working on. It had an especially sharp point. Amy and Evil Ed looked at it, horrified.

"That's murder, Charley," Amy said, her eyes wide.

Charley looked back at her with total seriousness. "You can't murder a vampire, Amy. They're dead, remember?"

"Charley, you're acting crazy," she said.

"I don't have any choice, Amy," Charley said. "The police won't listen to me. My mother and both of you think I'm crazy. Even Peter Vincent thinks I'm nuts."

"You actually went to Peter Vincent?" Amy asked, shocked that he actually did it.

"Yeah, Dandrige has to be stopped," Charley said with a nod. "Listen, I just taped this."

He hit the play button on his stereo Dolby Tape deck and a local newscaster played back over the speakers.

"Now, for the two o'clock news," the reader intoned. "Another body of a young woman was discovered early this morning near a construction site."

Charley hit the stop button, looking at his two friends. "See. After he attacked me last night, he went out and had his dinner." He turned, looking out his window at the Dandrige house. "I don't have any choice. Somebody has to stop him. I need to sharpen this knife..."

He rose and disappeared out the door in search of a knife sharpener. Evil Ed looked at Amy, his giddy humor gone, truly frightened for the first time.

"What are we going to do?" he whispered. "If we don't stop him, he's actually going to try to kill this guy." The thought really horrified him as he realized what Charley was suggesting. "With a stake through the heart!"

"I know, I know," Amy said, at as much of a loss as him.

"I don't believe this," Evil said, shaking his head. "It's like *Fright Night* — for real."

"That's it!" Amy said, her eyes lighting up.

"What's it?" Evil asked.

"We get Peter Vincent to prove to him that this Dandrige guy isn't a vampire."

"How are we going to do that?" Evil Ed asked.

"I don't know, but we'd better figure out a way if we don't want to be visiting Charley in jail."

Charley entered from the hall, carrying a knife sharpener. He plopped on the floor and went to work on his blade. Amy nervously cleared her throat.

"Charley, it's going to be dangerous going into that house all alone, isn't it?"

Charley nodded, satisfied his knife was sharp enough and returned to whittling the fence slat. "Yeah, I know. That's why I'm working so hard," he said. "I've got to do it before nightfall."

Amy, encouraged, plunged on. "You're going to need all the help you can get, right? Somebody like Peter Vincent, for instance."

"I told you, I tried," Charley said, looking up.

"Why not let me and Evil try before you do anything?" Amy said.

"Why would he believe you any more than he did me?"

"Maybe we're better talkers," Amy said, reaching for a reasonable reason and not quite making it.

"Fat chance," Charley said, continuing his whittling.

"What happens if you go into that house and he gets you?" Amy said, arguing as best as she could. "Who's going to stop him then?"

"Yeah, then he'll be able to suck his way through the entire town," Evil said, making a face as he glanced out the window. "Not that it would be much of a loss."

That stopped Charley, making him frown. "I don't know," he said slowly.

"Charley, it's gonna be dark soon," Amy said, continuing to push. "And you don't wanna go into that house then, do you?"

"No, you're right there," Charley said, looking out the window at the hulking house next door. He thought for a moment, taking the entire discussion with a grave seriousness. "All right," he finally said. "Try him again."

"Great," Amy said, brightening. "Now, you promise you're not gonna do anything till you hear from us. Okay?"

"Why? What're you going to do?" Charley said.

"Go to where he lives. Talk to him face-to-face," she said.

"I tried..."

"Yeah, but you're not a girl," Evil said, starting to get into it. "A pretty girl who'll be begging him to save her boyfriend."

"You think it'll work?" Charley asked, starting to weaken.

"It's worth a try," Amy said. "Are you cool with that?" Charley finally nodded. It made her feel even more hopeful she could avert this potential disaster. She looked at Evil Ed. "Come on."

Evil Ed hurried out the door, happy to be gone from the insanity as Amy followed him. Charley called after her.

"Amy." She stopped and turned back. "You don't believe me, do you?"

She looked at him, her heart overflowing with love and close to tears at the same time. "I love you, Charley," was all she could manage to say and disappeared out the door after Evil.

Charley went back to whittling his stake with a grave seriousness. One way or another, he was going to destroy Jerry Dandrige.

36
THE WAITING

Billy stood at the window, peering through the curtain at Amy and Ed as they hurried out of Charley's house. They hopped on her scooter, him in back, and sped past his house. Billy watched them go, hiding behind the flimsy shears of the window. At least they wouldn't be in the way when he and Jerry finished off the Brewster kid. There was still the mother to consider, not as a threat but as another body he may have to dispose of. Billy's concerns grew. He knew it had to be done, but it would draw suspicion and they may be forced to move before the ink on the deed to the house was even dry.

He checked his watch. 4 p.m., late afternoon. Two more hours until dark and then the master would awake. He turned and looked down the hall that ran beside the great stairs, toward the basement. It was the coffin that he and Jerry had carried in there only a few days before that had begun this.

He could go down there and do his best to wake the master, but he would be groggy without sleep and hardly able to think, much less move, at this early hour. Daylight did that to him; sunlight did even worse things, which was why he had made

Billy, his blood servant, reliant on his vampiric master for the gift of his blood in order to maintain his youth and power.

It had begun so long ago, over five hundred years ago, during the Ottoman incursions into Eastern Europe, at a time when Christian nobles sought to curb their trespasses into Moldavia, Wallachia, and Hungary.

Gellert had been tasked by his father to defend their lands in Wallachia. The land was mostly valueless, mountainous, and rocky. As such, it was ill-suited for farming and good only for goat herding. Gellert had few serfs to press into his armies and fewer lesser nobles to tax to pay for a war against the Turks.

It looked bleak, but Gellert was a smart, educated man. He sought fighting men without land looking for a fortune and a chance to trade their sword for gold. Gold the Turks had in abundance.

Billy Cole had been such a man. Born Wilhelm Von Bremen, he and his men were rural folk who'd clung to the old ways, forsaking the Christian God in favor of Woden the Sky Father, a God of War and Blood. A God that made sense to men in their line of work. But their choice made them exiles in their own land, so they had turned to selling their swords to other Saxons or even in far flung conflicts in Moldavia and Wallachia.

For nearly a year, Wilhelm and his men enjoyed wealth and success serving Gellert. Waging a campaign of terror against the Ottoman invaders raiding into their lands and attacking their supply caravans. But their successes had made them enemies, not only among the Turks, but among some of the other Wallachian Boyers who suffered the reprisals for their success. There was one, above all, who coveted the new wealth Gellert was amassing, Vlad the Second, a man recently released and restored to his position as Voivod of Wallachia.

Billy Cole reveled in memories of his past life, and the rush of meeting an enemy with a sword or an ax in his hand. Killing

Reg Douglas at the train station with the fire ax had renewed his longing to once again be unleashed upon the world. He and Jerry would have to have a serious talk about him finally being turned into a vampire. He'd been a faithful servant for nearly five hundred years. He'd seen Jerry turn dozens of others in that time, mostly on a whim. Billy wanted to know that power, that freedom.

37
IT'S A DATE

Peter let himself into his apartment, carrying a handful of mail, all bills he was sure. The place was small but neat. He insisted on orderliness, being very neat himself, but that didn't mean it wasn't packed. It was — with the mementos of his career. The walls were dotted with posters of his various movies, all in the horror genre naturally, some going back as far as three decades, all displaying his name very prominently.

Quite fitting. After all, he was the star.

The bookshelves and tables were filled with memorabilia, props, and awards from his various movies. He even had several clothing dummies stuck in the corners, wearing outfits from his movies. He had kept everything he could, knowing that it was an act of ego, self-glorifying, but, at the same time, sure that it pleased his fans — those who visited his abode, a number that had visibly fallen off over the years, much to his disappointment, which he never revealed, though he mulled it over late at night, fighting not to become bitter — and secretly he hoped his collection would grow in value, so if he ever had the need of money, which was all the time, he'd have something to sell, which was something he could never bring himself to do.

Goodness knows he'd never managed to make enough to put aside for the tough times, because they always kept coming. Now, he was fired and out of cash. What was he going to do this time? He didn't know, but hoped something would occur soon. *Very* soon.

He stopped by a table going through the mail. Bills and more bills, almost all of them unpaid, some paid a little, some not paid at all, until he came to...a notice of eviction for non-payment of rent. He had three days to comply or the sheriff would appear to put him and his belongings out on the street. The humiliation was overwhelming. This was what it had come to; this was what being a horror movie star had brought him: iniquity, disgrace, and hopelessness.

His chest collapsed in defeat and he was about to sink in a chair when there was a knock at the door. He could hardly summon the energy to answer. The knock came again, sharp and insistent, as if someone really cared if he was home or not. He felt just then he could have disappeared and his going would never have been noticed.

Fans? Ha. All he had was bill collectors.

He went to the door and carefully opened it, leaving the lock and chain on, just in case it was someone with a summons to appear in court for non-payment of just about everything. Instead, he found himself staring at the fresh faces of two teenagers, one a pretty young lady, and the other, a boy with spiky brown hair. Both were looking in at him through the crack in the door with something like awe on their faces.

Fans. Their appearance cheered him up.

"Yes?" Peter said.

"Mr. Vincent, could we talk to you for a moment?" Amy asked.

Peter's eyes slid to the unpaid bills piled on his table. "I'm afraid now is not the best time —" he began.

"Please, it's very important," Amy implored, her face pleading.

Peter stared at her and saw the desperation in her eyes. He knew just how she felt, even if his situation was different than theirs. It made him feel sorry for them, especially her. He stepped back, hurrying across the room, and slipping on his velvet smoking jacket. He looked for his black velvet slippers but couldn't find them. He might be broke, but at least he could act the part of a movie star for his fans. They deserved the best from him. Always.

"Well, if you would just wait there for one moment, I'll... um..." he stammered as he edged his way back into a hidden room. "Come in."

They entered, closing the door behind them and followed him.

Better to get rid of them quickly, he thought, so he said, "Now, what can I do for you? An autograph, perhaps? Or an interview for your school newspaper?"

"I'm afraid this is much more important," Amy said, turning to him.

"Really?" he said. "What could be more important than my autograph?"

He knew he was proud of his career and what he had accomplished, even if he wasn't on the uppers now, but others might find it self-centered, so he restrained his tongue.

"Saving a boy's life," Amy said, trying to make him understand the importance of their mission.

"Well, yes, I *can* see where that *could* be more important," Peter said, unable to keep a harrumph out of his voice. "Perhaps, you would care to explain."

"You remember a fruitcake kid named Charley Brewster?" Evil Ed asked in his imitable style. "He said he came to see you."

"No," Peter said with a frown.

He'd never been very good with names and considering the number of fans he had, he couldn't be expected to remember all of them.

"He's the one that believes a vampire is living next door to him," Amy said, hoping that would remind him. It did.

"Oh, yes," Peter said with a smile. It had upset him at first, but now he found it almost funny. Talk about letting fandom carry you away. "You know, he is insane." Then he focused on Amy's sweet, worried face and felt badly for her. "Oh, my dear, I do hope he's not a friend of yours."

"Yeah, she's got the hots for the creep," Evil said with a mischievous grin. He couldn't help giving it to Amy.

Amy flushed and gave Evil a whack on the shoulder, making him yelp. She was stronger than she realized, especially when she was upset. She turned back to Peter.

"We need your help to stop him, Mr. Vincent," she said. "You see, he really does believe his next-door neighbor is a vampire and he's planning to kill him."

"Yeah, with a stake through the heart," Evil Ed said, unable to hide his glee. He thought it was the funniest thing he had ever heard.

Peter stared at them for a long moment, trying to decide if they were pulling his leg or not. "Are you two serious?" he asked. Amy nodded and Peter saw honesty in her face. He shook his head sadly. "Oh, my dear, your friend needs a psychiatrist, not a vampire killer."

"Please, Mr., Vincent," Amy said, begging him, her desperation rushing to the forefront again. If he turned them down, she didn't know what she was going to do.

"I'm afraid not," Peter said, finally having decided on a way to get rid of them. He nodded at an open suitcase on the bed glimpsed through an open door. "You see, Hollywood beckons. I have just been offered a starring role in a major film. I have even had to quite *Fright Night*. And so you see..."

"I'll give you money," Amy said, cutting him off.

"How much?" he asked, quick as a wink.

"I have a five-hundred-dollar savings bond."

"I'll take it." It wasn't enough to pay his back rent, but he was sure it would give him a respite from being dispossessed of his apartment. Money in hand, green cash, was all to him now.

He sat in a chair opposite the two teens, turning on all his charm, which was considerable. "Now, how are we going to cure your little friend of this delusion?"

"I got it all figured out," Evil Ed said, stepping forward. And he did, too. He'd been thinking about it as he and Amy had ridden her moped across town. "We all go next door to this neighbor, and you perform some kind of vampire test on him to pronounce him human. You know, like in *Orgy of the Damned*. Where you looked in the mirror, the guy didn't have a reflection, and then you knew he was a vampire. Only this time, it'll prove he's human and Charley is wrong."

"Ah, yes," Peter said, getting a little misty eyed. He remembered it well. He still had a film career then. "That was one of my favorite roles. Do you know, I still have the prop?"

He rose and picked up a gold-plated cigarette case from a table. He flipped it open, revealing the mirror on the inside. He suddenly snapped it shut, dropping it back into the pocket of his smoking jacket. His mind was made up. Yes, he would do this.

"It sounds fine to me," he continued, "but how do we get the next-door neighbor to agree? I'm sure he's not going to be happy to hear about Charley's mania."

"Leave that to me," Evil Ed said confidently.

He picked up Peter's phone and pulled a piece of paper from

his pocket. He'd had the presence of mind to look up the number before he'd come to Charley's house, suspecting that he'd need it, even if he didn't know why. Now, he was ready to go.

He began to dial, Peter and Amy watching him. None of them had the presence of mind to look out the window, but if they had, they would have realized that darkness had fallen. Whether or not they would have realized what that meant was another matter.

38
SAVED BY THE BELL

In the Dandrige house, night had indeed fallen. At 6:17, exactly, all the clocks on the wall began to tick as one, signaling that dusk had fallen and it was time for Jerry to awaken. There was a phone on the portico table. It began to ring, seemingly unusually loudly in the house, silent except for the ticktock of all the clocks dotting the wall.

Billy Cole appeared down the hall, perhaps from the kitchen, and picked it up.

"Yes," he said, listening for the reply.

He turned, looking up the stairway. He knew his master had awoken a few minutes before and was undoubtedly in his room, dressing for the night. How he had gotten so swiftly from the basement to his room was no mystery to him. He had many shapes, smoke being one of them that would speed through all the cracks between the floors.

He was right about the timing, too. Indeed, Jerry Dandrige was walking down the stairs, dressed in a gray shirt with a lively black and white sweater and a pair of light-colored slacks. He was a picture of elegant unconcern, except for the fact that he was eating an apple.

Jerry was given to apples. He insisted he carried the genes of a fruit bat, part of being a vampire. Billy, being a ghoul, didn't know, but hoped someday to be able to make his own observations of vampirism, when he had finished his servitude and been carried over to the other side. It was just a simple matter of Jerry agreeing to turn him, but so far Jerry had not seen fit to do so. Billy was in no rush. He liked the half-life he'd been granted and the powers that came with it, but he did yearn to, one day, be his own master again. He knew his master's nature and kept his concerns to himself. The moment would come. He just had to be patient.

Billy held the phone out. "It's for you," he said, passing it to Jerry as he reached the bottom of the stairs.

Jerry took the receiver, seemingly unsurprised that someone might be calling him, as though it happened all the time, even though this was the first phone call he had received in this house.

"Yes?" he said, listening to a boy's reply. "Yes, this is Jerry Dandrige." He put the half-finished apple down on a tray on an end table, concentrating on the conversation as he listened. "I see." He began to smile. "Yes, of course. I'm always willing to help young people, but I'm afraid that crosses are out of the question." He thought for a moment and then his smile broadened. "You see, I've been reborn recently."

He smiled at Billy. Billy smiled back, easily guessing who might be on the other end of the line.

In Peter Vincent's apartment, Evil Ed cupped his hand over the receiver and looked at Peter as Amy watched anxiously. "He's a reborn Christian," Evil explained. "He thinks crosses would be sacrilegious."

"Ask him how he feels about holy water," Peter asked quickly.

He wanted Amy's five-hundred-dollar savings bond, and at this point, would be willing to make any compromise to get it.

"How about holy water?" Evil asked into the receiver. He listened for a moment and then looked at Peter with a shake of his head. "No, won't do either."

"Tell him it's just ordinary tap water. All he has to do is sip it," Peter said, running out of patience. He was all for believers in any religion. After all, faith supported morality and was one of the few things vampires truly feared. Still, he thought some people carried it too far on occasion, and this was obviously one of them.

Evil Ed spoke into the phone again. On the other end, Jerry listened attentively. This was like reeling in an unsuspecting fish, a fish that he had given a chance to escape the night he had faced Charley in his room. He had told him he would "give him a choice, something he did not have," but the boy refused, stabbing the wooden pencil through his hand instead.

It was his choice and he had made it. Now, he would have to pay.

"Well, yes, that sounds fine," Jerry said as Billy watched him, filled with admiration at Jerry's casual mastery of the situation. "But don't bring him over until six tomorrow. I'll be out until then." He took a pause to savor the moment.

He slowly hung up, looking at his faithful servant. "It seems we don't have to go out tonight after all. His friends are bringing him over tomorrow night to prove to him that I'm not," he paused to let the point sink in, "a vampire."

Billy smiled. Perfect. Jerry smiled back. Perfect, indeed, and they never had to leave the house to kill him. The only mystery left was how and when Jerry was going to do it, and, of course, how to make sure they were never suspected.

39
GOOD NEWS

It was later in the evening when Amy and Evil Ed pulled up on the scooter before Charley's house. She didn't like to drive in the night, especially when there was someone sitting behind her, but she didn't have a choice. She wanted to make sure Charley didn't do anything foolish, like go over to Jerry Dandrige's on his own and try to kill him with a stake.

They hurried inside and pounded up the stairs. They weren't worried about Charley's mother. They knew she was working the night shift. They came to a stop before his door, trying to open it only to find it locked.

Evil rattled it loudly, knocking on the door. "Charley, open up," he yelled.

"Who is it?" Charley called from within.

"It's me and Amy, stupid," Evil yelled, never known for his tact. "Now, open up."

A moment later, the door opened and Charley stood there, a stake in his hand, a carving knife in the other. Amy didn't wait. She threw herself into his arms, almost dancing him around the room in her joy.

"Charley, Peter Vincent said he'd come," she said.

"He did? When?" Charley asked, shocked by the news.

"Tonight, at six," Amy said, glancing at her watch. "Not even an hour away."

"But Dandrige will be out of his coffin by then," Charley said, frightened by the thought.

"Relax," Evil Ed said with a confident grin. "He's Peter Vincent, The Great Vampire Killer. He *must know* what he's doing, right?"

"I don't know," Charley said, getting more and more paranoid. "Maybe he didn't take it seriously."

"Oh, he did, Charley," Amy said, lying for everything she was worth. She was trying to save her boyfriend, assuage him of his worry, and do whatever it took to stop his vampire mania.

Charley looked at her, his eyes grabbing hers and drilling into her. "Honest?" he said, like he was a small kid again.

"Honest," Amy said, nodding solemnly.

"Then maybe we'll really have a chance to kill Dandrige tonight," Charley said, hope blooming in his breast again. Tears welled up in his eyes. "You don't know what it's been like, knowing there's a vampire living next door and having no one believe me."

Amy took him in her arms, holding him close like she would a small child. "It's all right, Charley," she said, doing her best to soothe him. "Really, it is."

Evil Ed turned away in disgust. The sappy stuff made him sick, but he couldn't help looking out the window at the dark window next door. Nope, nobody in there, least of all vampires.

But if he'd had X-ray vision, he would have seen Jerry Dandrige, sitting in the dark, rocking gently back and forth in a chair, catching the dim outlines of the three kids in the room across the way.

He smiled and if there had been anybody there to see it, especially the three next door, they would have run screaming in the opposite direction.

40
CALLING ON JERRY

Charley, Amy, and Evil Ed stood in front of the Dandrige house, waiting. Darkness had fallen and was now tightening its grip, driving even the shadows away in the gathering gloom.

Charley glanced at his watch, almost hopping up and down with nervousness. "It's six-ten. He said he'd be here at six, right?"

Evil Ed cut him a glance. "Relax, he said he'll be here. He'll be here."

Peter's old clunker Studebaker appeared around the corner, laboring its way toward them. Amy was the first to see it, calling out in relief. "Here he is."

The kids rushed to the car as Peter pulled up.

"Mr. Vincent, I cannot tell you how much I appreciate this," Charley said through the open window, not even waiting for Peter to get out.

Without answering, Peter slowly opened the door and stood to his full height. He wore his complete vampire killer regalia from *Fright Night*, the checkered Victorian suit, cape, and watch fob, and carried his kit, the wooden box with the thick leather strap, over his shoulder. There was something truly majestic about him, especially when he was playing his vampire killer role.

He looked at Charley, laying it on with a trowel. No, two trowels. "Charley Brewster, I presume?" he said with a studied formality as if he didn't want to ruin the moment. As Charley mutely nodded, awed in spite of himself, Peter formally shook his hand. "Now, down to business. Where is the lair of the suspected creature of the night?"

Charley pointed at the Dandrige house, finding his voice. "There."

Peter studied it with a frown, privately thinking that indeed if there was a house with monsters inside, it would be this one. It had a malevolent cast to it.

"Oh, yes," he said. "I see what you mean. There is a *distinct* possibility."

He opened his hunting kit and withdrew a small crystal vial of water and slipped it into a jacket pocket. He closed the kit and returned it to the front seat of the car, squared his shoulders, and turned back to the young people.

"Now, shall we go?" he said.

"Hey, wait a minute. Where are your stakes and hammer?" Charley asked without moving.

"Oh, I left them in my bag."

"You're not going in there without them?" Charley said with rising alarm.

"But I have to prove that he's a vampire first before I kill him, Charley," Peter said reasonably.

"Look, I *know* he's a vampire," Charley said.

"But *I* am the one who has to know, Charley."

"How are you gonna do that?"

"This is holy water," Peter said, holding up the glass vial.

"Now, if a drop touches him, he will blister. In this case, I've asked him to drink it while we all watch. He readily agreed."

"He did?" Charley said, shocked.

"Yes," Peter said, looking at Charley with a cocked eyebrow, "which doesn't exactly strengthen your case, does it? Now, shall we go?"

He took a step toward the house, only to have Charley grab his arm.

"But, Mr. Vincent, if I'm right and you prove he's a vampire, he'll kill us all right then and there."

"No, he won't, Charley," Peter said with a confidence born of countless movies (and he knew how this one ended). "Not with me here to protect you. After all, *I am* Peter Vincent."

He started up the walk, Amy and Evil Ed following him. Charley ran after him, increasingly worried.

"But, Mr. Vincent," he insisted, "you don't know how powerful he is. He can change into a bat and fly through the night —"

Peter came to a stop on the front porch, knocking on the door, listening to the boy with half an ear. "Of course, Charley, of course," he said dismissively. "But then, he's never dealt with me before either."

"But —"

Billy Cole opened the door, his face lighting up when he saw Peter. "Hey, Peter Vincent. Billy Cole," he said, shaking his hand warmly. "This is a pleasure. Won't you all come in?"

He stepped back and Peter, Amy, and Evil Ed entered the house. Charley had no choice but to follow, Billy Cole's easy manner disappearing as he gave him a threatening glare as he passed, quickly closing the door behind him. Slam. They were trapped inside, even if they didn't know it.

41

THE TEST

In the great room of the house, Billy moved past the guests to the bottom of the stairway, calling up. "Hey, Jer! They're here."

Although no one noticed, the clocks on the wall were tickling madly. The hour was 8:05 exactly, as though happily welcoming the all-enveloping night. Several seconds passed. Nothing happened. Peter looked at Billy,

"Perhaps he didn't hear you," the actor said.

"Oh, he heard me all right," Billy said with a smile.

Before anybody could say anything more, a step was heard creaking at the top of the staircase where the shadows were heaviest. Slowly, Jerry appeared, walking down the stairs into view. First, his elegant Italian shoes of the finest leather appeared, then his legs with their fashionable gray slacks, and finally the rest of him, beautifully turned out.

His handsome face stared down at them as he descended, making his entrance with an understated drama. Although no one said it, there was something truly majestic about him, both incredibly attractive and yet frighteningly intimidating at the same time.

Then he stopped, halfway down the stairs, his eyes fixed on Amy as though he was looking through her soul. He knew immediately who she was, but said nothing, not in front of this group.

Charley noticed. It was as though she had specifically aroused his interest. The teen felt a jolt of jealousy shoot through him. A much older man was interested in his girlfriend. Along with it, he felt a surge of insecurity. If the man on the stairs was interested in his one true love, how could he compete? Look at him. Jerry Dandrige was overwhelmingly attractive to any woman. Charley knew that and for the first time was worried not just for himself, but also for Amy.

Then, Jerry came unglued, as though recovering from seeing her, and continued down the stairs. He reached the bottom and turned to Peter with a blinding smile of perfect white teeth.

"Ah, Mr. Vincent," he said in a well-modulated voice that promised all kinds of wisdom and even more important secrets that only he would know. He shook Peter's hand warmly. "I've seen all of your films and I've found them...very amusing."

"Oh, thank you," Peter said, obviously pleased and totally missing the not-so-hidden subtext.

Jerry swung his gray-eyed gaze to Amy and Evil Ed. "And who are these two attractive young people?" he asked.

"This is Ed Thompson and Amy Peterson," Peter said, happy to make the introductions and get the evening moving.

After all, he wanted to get through the holy water test and go home. *Fright Night* was on and he wanted to see his appearance, although it was his last. He'd done a regretful goodbye and thought that he was appropriately touching, but he wanted to make sure. After all, he was his own best critic.

"Charmed," Jerry said, taking Amy's hand and bending low to brush his lips across it. He looked up at Charley with a wicked smile as he straightened. "Isn't that what vampires are supposed to do, Charley?"

Charley scowled at him. He knew when he was being made to play the fool, but the others laughed, Amy, Evil Ed, and worst of all, Peter Vincent. Jerry turned to an arched doorway. "Please, come in," he said and led them through the opening to another room.

"God, he's neat," Amy whispered to Evil, both of them totally captivated. She followed, Evil shooting a disgusted look at Charley.

"Some vampire, Brewster," Evil said and followed.

Charley was about to go after them when something amid all the packing boxes and furniture still covered by sheets caught his eye. It was a portrait, partially wrapped. He hesitated and looked closer, peeling a bit of the paper away.

He was shocked. It was a face he knew very well. "Amy?" he murmured.

It was her, but the clothes she wore were from a different era, a time long gone. Then, he felt Billy Cole closing in and starting to loom over him, so he moved after the others, into the other room. It was paneled with a large mahogany desk against one wall and a fireplace with a huge gleaming white ivory tusk on the shelf above.

In the study, for that's what it was, Jerry nodded at the packing crates and a few pieces of dusty furniture. "Please excuse the mess," he said. "I haven't finished unpacking."

"Where do you have your coffin?" Charley asked with a sour face. "Or do you have more than one?"

"Charley...," said Peter in a warning growl.

"It's all right, Mr. Vincent," Jerry said with a smile, being the model of graciousness. "I'm quite used to it by now. As you may or may not know, Charley even brought the police over a few days ago."

Peter, Amy, and Evil Ed all looked at their friend, shocked.

"Charley, you didn't?" said Amy.

Charley started to lose it. "Damn right, I did," he said angrily. "Only they didn't believe me any more than any of you." He looked back at Jerry, his face flushed. "But you'll believe me in a second. Mr. Vincent, give him the holy water."

"Charley, there's no reason to be rude about this," Peter said, polite by nature.

"It's perfectly all right, Mr. Vincent," Jerry said, raising a placating hand. "Where is it?"

Peter withdrew the vial, holding it up. Jerry regarded it warily, his voice was suddenly heavy with double meaning. "And are you sure that this is, uh, holy water?" he asked.

"Positive," Peter said, holding the vial high, playing it up with a bit of Irish brogue. "I saw Father Scanlon bless it down at Saint Mary's myself."

Jerry took the vial from his hand, pulled the stopper, and sniffed it. For the first time, nervousness crept into his manner.

Charley sidled up to Amy, whispering in her ear as Jerry prepared to drink. "Get ready to run. I'll protect you with this."

He inched a cross out of his pocket, giving her a glimpse of it. He glanced up as Jerry threw his head back and downed the contents of the vial in one swallow.

Nothing happened. He turned to Peter with a big smile. "There, satisfied?"

"Totally," Peter said with a happy smile all his own. He looked at Charley. "Well, now, Charley, you saw that. Are you convinced now that Mr. Dandrige is not a vampire?"

Charley stared at Jerry and the vial, stunned almost into speechlessness. "But it can't be..."

"But, Charley, you saw it," Peter insisted. "You know as well as I do that no vampire can drink blessed water."

"Then it wasn't blessed," Charley snapped.

He was sure something was wrong and it had to be the water. He *knew* Jerry was a vampire. He'd seen him turn into a monster when he'd attacked him in his room.

"Are you calling me a liar, young man?" Peter said in a huff, insulted by the implication.

Charley looked at Jerry. The vampire stared back with that ever-present smile. Charley suddenly whipped the cross out of his pocket and held it up.

"If he's not a vampire," he cried, "then have him touch this."

He took a step toward Jerry even as the vampire edged back and Billy Cole began to launch himself at Charley, only to have Peter step up and snatch the cross out of the teen's hand.

"Charley, you've already made a fool of yourself once. There's no reason to compound the error."

"Yes, Charley," Jerry said, stiffening with barely suppressed rage. "You've already caused your friends quite enough pain."

He'd had quite enough of this boy. If he had to attack and tear him apart now, so be it. Of course, he'd be forced to do that to all his friends in the room, but the joy of killing his attacker would be justification enough. But he restrained himself, his eyes burning into the young man as he hammered his point home.

"You wouldn't want to cause them any more, would you?"

Charley watched him, seeing his body tense, coiling to spring. Billy Cole slid into place, blocking the doorway so that none of his friends, much less himself, could escape. The tension in the room became unbearable. Peter, Amy, and Evil were aware of it, although they missed the reason. They found it impossible to really believe that Jerry Dandrige, their charming host, was a supernatural creature.

"No, no, of course not," Charley said, his shoulders sagging in defeat as he realized that if he didn't defuse the situation, they were all going to die.

"And you're finally convinced I'm not a vampire either, right?" Jerry said, hammering the point home.

Their eyes locked, his and Charley's, the two staring at each other, both knowing the stakes.

A moment passed. Then, "Yes," Charley said with a hiss.

Jerry smiled at him and the tension rushed out of the room in a whoosh that all of them felt, even Billy Cole.

"Well, I'm glad that's settled," Jerry said as he ushered them toward the portico.

They all stopped before the front door, Billy Cole hanging in the background, keeping a careful watch as Jerry turned to Peter. "I can't tell you how much I appreciate this, Mr. Vincent. You've been a great help," he said.

"Not at all, Mr. Dandrige," Peter said, pleased at the praise. It was so nice to be appreciated. "Glad to be of service."

Jerry ignored Charley, turning to Amy and Evil Ed as Peter stepped back, reaching into his coat pocket for the cigarette case from his apartment. It was the very prop he'd kept from *Orgy of the Damned*. He brought it along, thinking the kids might get a thrill out of it. He opened it, fishing for a smoke, something he very seldom did but this felt like a celebratory moment. At last, he'd freed the boy from his mania about Jerry Dandrige, the charming host of this house.

Closer to the front door, Jerry was speaking to Amy and Evil Ed. "It's been very nice meeting both of you. Please, feel free to drop by anytime." His gaze singled Amy out, burning into her eyes. "You'll always be welcome," he said, willing her to do as he said and come back soon, perhaps even that night.

"I'd, I'd like that, Mr. Dandrige," Amy said, stumbling over her words as her eyes began to glaze over. She wasn't sure what was happening, but she felt like she was sinking into the other man's gaze.

"Please, call me Jerry," he said, his eyes still drilling into hers.

She was falling under his spell. They all did, but this one he particularly wanted. She reminded him of the girl in the portrait Charley had spotted earlier. Yes, from a different time, but he knew who she was, reborn once again, just for him.

Damn the curse that kept torturing him. This one, he would keep close. He would make sure she didn't die. He hoped.

Charley noticed Jerry looking at her in alarm, remembering the girl he saw in the window the other night before Jerry attacked her. She was totally passive, under his spell as he pushed her hair back and sank his fangs in her neck.

Amy was slipping away, just like her.

"C'mon, let's get out of here," he said, grabbing her arm and tugging her toward the front door.

Amy pulled away from him, falling into Jerry's gray eyes. Or were they green? They kept changing colors.

"Just a minute, Charley," she said, almost stepping forward and falling into Jerry's arms, and those eyes, oh, those eyes.

Behind them all, Peter had his cigarette out, about to tamp it down on a thumbnail and light it when he glanced at the mirror on the inside of the lid. He saw Amy, Evil Ed, and Charley grouped around where Jerry Dandrige should be standing — but he wasn't there. In the mirror, it was as though the kids were talking to thin air.

"The same goes for you, Ed," Jerry said, talking to Evil as he moved them toward the front door. "I suspect we have many of the same interests. You know, in such things as horror movies and the occult."

Peter's head jerked up and he looked at the doorway. Now, he saw Jerry standing there, talking to the young people. Peter looked back down at the mirror again. No Jerry. Peter's face went chalk white, and his jaw became unhinged as it dropped open. He gasped for air as the truth hit him, and he dropped the case to the hardwood floor with a crash.

Everyone turned and looked at him.

"Something wrong, Mr. Vincent?" Jerry said with a frown, taking note of his horrified expression.

Peter hurriedly scooped up the case, trying to hide his shaking hands and keep the tremor out of his voice.

"No, no, just my clumsiness." He had a quivering smile on his face.

"Are you sure?" Jerry asked.

"Oh, I am positive. Oh, look, we have been taking up much too much of your time. Thank you so much. Come along now, everybody," he said to the kids, herding them out the front door as quickly as he could.

His voice trailed back. "Thank you again, Mr. Dandrige, thank you," and they were gone.

Jerry looked after them, puzzled by Peter's sudden change in attitude. His frightened panic could also be described as terrified. Something had happened, but what?

42
BROKEN PIECES

Outside the house Peter plunged down the walk to his car, the kids hurrying to keep up with him. Charley rushed along with him, trying to make eye contact.

"What's wrong with you?" he said.

"Nothing," Peter said, wanting nothing so much as to be gone from there.

"Then why are you shaking?" Charley asked as they stopped by Peter's old Studebaker, the actor fumbling to get his keys out.

"I'm not shaking," Peter snapped, looking up, his hands shaking worse than ever.

He finally got the door open and hurriedly slid behind the wheel. Charley leaned down, yelling through the open window.

"You saw something in there, didn't you?" he said, "You saw something that convinced you he was a vampire?"

"Will you be quiet," Peter almost begged as he tried to fit the key into the ignition. In his panic, nothing was working.

But Charley wouldn't let go. "Is Jerry Dandrige a vampire or not?" he said, pushing for an answer, Amy and Evil Ed hanging by his side, hearing every word.

"No, no, of course not," Peter said as he turned the ignition.

The damn car wouldn't start. He'd probably flooded the engine. It only made him more desperate to be gone.

"Please, Mr. Vincent," Charley begged, "you have to tell me. Our lives depend on it."

"All right," Peter said, looking up, realizing the boy was right and his basic decency pushed through his panic. "He didn't cast a reflection in my mirror. Satisfied now?"

"Mr. Vincent, you have to call the police," Charley said, pushing even harder now. He needed help. He needed an adult to tell the police what he already knew. He needed Peter Vincent.

The engine finally caught and Peter roared away in a cloud of burning rubber without replying. Charley stood there, watching him go, so frustrated he almost screamed.

"Shit!" Charley yelled, stomping his foot and whirling because there was nothing else he could do.

Inside the house, Jerry and Billy peered out the window, watching the kids walk away from the house. "Looks just like her, doesn't she?" Jerry murmured to himself, his eyes on Amy. "I could teach her so much."

"What?" Billy Cole said, looking at him.

"She reminds me of my Maria," Jerry said.

Billy had seen the resemblance, but had hoped he'd been wrong. He knew of Jerry's curse and everything that came with it. They had met shortly after Jerry had wed Maria, so many centuries ago, and he knew that every time she had been reborn and found by the master, she would tragically be lost again. Could this callow girl really be her reborn?

"Are you sure she is her?" Billy asked.

"Not yet, but I will be before this is through," Jerry said, turning away and walking back toward the great staircase.

Billy followed with a smile. "One good thing, they'll never believe him now."

Crunch, something went under Jerry's foot, making him stop and look down. He bent and picked up a sliver of the mirror Peter broke, looking at it. Of course, he was not in the reflection. He held it up for Billy to see.

"No?" he said, putting the sliver on a table, his face tightening with determination and something else perhaps: blood lust. "Time to find out if she is my love reborn. And put an end to this troublesome group of young people."

"What about The Great Vampire Killer?" Billy asked, amused by the name.

"Him, too. Let's show him what a real vampire can do," Jerry replied. "Let's go."

With that, he started for the back of the house where their vehicle was parked. An equally grave Billy Cole followed.

43
THE LONG WALK HOME

The kids walked down the street, away from the Dandrige house. The darkness pressed in on them. Even the houses they passed were all dark, the inhabitants long ago asleep.

"Well, at least you two heard him," Charley said, trying to cheer himself up.

"Heard who?" Evil Ed asked.

"Peter Vincent. He said Dandrige had *no* reflection," Charley reminded him.

"Probably just a trick of the light," Evil Ed said, shrugging it off.

"You felt how evil Dandrige was, didn't you?" Charley asked Amy, looking for support. "Remember the way he looked at you?"

"Yes, sort of —" Amy said, confused by her memories. She did remember his eyes; they were so beautiful, but she didn't want to say that to Charley.

"Oh, for God's sake —" Evil groaned, bored with it all at this point. He turned, about to duck between two houses.

Charley shot him a look. "Where are you going?"

"Home," Evil said. "I'm hungry and the only thing open in this burg at this time of night is my fridge."

"Wait a minute," Charley said. "We walk Amy home first."

"Why?"

"Because it's after dark, pencil dick, and there's a vampire back there," Charley nodded over his shoulder.

"Oh, ahhhh," Evil laughed, looking down at his crotch before he looked up again. "Kid me all you want, Brewster," he said, "but you're still certifiable."

They kept walking, no one saying anything for the moment, all of them too overwhelmed by what they had experienced so far. Ten minutes, later they were strolling through downtown Rancho Corvallis. Not exactly a lot of tall buildings around, but a few. Street lamps cast pools of bright lights, making the shadows even deeper and darker. It didn't bother the kids. There were a few pedestrians out and a car passed every now and then, but not many.

Evil Ed came to a stop before a shadow-encrusted alleyway.

"Hey, let's cut through here," he said.

"Hey, no way," Charley said as he eyed it. "C'mon, we want people and lights. The more, the better."

"Ugh! Listen, Brewster," Evil Ed said, getting irritated, "vampires *don't* exist. Haven't you gotten that through your thick head yet?"

"What if you're wrong, Evil?" Charley asked. "What if Dandrige is a vampire and he *thinks* you know it? Would you walk down that alley then?"

The hair on the back of Evil's neck started to stand on end. No, his buddy was right. He wouldn't be happy about it, but he wasn't about to show him.

"Aw, fuck you, Brewster," he said and took a step toward the alley anyway.

"Look," Charley said, grabbing him. "C'mon, Evil, please. Just stick with us, okay?"

"Forget it! You may be chicken shit," Evil said, "but I'm not."

With that, he pulled free and disappeared into the darkness of the alley. Amy and Charley stared after him, not liking what he did, but not going into the shadows after him either.

"What do we do?" Amy asked with a worried frown.

"Let him go," Charley said, finally having had enough from his friend. "No vampire's gonna want him. Probably give him blood poisoning."

They were just turning away when there was a blood-curdling scream from the alley. Without thinking, they both charged headlong into the darkness, pounding down the narrow passageway only to skid to a halt on the slick pavement, looking around.

"Where is he?" Charley said.

Amy spotted Evil Ed lying crumpled against a brick wall. "Over here."

They dashed to his side. Evil's eyes were closed, his breathing shallow. Charley knelt, trying to shake him awake.

"Ed, Ed, are you all right?" he said. Nothing from the boy. Charley looked up at Amy. "Jesus, I warned him —"

Evil Ed's eyes suddenly snapped open, staring up wildly at Charley. "He got me, Charley. He bit me." He grabbed him by the collar, jerking him close. "You know what you're gonna have to do now, don't you?" Charley shook his head, staring at him, only inches away, really scared. "Kill me. Kill me, Charley. Before I turn into a vampire and..." he suddenly heaved himself at Charley, his mouth open, going for his throat as Charley tried to pull back, terrified, "give you a hickey!" he yelled in his startled friend's face.

He suddenly let Charley go, rolling on the pavement and

laughing like a maniac, perfectly all right. Charley sprung to his feet, furious with him.

"You asshole!" he yelled at him, his voice echoing down the alley.

Ed rolled on the ground in hysterics, pointing and laughing at him. "Ha-ha, really fooled you." He finally climbed to his feet, dusting himself off, enjoying Charley having fallen for it. "You really believed me, you poor dope!"

"You're gonna get yours someday, Evil," Charley said, flushed with anger.

He grabbed Amy by the hand and dragged her back down the alley toward the streets and the welcoming lights. Evil Ed stood behind them, yelling after them.

"Oh, yeah? When? When I'm bit by a vampire? There are no such things as vampires, fruit cake!"

Still chuckling to himself, he turned in the opposite direction and disappeared down the alley into the darkness. A moment passed. Silence and more silence. Then, suddenly, somebody was looking down at him from the fire escape above — or something. Until it took to the air and somersaulted through the air, landing in the alley below and straightening. It was a man and he looked behind him, in the direction that Amy and Charley had taken.

It was Jerry Dandrige, looking cooler and more in control than ever. With a smile, he turned back and started down the alley — after Evil Ed.

44
DEAD END

Evil Ed walked through the alley, knowing the street was not very far ahead. The last thing on his mind was vampires. He'd discarded that silly notion along with his friendship with Charley, at least for tonight. He figured Charley would be over his anger at him by tomorrow in school, and if he wasn't, he could deal with it. There were so many kids who thought he was weird with his love of horror. They just forgot he loved it for the fun it provided; not because he believed in any of it.

There was something else, too, if he was honest with himself. And he hated being honest with himself, especially about his other feelings. He wasn't like Charley. He liked girls, but as people, not as females he wanted to have sex with. Nobody would have given him credit for his level of sophistication and with good reason; he kept it hidden, but he'd come to realize he was different. It was 1985 and being gay wasn't cool. He wasn't even sure he was gay, but he didn't lust after girls like his schoolmates. Yeah, some were cool to hang with, but he didn't slobber after them with the hope of making out and feeling them up.

No, he felt those things were for other boys. Not that he wanted to kiss Charley. He didn't. Too boring, but he'd gone with his parents to San Francisco a number of times and seen gay men. You couldn't miss them, a lot of them anyway, and he'd felt their eyes on him. He hadn't looked back, but once, the last year or so, he hadn't been so shy. He could see what they were offering in their appraising glances and it excited him. He just wasn't sure what to do about it.

No, that wasn't true. He knew what to do about it; he just wasn't ready. But Jerry Dandrige had been different. The way he'd looked at Amy, Ed was sure he was attracted to her. He could see Charley stiffening as he noticed, too. Jerry was fascinating, beautiful in a way no other man had ever been to Evil, but he hadn't seemed to notice him. Then he had turned that piercing gaze on him and mentioned how they shared mutual interests, perhaps even in horror. But there had been something under it, something Ed couldn't identify. He liked him, liked how he looked, no, it was more than that, but what? Ed supposed he'd learn in time. Jerry wasn't a vampire, but he was someone he was pretty sure he'd meet again. It was in the man's eyes and truth be told, Ed had been attracted to him.

He was so cool, he thought admiringly.

Then he heard the footsteps behind him, coming through the dark, slowly catching up to him, deliberate footsteps, slightly faster than his own. He stopped and looked back. He couldn't see anything.

"Charley, Amy, that you?" he called out.

He heard nothing in return except the footsteps, now quickly gaining on him. The fear started to work at him, twisting up in his guts and making his forehead glisten with sweat. Vampires couldn't be for real. That guy, Jerry Dandrige, he couldn't be a creature of the night. Not someone that handsome. He couldn't have followed them.

Could he?

He stepped forward, yelling out with false bravado. "If that's you, it isn't working. I'm not scared!"

But he was. The footsteps were getting louder and closer. Then, Jerry emerged out of the shadows, smiling at him as he came, like Ed was some delicacy he was about to taste.

Oh, shit, went through Evil's mind. *He's for real. He is a vampire.* He whirled and raced down the alley in the opposite direction. As he did so, he glanced over his shoulder. Jerry Dandrige was closer to him, still walking at the same steady pace. But how could that be? Evil was running, but Jerry was still walking. Another glance and he was closer still.

It was crazy, it couldn't be. But it was.

Evil picked up his pace, running like he never had before, smashing into a pile of metal garbage cans and going down with a clatter. He leaped to his feet, ignoring the pain in his skinned hands and bruised knees, and taking off again, running for his life and knowing that was exactly what he was doing.

He had to escape or he was dead and maybe not in a good way if Jerry needed another slave. That's what Billy Cole was, Evil knew it for sure in that moment, and he didn't want to be anybody's slave, especially not that of a blood sucking vampire.

Was that what he was? Had to be. It was the only explanation for the way he was gaining on him without ever changing his pace.

He suddenly skidded to a halt, facing a tall brick wall. There was no way over it or under it. He was in a blind alley. He whirled, looking back the way he came. Thick fog obscured his view. Then, it reversed direction, as if there was a huge wind machine sucking it back toward him. Evil took a step forward to see better, and at that moment, Jerry Dandrige stepped out of the darkness behind him where there was nothing but a brick wall. It was certainly no way for a man, supernatural or not, to appear. Yet there he was.

He leaned down and whispered in Evil's ear. "Hello, Edward."

Evil whirled with a scream to find Jerry standing right next to him. Almost insane with fear now, slobbering like a wounded animal, he backed away from the shadowy figure, hitting the other side of the brick wall, and sliding to the cold pavement. He curled up in a fetal ball, tears streaming from his eyes. He was ashamed of himself, but he couldn't stop it.

Dandrige stepped over to him, staring down with something like pity in his eyes or revulsion; Evil wasn't sure.

"You don't have to be afraid of me," he said in a voice that flowed like honey. "I understand what it's like being different. Only they won't pick on you anymore or beat you up. I'll see to that." He paused. Now Evil could see sympathy in those gray eyes, caring even. "All you have to do is take my hand."

He reached down to Evil, a slight smile on his face, gentle, seductive, and beguiling. "Here, Edward," he repeated. "Take my hand."

Evil looked up at the hand outstretched to him. It was beautiful, perfectly shaped with thin elegant fingers, almost womanly, with nails impossibly long, perfectly shaped, and tapering to five gleaming, razor sharp points.

Evil Ed slowly reached out, he couldn't help himself, and took the vampire's hand. Jerry smiled down and slowly lifted him into the last embrace Edward Thompson would ever know — as an air-breathing human being anyway.

A long cloak swept over him, burying both of them in blackness. A sharp puncturing sound as fangs sank deep into Evil's neck was heard and then his scream broke out and echoed down the alley — which subsided into sobs of pure ecstasy.

45
ON THE RUN

Charley and Amy walked rapidly along the street, heading toward Amy's house. Charley cut a glance at her. "How much farther?"

"About ten minutes," she answered.

A scream, long and high-pitched, reached their ears, only to suddenly come to a sharp end. It could have been either a death rattle or a cry of ecstasy. It was crazy, she couldn't tell which, but it *echoed* through the town streets, down alleyways, across apartment buildings, and past houses, faint yet filled with so much terror it stopped them cold and left them staring fearfully at the shadows.

"What was that?" Charley said.

"It was just Evil messing around again," said Amy, not because she was so sure, but because she wanted to reassure the two of them. She raised her head and yelled back into the darkness. "Cut it out Evil! It's not funny!"

Her voice bounced off the walls and down the street and then died, leaving them staring at the darkness. They were both trying to act brave and failing.

"C'mon," Amy said and grabbed his hand, the two of them starting down the street again.

Charley glanced nervously over his shoulder as they walked. "Amy, what if Evil was really in trouble?" he said.

"Charley," she said, "you're not gonna let him sucker you in again, are you?"

All the street lights suddenly went out, up and down the street, plunging them into almost total blackness. They whirled, looking around, slowly backing away from the darkness, only to find themselves in more blackness.

"Don't tell me," Charley said in a hoarse whisper, "this is a power outage."

"Well, what else would it be?" Amy said, just as scared as he was.

He stopped with a jerk, grabbed her and nodded at a light pole opposite them. There was a transformer on the pole and its front had been ripped open. They could see claw marks dug deep into the metal. The wires inside had been shredded and it was fitfully sparking.

Before they could even gasp at the sight, huge bat wings beat overhead, and a shadow flew across the building wall opposite them.

That's all it took. They whirled and dashed down the street, running for all they were worth. Within moments, they were under a bridge and panting their way up the hill to it. They started to cross, slowing to a fast walk as they gasped for breath, feeling safer if only because houses and tall buildings weren't crowding them anymore.

"I think we lost him," Charley said.

"Yeah," Amy said, stopping and turning to him, her face wreathed with guilt and regretfulness. "Charley, you were right about the holy water. We faked it. I paid Peter Vincent to be there tonight. I'm so sorry I didn't believe you."

"It's all right, Amy," he said.

Just hearing her say she believed him now was an enormous relief to him after what he had been through. He had even doubted his own sanity, but no more. No, no more. He kissed her and took her hand and they began their walk across the bridge.

"We've got it made," he began to say only to stop with another gasp.

There, high above them on one of the arches of the bridge, so high nobody could possibly get there unless they flew, stood Jerry Dandrige. He was staring down at them, a solitary unmoving figure with a gray leather overcoat, framed against the moonlight. Without waiting, the two teens whirled and dashed off the bridge and down the street.

But there was no way they could feel safe this time. They turned the first corner, only to skid to a halt. There, standing on the sidewalk, was Jerry Dandrige. He was smiling, amused by the horror on their faces.

"Run!" Charley cried and they whirled, racing down the street in the opposite direction.

They whipped around another corner, only to jerk to a halt again. There stood Jerry Dandrige once more, smiling at them. He took a casual step toward them and they turned, diving down a side street, anywhere to get away from him.

They started to stagger with the effort of running non-stop, only to see the neon sign of Club Radio at the end of the street. Rancho Corvallis' first and only night club, they'd opened recently to cater the growing influx of 20 somethings and tourists looking for late night kicks. Its entrance was jammed with people waiting to get in, all of them dressed to the nines in whatever the fashion magazines told them was hip to wear.

"Over there," Charley gasped, dragging Amy toward the club just as Jerry appeared down the street behind them, walking after them with a steady relaxed gait, in no hurry, a hunter sure of his kill.

They reached the crowd around the entrance, fighting their way through them to the front door where they met a bouncer checking ID's and collecting the cover charge. He hardly gave them a glance as the two breathless teens stepped up.

"Five bucks apiece," he said.

Charley frantically searched his pockets and came up with change and nothing else. Why hadn't he thought to bring money? Because he couldn't think about anything else but exposing Jerry Dandrige and killing him. Now, he was fleeing him with Amy and needing shelter and he was dead broke.

Amy pulled out a ten-dollar bill. "I've got it," she said and gave it to him.

She was keeping an eye on the street and wondering where Jerry Dandrige was going to show up next. She was sure he was after *her*. She knew that from the way he had looked at her in the house and the tug she had felt when their gazes met.

What did that gaze mean? She shuddered with a combination of fear and expectation and then banished it from her mind.

Charley took the money only to spot Jerry moving his way through the crowd toward them.

He shoved the money at the bouncer hurriedly. "Here..."

The man took it and Charley grabbed Amy, pulling her toward the door, watching over his shoulder as Jerry closed in on them, but they were going to make it. They were going to get inside where there were a lot of people and Jerry couldn't afford to cause a scene.

Suddenly, the bouncer reached out and collared Charley, Amy with him. "Just a sec. How old are you two?"

"Eighteen, both of us" Charley lied, his eyes on Jerry who was now only a few people away.

"Let me see some ID," the bouncer said, doing his job.

Charley glanced back, about to make a run for it without flashing ID he didn't have. Jerry was only an arm's length away now, about to grab Amy which would make Charley stay, trying to defend her, even though he was sure he'd lose.

Just as the vampire's hand was about to close in on her, a man suddenly shouldered him aside.

"Hey, wait your turn," the guy said, not having a clue who he was dealing with.

Jerry stopped and stared at him. Whatever the man saw in his eyes gave him the cold sweats and he backed hurriedly away. Charley used the moment to yank Amy down the street, the entrance to the club forgotten in his panic to be away from Jerry.

"Hey, what about your money?" the bouncer yelled after them, but Charley was no longer listening.

All he wanted was the two of them out of there and away from the vampire.

They emerged from the crowd, backing away from the entrance as Jerry emerged, stepping after them. He was only a dozen feet or so away now, smiling as he approached, both Charley and Amy realizing it was futile to run at this point. They continued to back away, crossing the mouth of an alley.

There was a *crash* of a garbage pail and Charley glanced down the alley to see a dish washer from the club dumping garbage, the bright lights of the door into the club kitchen spilling into the alley like a beacon in the night. Charley grabbed Amy's hand and ran down the alley.

He and Amy burst through the door, racing through the madhouse of the kitchen as one of the cooks looked up from chopping lettuce.

"Hey, you can't go in there," the chef yelled, waving his butcher knife at them.

But it was too late for him. They burst through the door to find themselves in a packed video disco with four huge screens overlooking the floor. All of them were synced to play the video of whatever song the crowd was dancing to.

Charley and Amy disappeared into the heaving crowd of dancers. A moment later, the cook appeared from the kitchen, signaling a bouncer circling the floor, keeping a wary eye out for trouble.

At the same time, Charley and Amy fought their way through the sea of dancers while Charley looked about. He saw a sign above a hallway reading "Restrooms and Phone." He dragged Amy in that direction. On the balcony above the dance floor, the cook could be seen gesturing to the bouncer, pointing in their direction.

Charley and Amy broke through the crowd and down a short hallway to a bank of pay phones opposite the restrooms. Charley dug a dime out of his pocket, dropped it in the slot, and dialed.

"Who are you calling?" Amy yelled to make herself heard above the din of pulsating music.

"The police," Charley yelled back, only to speak loudly into the receiver. "Yes, give me Lt. Lennox, please. It's an emergency. I have information about the murdered girls."

In the Corvallis Police Station, Lt. Art Lennox reacted immediately when the dispatcher called him, picking up the phone and answering.

"Lennox here," he said quickly.

"It's Charley Brewster," Charley said from the club. "I'm the kid you met at Jerry Dandrige's house, the one next to mine."

"Yeah, right," Lennox said, concentrating, trying to hear over the throbbing music in the background. "Where are you?"

"Club Radio. My girl and I are inside, trying to escape Jerry Dandrige. He followed us in here and he's hunting us right now."

"What?" Det. Lennox said, trying to understand.

This was the same kid who'd made a fool of him the day before with his crazy story about a vampire in a coffin in the house next door. The roommate thought he was crazy. So did Art.

"You've got to believe me," Charley said, his voice choked with desperation. "He is a vampire. He's awake and now he's after me and my girl."

"Listen, you nut case," Art said, having had more than enough of the kid. "We're dealing with real murders here by a very real killer. They don't have anything to do with vampires and if you call me again, I'm going to arrest you!"

In a fury, he slammed the phone down and sat there, steaming. *This kid just will not give up,* he thought. *He must really be crazy.* Still, this felt like more than just some kid's wild fantasy. He could hear it in the Brewster kid's voice; he sounded genuinely scared. He really believed what he was saying. Vampires? He needed a shrink, not a cop. With that, he tried to go back to work, which wasn't easy.

The kid had really upset him.

Inside Club Radio, Charley turned back to Amy, his face swept with hopelessness.

"He didn't believe me."

"What do we do now?" Amy asked, looking down the hallway at the sea of dancers on the floor, afraid that she was going to see Jerry Dandrige at any moment.

"I'm going to call again. Maybe the Chief of Police," Charley said and dropped another dime while Amy watched the dance floor.

She suddenly realized with a start that she was wishing Jerry did appear. Something had happened in his house when they had met and he'd kissed her hand. Something unlike anything she'd ever experienced before. She wanted him, she realized, just like he wanted her. But what did that mean? Wanted what?

Maybe Charley was right, she thought. *Maybe Jerry Dandrige was a vampire and had power over her. Could that be true? What was she going to do when they met? What?*

But she didn't hear an answer in her head, just the question she kept asking herself again and again. What, what, what???

46

EVIL AWAKENS

Ed Thompson's eyes suddenly popped open and he found himself staring up at the night sky. He sat up to find himself at the end of the blind alley, right where Jerry had left him.

His eyes widened as he remembered. He had taken his hand and Jerry had drawn him into his arms. It was the first time he had willingly embraced another man. He saw hope and caring, perhaps even love, in those smoky gray eyes, and as he had thrown his cape over him, covering him in darkness, Edward had willingly offered his neck.

It was then he had felt the fangs slipping into his neck and sucking his blood and with it had come feelings of ecstasy, but not death. At the same time, Jerry had sliced his palm and pressed it to Ed's mouth. Without thinking, he had greedily sucked at it even as Jerry was drinking his blood from his neck.

Then, he had slipped into the blackness of a coma, only to awaken now.

He stood up and, as he did so, he felt the difference in his body. It was a surge of strength, of vitality, and of powers that he could only dream about. But no more. Perhaps, he even had those powers now.

He raised a hand, looking at it, realizing his body would change if he willed it. He did so. He wanted to be a vampire. He embraced it. He wanted to revel in it. His hand began to transform with the nails elongating, the palm turning gray with a scaly hide, and something poking out of his clothes on his back.

He was startled to realize they were the beginning of wings. He could transform into a bat if he willed it. Indeed, he was no longer simply Ed Thompson. Oh, no. He was now truly "Evil" Ed Thompson, and with that realization, a command filtered into his consciousness.

His master had told him to find and kill Peter Vincent. To attack the horrid old fool of an actor and show him what a vampire truly was; one who would drink his blood until he was but an empty vessel. He knew where he lived already. After all, he and Amy had been there only a few hours earlier when they had ask him to convince Charley that Jerry Dandrige was not a vampire.

Ed giggled. How silly they had been. It seemed so long ago, but now he was to have the opportunity to exercise his newfound powers. Not as a bat. No, that was too clumsy. He would go another way, riding the night breeze to Peter Vincent's. He raised his hands high in the air, stiffening his body as if he wanted to reach out to the moon, and, as he did so, his body began to dissolve into a stack of gray smoke.

As he finished the transition, he rose into the air and was picked up by the breeze which wafted him across town toward a certain four-story brick apartment building he still remembered.

Peter Vincent, the great vampire hunter lived within, and soon he would face a real vampire. Him, Evil Ed Thompson.

47
CLUB RADIO

Charley slammed the phone back in place, more frustrated than ever. Amy was watching him worriedly.

"The police don't believe me," he said.

"I'm scared, Charley," Amy said, sinking back against the wall. "I'm *really* scared."

"I won't let him get you, Amy," Charley said, touching her shoulder and looking at her with a worried frown. "I promise you."

"We haven't got a chance, Charley," Amy said, looking up at him. "Not the two of us against *him.*" She suddenly thought of someone else that might help them. "What about your mother? Call her."

"She can't handle this, Amy," he said with a shake of his head, only to think of another person. "You got Peter Vincent's number?"

"He doesn't care about us," she said, looking away. "I told you. I paid him to be there tonight."

"It doesn't matter, Amy. We don't have any choice. Now, give me his number."

She reluctantly dug a piece of paper out of her pocket as Charley dropped another dime.

Outside the club, Jerry stood at the edge of the crowd, thinking how panicked Charley and Amy must be inside. He wasn't worried. There was no way they were escaping him, not that he was concerned with the boy. He was an annoyance, nothing more.

It was Amy he wanted. Jerry's thoughts raced. *Could she be his one true love reborn? His love down through the centuries? Could she have come back in the person of a teenage girl in small town America? Could it be his curse taunting him once more and in the most banal of ways?*

He would have to see. With that, he started for the entrance to the club, shoving people out of his way. A few went to object, but then they caught a glimpse of his dark enraged face and decided it was best to step out of his way and keep their mouths shut.

Good move.

Inside the short hallway in the club, Charley stood at the phone, Amy beside him, watching anxiously as he listened to the phone ring on the other end.

"C'mon, Mr. Vincent," he said, "answer. Please, answer."

Unseen by either of them, Jerry appeared on the balcony above, overlooking the dance floor. He slowly came down the steps to the party goers below. With eyes glowing a faint red, he reached the main floor and disappeared among the dancers.

At the same time, Peter Vincent sat in his apartment, staring at the ringing phone, terrified to pick it up and answer. It kept ringing, mocking his fear.

Inside the hallway, Charley turned his back to the dance floor, trying to hear better if Peter should dare to pick up.

"Answer me, damn it," he said, urging the vampire hunter to pick up. "Answer me, please."

Behind him, Amy stiffened, staring out onto the dance floor at the sea of heaving people. Moving through the dancers, like a golden god among mere mortals, walked Jerry Dandrige. The hot colored lights hung on the ceiling above highlighted his hair, accentuating his gracefulness, making him seem even more beautiful.

Amy lost him in the crush a good twenty feet away and stepped further out of the hall for a better look, only to be stopped as Jerry appeared right in front of her. She hadn't seen him approach that close. He held his hand out to her, the orgiastic song "A Good Man in a Bad Time" washing over both of them. His eyes burned into hers, willing her to come with him.

Terrified, Amy turned back toward Charley. At that moment, Jerry disappeared from the mouth of the hallway. Amy glanced back as she was about to grab Charley, only to see he was gone.

She stopped, more intrigued than frightened, by the beautiful man holding out his hand toward her. She took a step forward, continuing down the hall until she had a clear view of the dancers again.

Jerry was nowhere to be seen.

Behind her, Charley was just about to look in her direction when a voice answered on the other end of the payphone.

"Yes?" said Peter Vincent.

Charley cupped one hand over his ear, bending down to hear better. Behind him, Amy disappeared onto the dance floor.

"Mr. Vincent, this is Charley Brewster," he said into the phone. "You gotta help us. Jerry Dandrige has me and Amy trapped in this club —"

In his apartment, Peter moved to the window, the phone in his hand. He pulled back the curtain, peering down at the street below.

"I'm sorry, Charley," he said, trying to stop the quiver in his voice. "I can't do that."

"But you have to, Mr. Vincent," Charley begged. "Please, you're the only one who knows what's really going on."

"You have to understand, Charley. They're more powerful than I'll ever be." Peter turned away from the window, pacing the room with the phone. "If I go out now, Jerry Dandrige will kill me for sure."

"If you don't," Charley yelled, almost in tears, "Dandrige will kill us!"

Charley spun about, trying to figure out what to say to convince Peter, so desperate he didn't even realize that Amy was gone.

"I'm sorry, Charley," Peter said, almost in tears himself. "I just can't."

With that, he hung up the phone, sinking into his easy chair, his shoulders slumped forward, and his hands covering his face in total defeat. He couldn't stand himself and what he'd just done, but he couldn't help it. He didn't want to be killed by a vampire. He knew what that would be like. He'd done enough movies about it. More terrible than being dead was a living death, an eternal living death under the control of the one that had supped on your blood.

In the club hallway, Charley slammed the phone down, turning to Amy. "Damn it! He won't help us —" he began, only to realize Amy was gone, and the hallway empty.

48

EDWARD?

There was a knock at Peter's locked and chained door. He slowly rose from his chair, a cross clenched tightly in his hand, terrified. After he'd fled Charley and the other two teens, he'd hurried home, meaning to pack his bags and flee. He had Amy's five hundred dollars, not that it would get him that far, but at least back to the city. He could take shelter there. Perhaps, Dandrige wouldn't be able to find him in the mass of people.

However, he'd only gotten as far as pulling his bag from the closet and opening it on his bed when he was assaulted by guilt. He was being a coward, totally and hopelessly, and that made everything he'd thought of himself a lie.

Then, Charley had called him from that dance club and really put it to him. He and Amy were trapped inside and Jerry Dandrige was after them. Peter had to come and save them, but he hadn't had the nerve to even leave his apartment.

He wasn't The Great Vampire Killer. He was a coward, through and through, and finally had to admit it to himself. He was an aging washed-up actor that nobody, certainly not Hollywood, wanted. Worse, he was fleeing and leaving three teenagers to face the most powerful and terrifying of supernatural beasts, a vampire.

He'd thought they weren't real, and that none of that horror nonsense was, but now he'd suddenly found out he was wrong, and he was as afraid as any civilian would be.

His whole life was a lie and he couldn't stand himself. Instead of fleeing, he'd sunk in his chair in despair and deep despondency.

Knock, knock, knock it came again. Who was out there? Jerry Dandrige, about to make sure he never talked, or perhaps that servant of his, the huge hulking muscle-bound Billy Cole?

Knock, knock, knock. Well, he could stay there in the dim light or go and answer it. Better to find out his fate than to wallow in self-pity.

As the knocking came again, he crossed over to the door and called out, "All right, I'm coming."

He stopped before the door, his hand raising to unlock it and fling it open when he thought better of such a vainglorious gesture. Better to be careful so he could prepare himself for whatever was on the other side.

"Who is it?" he asked, putting his lips close to the door and whispering.

"Me, Evil Ed," came the voice from the hall.

Oh, my God, thank you, his mind said, but he was still cautious. "What do you want?" he asked.

"There's a vampire out here. Let me in," came the answer.

Oh, no, the boy was in danger! Peter shoved the cross back in his pocket, unchained the door, threw the lock, and opened it. He pulled Evil Ed into the room, hurriedly locking and chaining the door behind. He whirled to face him, only to hesitate.

Something was wrong. The boy had changed, and not for

the better. His skin was sallow and there were huge dark circles under his eyes. His lips were bloodless, and his collar was turned up tightly about his neck. He looked sick, very sick.

"What are we going to do?" Peter said in a burst. "Jerry Dandrige *is* a vampire. I made a terrible mistake and put you all in danger."

"What are *you* gonna do? Not me!" Evil said with a disconcerting eagerness, as though he knew something the older actor didn't.

Peter stared at his nasty grin, at a loss for words for once. Evil Ed slowly reached up and pulled down the collar of his shirt, revealing two small reddish puncture wounds on his neck. They had definitely not closed yet.

Peter's eyes widened in horror. Evil Ed's smile only grew wider.

"I used to admire you, you know that?" he said. "Of course, that was before I found out what a fake you were."

He advanced on Peter, looming over him for he was an inch taller. Peter stared up at the boy in growing mute terror. Evil Ed smiled at him, revealing two huge sparkling white fangs.

Peter whirled for the door, fumbling to undo the chain and lock. He wanted out of there and away from the horrid teen. Evil Ed watched, his rictus grin just growing wider.

"Peter Vincent, The Great Vampire Killer, indeed," he laughed and with that, he grabbed Peter from behind, opening his mouth wide to sink his fangs deep into his neck.

Peter straightened, grabbing the cross from his pocket and slamming it into the boy's forehead between his eyes. The teen's skin crackled and sizzled, and smoke rose until Evil Ed pulled away from the cross, taking strands of skin with it. He screamed in ear shattering pain as his hands held to his face.

He slowly looked up as Peter watched, frozen in horror. Evil dropped his hands, revealing a smoking sign of the cross branded into his forehead. Peter could only stare at him, open-mouthed.

"What have you done to me?" Evil Ed wailed.

He turned to look at himself in the wall mirror, but, of course, there was no reflection for him to see. He whirled on Peter, screaming like the spoiled brat he was.

He took a step toward the actor, his hands no longer hands, but now claws with long deadly fingernails, coming up to attack. Peter thrust the cross at him, as smoking pieces of his flesh still clung to it.

"Back," Peter commanded.

Evil Ed took a step back, recoiling at the sight. Peter advanced on him, and Evil backed across the room.

"The Master will kill you for this," Evil said, spitting his venom at the older man, "but not fast. No, slowly. Oh, so slowly..."

Peter continued forward, the cross held out with his shaking hand, backing Evil toward the window.

"Back, I say! Back!" Peter kept repeating.

Evil Ed snarled like some trapped feral animal and suddenly spun about, throwing himself headlong out the window in an explosion of glass and torn drapes. Peter rushed to the window, staring down at the street below.

Nothing to be seen, certainly not a body. Far above, he heard the flapping of wings, signaling Evil Ed undoubtedly escaping. He knew if he was shapeshifting, he was now a fully made vampire, a gift from Jerry Dandrige.

Peter drew his head back in, leaning against the wall, gasping for breath, with his hand on his heart, feeling it about to leap out of his chest.

He didn't know what to do. He couldn't leave. He'd never

escape anyway. Not now that he knew Jerry Dandrige was really a vampire. And he couldn't fight him, not really. He wasn't strong enough; he'd lose.

What could he do?

49
BACK AT CLUB RADIO

Amy was gone. Where was she?

Charley rushed out onto the jammed dance floor, looking about in the crush of people. Nothing. He didn't see Amy, but she had to be there. She had to be. He plunged into the crowd, weaving in and out among the dancers, as he searched for her.

He passed a bunch of drunken teenagers his own age, none of whom he knew, accidentally bumping into a table. A man looked up, yelling at him angrily.

"Hey, asshole, watch out!"

Charley looked down. The man was snorting up lines of white powder. Charley had never used it; he didn't do drugs of any kind, but he knew what the powder was. He was a junior in high school. How could he not? But what did that say about Club Radio? What kind of a place was it? He already knew the answer. An "anything goes" kind of place.

Across the dance floor, hidden from Charley by the swirling crush of dancers, Jerry Dandrige came to a halt with Amy, holding up her hands, looking down at her with a smile. She felt the cold touch of his hands and tried to pull away, but he held her firm. As she looked up, and their eyes met, a wave of pleasure passed through her, given away by a flickering smile on her face. The two of them stood still among the twirling dancers. The music changed to a new song, "Come to Me." They began to dance, gentle, close, and oblivious to the other dancers. His eyes never released hers. Amy no longer felt the chilling touch of his hands, only a mounting desire for his caress.

Across the club, Charley hurried by a wall of people, men and women, young and older, standing self-consciously about, eying anyone who passed. Charley spotted a girl who looked from the back to be Amy's age.

"Pardon me," he said, "have you seen a girl, light-haired —?"

The woman swung about, revealing herself to be well into her sixties, if not past it. She was dressed like a teenager, but years of sun worship and cigarettes had given her skin a leathery appearance. She gave him a yellow-toothed smile, displaying a desperate need for dental work.

"Forget her. Take me instead," she said, licking flaccid lips.

She reached out to kiss Charley who fled into the flesh watchers, most of whom laughed at him.

On the dance floor, someone bumped Amy as she danced with Jerry, bringing her back to her senses for a moment. She whirled to move away. He stepped forward, his movement confident and languid, laying a single hand on her shoulder. She stopped with a jerk as he came up behind her, taking both her hands and crossing them in front of her, and holding her in his arms from the back.

They began to move in unison, him behind her, moving his body with hers, and his pelvis rubbing against her. Her eyes widened with the desire he was awakening in her.

Across the dance floor, Charley stopped in front of several

masculine women, several of them much more feminine than the others.

"I'm looking for a girl..." Charley began.

"So am I," replied one of the women, dressed in black leather and silver chains, with the hint of a mustache on her upper lip.

The other women broke into laughter, as a girly girl embraced and kissed her deeply. Charley backed away. This wasn't what he was looking for at all. What was going on in Rancho Corvallis? The town was so boring. Or was supposed to be. He bumped into a heavy metal biker, a bushy-faced male who wore a knuckle duster across one clenched hand. He was the kind of guy who worshiped Judas Priest.

The biker pushed Charley roughly, sending him stumbling into several step dancers who pushed him again, sending him stumbling like a cue ball banking wildly off every side of a pool table.

They were all laughing at him as Charley regained his balance and fled to the stairs to the balcony above, stopping several steps up, searching the heaving crowd of dancers as the music continued to throb.

Toward the other side, the dancers spun about. Jerry and Amy, still in their own world, fixated on each other as she turned into his arms, and slid down his body. He looked down with that smile which never seemed to leave him, and took her hands to lift her back to her feet.

Her hair seemed to have changed. It looked more daring, slicked back, revealing the smooth curve of her, oh, so white, delicious neck. It was the same with her clothes; teenage cotton transformed into womanly silk, making her that much more desirous. How was all this happening? Who knew? They were both falling into each other as he leaned down, his mouth opening.

Her head jerked back, looking up at him, now denying him her neck, and they started to whirl once more, their arms wrapped around each other.

Then, Charley caught a glimpse of them, rushing down the stairs and pushing his way through a clot of dancers. He saw them, appearing and disappearing on the floor, Amy dancing with Jerry. He weaved his way through the dancers, working his way toward them.

On the floor, Amy moved with Jerry; their bodies were locked together now. She was slowly falling into his eyes once more, dancing slower and slower with him until finally she had no will left of her own. She was now madly in love with him. It was at that moment that she looked up and pulled back the collar of her blouse, exposing the smooth whiteness of her neck to him once more, this time without reserve.

He smiled and for the moment ignored her offer as he spun her slowly about, her eyes gazing at the wall of mirrors they were passing. For his part, he bent down toward her exposed neck, his mouth opening to kiss her. It was then that Amy saw her reflection in the mirrors against the wall; *she was dancing alone.*

Shocked back to her senses, she went rigid in Jerry's arms, looking up to see the exposed fangs in his mouth. She tried to pull away from him, screaming as the music ended with a sudden crescendo and dancers came to a welcomed halt for a moment's breath.

"Charley!" Amy called loudly.

Across the dance floor, Charley heard her scream and pushed his way through the sea of humanity, fighting his way to her side where she stood with Jerry, once again caught in his eyes. Charley grabbed Jerry by the shoulder, trying to pull him away from Amy.

"Let her go!" he said in a fury.

Jerry, the taller man, looked down at him, mocking him with a smile as the music started again and Amy swayed in his arms, her eyes locked adoringly on his handsome face.

"What's wrong, Charley?" the vampire said. "Jealous?"

He ground his pelvis against Amy, dry humping her in front of Charley. She threw her head back, her mouth opening in something close to ecstasy, giving herself to him as she cocked her head to one side once more, exposing her tender young throat.

"You filthy son-of-a —" Charley said, rage and jealousy hammering him.

He swung at him only to have Jerry release Amy, easily catching the teen's fist in the palm of his hand. He stared at the boy.

"You shouldn't lose your temper, Charley," he said with that same cool smile. "It isn't polite."

He tightened his grip, slowly squeezing Charley's closed fist. The bones in his hand ground together in a horrible sound. Charley's face contorted in agony, driving him to his knees before Jerry. The teen looked up at the vampire, tears of pain streaming down his face.

"You can't kill me here —" he said, gasping in pain.

"I don't want to kill you, Charley," Jerry said, leaning down to look him more closely in the face. "I want you to bring Peter Vincent to my house, just the two of you. That is, if you ever want to see Amy again."

He shoved Charley, forcing the teen to the floor, and disappeared into the swirling mass of dancers with Amy. Charley struggled back to his feet, ignoring the pain in his hand, and plunged after them.

Charley broke free of the swirl near the bar, looking every-

TOM HOLLAND

where and not seeing either of them. Suddenly, he was grabbed by a strong pair of arms. He looked up to find himself staring into the face of a huge bouncer, who looked like he was a guard in the NFL.

"Let me go," Charley said, struggling desperately and not able to loosen the man's grip.

"Hey, Donny, this the one?" the man called, ignoring him.

Another bouncer, the one the cook talked to and just as big, if not bigger than the other one, broke out of the dancers, staring at the teen.

"Yeah, it's him," he said with a nod. "Where's your girlfriend?"

Charley suddenly saw Jerry and Amy breaking through the crowd, heading for a stairway. He shook free of the man holding him, pointing after them.

"That's her, there with the older guy," he said.

"C'mon," Donny said to the other man, and they cut across the floor to intercept Jerry and Amy.

The former NFL bouncer dragged Charley with him. They broke through a gaggle of people, blocking Jerry's way. Donny jerked Amy out of Jerry's hands, passing her to the other bouncer, nodding at her and Charley.

"Get the two of them out of here," he ordered.

Jerry stepped toward, his face beginning to darken. The music pulsated around them, oblivious people swirling by on all sides.

"She's mine," Jerry said.

Donny put out a hand, stopping Jerry as the other bouncer dragged Charley and Amy toward the front door.

"You want chicken, man," Donny said, "you go someplace else."

Jerry snarled, his eyes beginning to glow, and his hair slicking back. The hint of fangs protruded over his lower lip as

206

rage overtook him. He raised his right hand, holding it out in front of him so the bouncer could clearly see what was happening. The nails on the four fingers popped out, literally elongating several inches in front of the man's startled eyes. They were now razor-sharp claws that sparkled in the overhead lights that spun off the walls and floor.

The bouncer, no fool, screamed for his companion. "Hey, Leon! Get back here!"

Toward the entrance, Leon released Charley and Amy, hurrying toward his buddy. Charley grabbed Amy, who was watching, not wanting to move, and hustled her toward the door.

"C'mon, quick," he said.

But it was already too late. Donny screamed as Jerry's talons whistled through the air, tearing out his throat in one swipe. Blood flew everywhere, blinding the dancers swirling by, hitting people drinking at the bar, and a couple necking in the corner, as blood went flying everywhere.

Jerry stepped around the corpse as it toppled backward over a table of people snorting white powder. The bouncer's dead eyes stared up at them. Leon dashed up, lunging for Jerry. Bad idea. The vampire's hand snapped out, grabbing him by the throat and squeezing it. He lifted the huge man several feet off the floor, as his claws dug deeply into his skin.

More blood flew as Jerry tossed him through the air, his body smashing into a table and collapsing it as he skidded across the floor. The multi-colored lights picked him out as he halted in the middle of the dance floor. The dancing and the music came to a shrieking halt as people froze, staring at the dead body.

Pandemonium erupted throughout the club. People screamed and ran for the exits. The fear contagious, many streamed into the bottleneck of a hallway leading to the front door. It turned it into a battleground of panicked, terrified people, clawing and screaming to get out of the club.

The front door was closed by the crush, so Charley and Amy fought their way to a stairway providing another exit. They were crushed by people having the same idea, as a mash of panicked individuals swept them down the stairs.

"Hold on to me —" Charley cried out, only to have Jerry suddenly step out in front of them and sweep Amy away from him, carrying her down the stairs.

Charley fought to get to her, peering over the balustrade at the stairway below.

"Amy!" he screamed down the stairs.

Jerry stopped, with Amy in his arms, and he looked up at Charley with a million-watt smile. Charley reached over the railing for her, but it was too late. Jerry carried her down the stairs and out of sight as Charley was buffeted from side to side by the sea of humanity.

A moment later, Jerry was outside, lifting Amy into the front seat of the Jeep. Billy Cole was behind the wheel, and Evil Ed was in the back. Jerry pushed Amy over, swinging in beside her. His gaze landed on Evil who had his face averted. "What's wrong with you?"

Evil didn't answer, turning away even more, hiding his face. Jerry's hand snapped out, grabbing Evil and pulling him forward into the spill of a street light so he could see him better.

The sign of the cross, red and angry, was clearly visible on his forehead. Jerry stared at it in revulsion.

"What is that?" he snarled.

"The actor had a cross," Evil Ed cried out, begging for pity.

It was compassion he was denied.

"Fool!" Jerry said, slamming him back into his seat with such force it bent the crossbar that held it in place. With that, he looked at his driver. "Go."

Billy Cole put the Jeep in gear as Charley finally fought his way out of the club just in time to see the black Jeep roar down the street. Evil Ed had recovered and was peering out the back, hooting and grinning wildly, mocking him with his full set of fangs. Charley came to a breathless halt, staring after the disappearing Jeep, totally defeated.

50
CHARLEY AND PETER

Peter was hurriedly packing, shoving the bare necessities into his suitcase. He had finally decided he had no choice but to flee. He knew he had no chance of fighting Jerry Dandrige. He was much too powerful.

Peter couldn't even imagine how old Dandrige must really be, but given the ease with which he had fooled them all, very old, indeed. Furthermore, Peter knew the older the vampire, the more powerful.

As for his mementos, such as his screen-used props, he was afraid he had no choice but to abandon them for the moment. Perhaps, when he was safely away and had made some money, he could contact his landlord and get them back. He hoped so. He loved his collection.

In many ways, they *were* him. They were his favorite memories of his movies and the effort it had taken to make them. The friendships that he had made and the talent and craftspeople he had worked with were all recalled each time he looked at each piece. He adored them all, because they had helped him so much in making his character, Peter Vincent, The Great Vampire Killer, come alive.

It had been an act of love. Self-love to be sure, but also love for the audience and his fans and those of the horror genre. All that love was somehow encased in his props and to lose them was to die a little bit if not a lot.

There was knock at the door. It was loud and quick, as though the person on the outside was as desperate as he himself felt.

He looked up, terrified. "Who is it?" he called, remembering his last visitor and staring wide-eyed at the door.

"Charley Brewster," came the answer. "Let me in."

Peter hurried to the door, throwing the lock and cracking it open, a chain across the latch. He peered out at Charley.

"Are you one of them, too?" he asked.

"What are you talking about?" Charley asked.

Peter pulled his cross and thrust it through the crack. "Here, grab this," he said.

Charley did as told without hesitating. Peter peered at the teen's hand. No smoke, no crackling skin. He hurriedly slipped the chain and pulled Charley inside, slamming the door shut behind him, chaining and locking it closed before he hurriedly returned to packing his suitcase which he'd left on the bed in the other room. Charley followed.

"Your friend Edward showed up earlier!" Peter said. "Very intent on making a late night snack of me."

Charley had seen the cackling Evil Ed with his fanged face pushed up against the rear window of Jeep as Jerry sped away with Amy.

"But he was no match for Peter Vincent..." Peter let the words trail off. He'd started them out of years of fake bravado, but the evidence was in; he was all roar and no courage.

Peter turned back to his packing.

"What are you doing?" he asked.

"I'm leaving," Peter said, not in the mood for talk at this point. He had only one thing on his mind: fleeing.

"You can't," Charley said, shocked at what Peter was doing.

"Watch!" Peter said, slamming the suitcase shut and turning for the door. Charley stepped in front of him.

"Look, Dandrige has Amy," Charley said. "He says he's gonna kill her unless we come to his house."

Peter stopped, staring at Charley, stunned. The blood drained from his face.

"Oh, my God," he said. He quickly reached for the phone. "The police, I'll call the police."

Charley grabbed the receiver from him, slamming it back in its cradle. "No, Peter, no! They won't believe you," he said. "I've tried."

Peter collapsed in his chair, staring blindly ahead. Charley knelt by his side, looking at him, speaking the truth.

"Peter, it's just us. *We're* going to have to save Amy."

"I can't," Peter said, finally admitting the truth. "I was paid to be there tonight."

"I know," Charley said quietly, realizing how hard it was for Peter to say that.

"And you still want me to help you?" Peter said, looking at him in surprise.

"Yes," Charley said, meaning every word. "You're Peter Vincent, The Great Vampire Killer."

Peter looked up at him, wishing it were true but knowing it was not.

"That is a character in a movie!" he shouted. Then, softening, he said, "That's not even my real name." He sat there, trying to repress a sob. He wasn't even sure *he* was real anymore, not to mention his name. "I'm terrified. I'm sorry, Charley, but I am."

"I can't do it alone, Peter. If you don't help, Amy is gonna die.

Me, too, probably." Peter said nothing, not able to meet Charley's eyes. "Please, Peter," Charley said, trying one last time.

"I'm sorry, Charley," Peter said, still not able to meet the young man's gaze.

"Yeah, me, too," Charley said, finally accepting Peter wasn't going to help him.

What was he going to do now? He realized there was only one thing he could do. His father had run back to a burning car to save strangers and it had cost him his life. Charley's dad had set the bar high. He loved Amy. If trying to save her cost him his life, well, then, he had no choice. He knew that people might think he was crazy, but he was sure, somewhere, his father was looking down at him right now.

He couldn't fail either Amy or his father.

He walked to the door, slipping quietly out of the apartment, leaving Peter staring miserably at the floor.

51
POLICE AT CLUB RADIO

Detectives Dent and Deshawn stood on the balcony overlooking Club Radio, surveying the aftermath of the two killings. The uniformed officers questioned the few remaining club goers and staff, taking their statements before releasing them into the night.

Dr. Greenleaf had moved from the first body to the second. Gonzales and the rest of the Criminal Science teams tagged and photographed the scene. The body of the huge bouncer that had been tossed from the stairs still lay on the dance floor. A second body, that of the first victim, lay on an elevated platform, his throat cut open like a second mouth.

"About thirty feet, I'd guess," said Det. Deshawn, estimating the distance from the steps to where the body lay.

"Guy looks, what, six-two, two-fifty?" Dent said with a grimace. "How the hell could anybody throw him from here to there?"

"Judo?" Deshawn offered.

"What about the guy whose throat was torn out?" Det. Deshawn asked, nodding at the blood splattered across the dance platform.

"Doc Greenleaf said his throat was cut, and had multiple cuts, but one hit the carotid, spilling blood everywhere," Dent offered.

"You think it had to do with the other killings? You know, the ones that Lennox is looking into?" Deshawn asked.

"Nothing about them seems related. Even so, it's weird that we've suddenly got a rash of murders on our plate," Dent offered.

Sgt. Gonzales walked over to the two detectives. He held his notebook in his hand as if it contained the answers to all their questions.

"What do you have?" Dent asked.

"Not a lot. Initial interviews are sketchy, but this is what I've pieced together. A well-dressed man in his thirties, dark hair, intense eyes, was dancing with a girl, a bit on the young side. Some kid rolled up and took a swing at our well-dressed man and he caught the punch mid-swing," Gonzales paused.

"Bullshit," Det. Deshawn managed.

"I've seen it, once or twice, an amateur swinging on a pro, but yeah, it's rare outside the movies," Gonzales said. "But that's what the witnesses say happened."

"Anyways, next thing is this guy," Gonzales pointed to the bald bouncer, with his throat slashed open. "He walks up and confronts the well-dressed guy and calls out for back up. Before help can arrive, he goes down, throat opened to the bone."

Gonzales points at the second bouncer laying face up on the dance floor.

"Witnesses say the well-dressed guy grabbed this one by the throat, lifted him off his feet, and tossed him thirty feet across the dance floor."

"That's got to be hyperbole," Dent said.

"Hyper-what?" Gonzales asked.

"It's bullshit," Deshawn replied.

"Well, that's what I got. Talked to half a dozen witnesses and they said the same thing," Gonzales said. "Another group of witnesses outside say the well-dressed man got into a Jeep, or a truck, with a girl. The vehicle was driven by another man and there was some kid laughing his ass off, hanging out the back."

"So, we have a double murder and a possible kidnapping?" Det. Deshawn asked.

"Could be. Maybe we should wake up the chief," Det. Dent said.

The three men looked at their watches, and noted the time half past eleven.

"He ain't going to be happy," Det. Deshawn said.

52
AMY AWAKENS

Amy slowly regained consciousness, opening her eyes to find herself lying on the floor. Jerry Dandrige loomed over her, watching. She cowered back, looking about the room, and stiffening as she saw a portrait of herself on the wall. Then, she realized it wasn't her face, but one similar to hers. She was wearing clothes from a different era, a much earlier era.

Then she looked down and saw she was wearing a flowing white chiffon dress. But how? She wasn't wearing it in the club when he'd taken her. He must have changed her clothes while she was unconscious. A blush rose to her cheeks, making them hot, but then she knew he had seen her in a way she'd never been seen before, and it wasn't just because she'd been naked as he undressed and dressed her. He had seen into her heart. No, that wasn't quite correct. He had seen into her passion, and into her need — for him. She reached down and picked up the hem of the dress. It was a soft cloth, rich, lovely, and flowing, and clinging to her body.

She looked up and saw that she was in his bedroom. Then, she realized with a start, that she was dressed for love.

"Where am I?" she said, already knowing.

"Where you wanted to be. In my bedroom," he said, reaching out a hand to her.

She cowered back, finding the outrage to look up at him.

"Liar, I don't want anything to do with you," she said. "Where is Charley?"

"You don't really care," he answered and moved to a shelf in the room, hitting a button on the tape deck.

Music, slow and sinuous, hot, and hypnotic at the same time, snaked out of the speakers. The words caught her attention.

"Come to me when you're lonely," sang a haunting voice, low and seductive. "Come to me when you need something new..."

He flowed across the room to her, unbuttoning the fine gray cotton shirt he wore, his movements as sinuous as the song. She looked away, but found her eyes drawn back to him, only to find herself trapped in his gaze. She stared at him, fighting to break free and finally managed to turn her head aside as he knelt in front of her, his eyes now level with her own.

"I do care for Charley," she managed to say, her voice constricted by her passion, rising unbidden inside her. "I love him..."

"You do? I don't believe you," he said, leaning in, his tongue wetting his lips. It was beautiful, his tongue. Could a tongue be beautiful? It could be when it was licking his beckoning lips. "Am I lying, Amy? Am I?" he asked, but she couldn't answer. She could feel his breath, stroking her face.

"I can show you the world in a different light," the song's lyrics penetrated her brain, reminding her of what he was offering. "Keep your heart to yourself, give your soul to the night."

He leaned in even closer. In a moment, she was gone, as his

eyes drew her in and swallowed her, drowning her in their faint red glow as the music continued.

"Come to me when you're restless," the singer crooned, "Cuz I've got something just for you, just for you..."

He held his hands out to her. She slowly took them, and he pushed her head aside, exposing her tender young neck, surrounded by the loose white dress. He reached down, loosening the upper part of the chiffon dress, letting it slip to the floor. It left her bare-breasted before him, the whiteness of her back exposed.

Then, he slowly bent down to kiss her, revealing two razor-sharp fangs with their faint alabaster cast. He delicately slid them beneath her skin, his mouth enveloping her lower neck.

She stiffened in pain. No, it wasn't pain. It was something else, something — wonderful. He began to suck and slowly two thin lines of blood ran out of either side of his mouth and down her back, creating a beautiful red mosaic against her naked pale skin.

Her body arched, both arms pressing him to her, clinging to him. Her head threw back and she gasped as she felt a rush toward a desire she had never known. Then, she screamed like she was having a sexual climax, only it was better. Much, much better.

And just under her scream was the horrid, greedy *sucking sound* of Jerry Dandrige, feeding on her.

53
JUDY HEARS THE NEWS

Judy stopped inside the tasting room in the winery. It was nearly midnight, just a few minutes before closing time, and people were filing out from the attached bistro headed home or somewhere else to keep their night going. They'd taste the different wines here first and decide what to have with dinner before they went in, but she wasn't thinking about that. Not anymore. Her eyes were glued to the small TV set up in the corner. The volume was low, but she leaned over, turning it higher.

"A double murder was reported at Club Radio in downtown Rancho Corvallis. The police have not yet made a statement, but eyewitnesses emerging after being questioned report a scene of mayhem, with people panicking in their rush to escape the violence."

Nora Pace, another lady in her forties who worked with her, walked over, watching the TV. "Oh, no," she said, "not more murders."

"At least these weren't young girls," Judy nodded, picking up the phone. "I'm calling, Charley to see if he's watching."

She was thinking how grateful she was the killings were of

two men and apparently the result of violent conflict. At least Charley wouldn't try to blame these on some vampire.

"Just as long as he's not there," Nora said, meaning Club Radio.

She was still watching the screen as the reporter questioned witnesses emerging outside the club. They were telling all kinds of stories about a fight between the bouncers and one of the dancers. Apparently, it was over a woman.

"I doubt he's ever been there. He's not old enough to go to nightclubs," Judy said with a frown as she listened to the phone ring on the other end.

"What's wrong?" Nora asked, noticing.

"Nobody home," Judy said as she hung up and checked her watch. "Almost midnight. Maybe he's out with Amy Peterson or already in bed."

"I'm sure it's nothing," Nora said, still watching the TV. "You want to grab a bite after we close up?"

"I'm hungry, that's for sure." Their options were limited this late at night. "The Four Star again?" Judy asked, referring to their usual restaurant of choice, a small diner out by the truck stop.

"Sounds good," Nora said, tearing her eyes from the TV news as customers, wanting to get one more bottle of wine before they closed for the night, walked in the front door.

Nora went to greet them as Judy turned to restocking the Merlot. Their bottles were low from the tastings. People really liked Merlot. Too bad she couldn't have a sip; she could use it. Her mind drifted from the recent killings at the club to the serial killer stalking Rancho Corvallis.

There had been no suspect in the serial killings of the young girls. How many now? Four, no five, and still no suspects. Now, there were two more random killings. Rancho Corvallis was turning into the murder capital of northern California and she didn't like it at all.

It was obviously making her son a little crazy. Vampires, humph. She hated horror movies and Peter Vincent. A lot. They were responsible for her son's madness, but there was a real killer loose in town and he had to be stopped. She just hoped someone figured it out and quickly.

54
PETER STANDS UP

P eter placed his suitcase in the trunk of his Studebaker and slammed the lid shut. He'd called his landlord to tell him he was leaving, but he wasn't there, so he'd had to leave a message. He'd use the five hundred dollars Amy had given him to pay a moving company to put his props and possessions in storage. He just couldn't bear parting with them, but he had no choice but to leave. No, *flee* was more like it. After he'd been attacked by Ed Thompson, who, indeed, had become "Evil," he saw he had no choice, not if he wanted to live.

There was no way he could win a fight against an ancient vampire like Jerry Dandrige, for that was surely what he was. He'd barely fended off the newly turned Ed Thompson. Dandrige would drain him of blood and kill him, or worse, make him a slave or a ghoul, like his companion, Billy Cole.

It was the attack by Evil Ed that had convinced Peter he was helpless before him. He was lucky to have survived the teen's assault. He felt sorry for Jerry making him into a vampire, which was an irrevocable condition, but he still had almost killed him and that tempered his sympathy.

He got into his car, slamming the door behind him, and

leaned forward to turn the ignition, only to be swept by feelings of helplessness. Tears welled up in his eyes. He'd been wrong about everything he had thought about himself. He wasn't a great vampire fighter. He wasn't a hero. His entire acting career had been a lie. Forget the quality of his work. Yes, he knew he was a ham actor, but he had taken the part seriously. He had done his best to inform himself so he could play the character as truthfully as possible, only to learn in the end he did not have the backbone that was called for it.

He couldn't forgive himself, but Charley's last plea kept ringing in his ears: "If you don't help me, both Amy and I will die." He knew the boy was right. Even worse, he was so brave he made Peter feel ashamed of himself. There was no doubt in his mind that, even now, the boy was preparing to go into that house by himself.

There was no way the teen would survive, Peter was sure of that. He had also seen the way Jerry Dandrige had looked at Amy Peterson. It wasn't lust in his eyes. Oh, no, it was something worse than that. He wanted her so badly there weren't words for Peter to express it. Charley was right. If he didn't help him, both he and his teenage love would be gone, destroyed by the power of Jerry Dandrige or worse. And it was all his fault, for having failed them.

But if he tried to help, what then? It would be all three of them that would be dead or under Dandrige's power. What could he do? He turned the key starting the car. He had to get out of Rancho Corvallis and now. Given enough time, he would forget his failure. Perhaps, he could find theater work in San Francisco, or even more likely in Los Angeles, the center of the movie industry.

All he needed was an agent to represent him. But, truth be told, he hadn't been able to get an agent interested in representing him for more than a decade. Damn, it was more like two decades. His last three films had all failed and they were terrible. Not even Roger Corman would have done them in his time. He, Peter Vincent, had sunk so low that even Ed Wood would have felt sorry for him. Worst of all, no one cared about him anymore and that was all he ever really wanted, to have people actually like and care about him.

Vampire films? They were so yesterday. All anybody was really interested in now were the "kills," and how violently the characters were murdered by whatever monster it might be. Hell, even a stupid red-haired doll was more commercially viable than vampires were. Without vampires, who needed a vampire killer?

He put the car in gear and drove down the street toward the road out of town. He made it to the end of the block when he suddenly slammed on the brakes. Better he was dead than live with the shame of what he was doing. Yes, everything about him was a lie. He was born in shame, a bastard who never knew his father. His childhood had been terrible. Whose childhood wasn't, especially if they were creative? Nothing in his life had been good or even bearable except his time as Peter Vincent, and he had held onto it desperately.

How could he make up for all his failures? He looked at his reflection in his rearview mirror. There was only one way and that was standing up with Charley Brewster and saving Amy Peterson. He was doomed either way, but better to die doing what was right than living with disgrace and cowardice.

Biting down so hard on his lower lip that he bled, he suddenly executed a U-turn and headed back in the other direction toward Charley Brewster's and the terrible house next door.

At least if he were to lose and be killed, Charley and, hopefully, Amy would know that he had died trying to defend them by stopping the curse of Jerry Dandrige. After all, he was Peter Vincent, The Great Vampire Killer.

55
CHARLEY INTO THE FRAY

Charley stood in his room. It was dark and all the lights were turned off. He was staring at the room across the way, Jerry Dandrige's room was how he thought about it, but it was dark, too. The shade was pulled shut. The phone had rung a few moments before. He was sure it was his mother, so he hadn't picked it up.

She was working the late shift tonight, and wouldn't be off until eleven. She had probably heard about the killings at Club Radio. He hadn't listened to the news. Why bother? He had lived it, and knew that Jerry was next door with Amy, guarded by the monstrous Billy Cole.

He was alone. Peter wouldn't help him. He'd seen Evil being driven away from the club and knew he'd been taken to the Dark Side, even before Peter Vincent had told him he'd been attacked.

If Amy was to be saved, he was going to have to do it, all by himself. He turned, picking up several well-sharpened stakes he had laid out. He put two to either side of his belt and one each in his jacket pocket. He picked up the wooden mallet. Now he was ready.

Did he have the nerve to go next door and face the vampire? He would soon find out. He turned and walked out his door, down the hall, and down the stairs to his front door. He stepped outside, looking at the Dandrige house. There seemed to be a low light on in the side window of the first floor, but he didn't know what room it was.

He hadn't been in the house in years until tonight when Peter had run the fake holy water test on Jerry Dandrige. When he was a kid, a nice family had lived there for a while, only to move away. Since then, it had either been abandoned or people moved in to fix it up and sell it only to give up and leave. There was something about it that had always repelled people, but it hadn't been pronounced enough to get a reputation as a "haunted house." It was just seen as a place that was more of a money pit than a home.

He moved across the street, wanting to view it from the front, so he could see what he was getting into as he mounted his attack on it. Perhaps, he could get a hint of where Amy was being kept. After all, she was his reason for venturing into the vampire's lair.

He walked through the darkness, pulling a stake, the hammer in his other hand, studying the Dandrige house from a side yard across the street. Only he could save Amy and he was determined to do it, even if it cost him his life.

The shadows loomed over him, as the wind caused the tree branches to rustle, making Charley more and more nervous with every passing second. He didn't want to be alone. He didn't want to face Billy Cole and Jerry Dandrige all by himself, but he had no choice. He loved Amy. He couldn't let the vampire destroy her, murder her, or make her his slave, or whatever he intended for her. Charley had to stop him, even if he couldn't think of a better way than to face him in his lair all by himself.

No matter how hopeless it seemed, he had to try.

He stepped out of the darkness of the trees, stopping to stare. The house was huge, silent, and dark, no longer looking like every other house on the block, certainly not like Charley's house next door. It seemed to have a life of its own, turning into a brooding monster, and still looking like it was ready to leap forward and pounce on him.

Well, nothing for it. He had to face his fate and kill the monsters and save Amy if he could. He gripped his stake and hammer, checked the cross in his jacket pocket, took a deep breath, squared his shoulders, and started the slow walk across the street toward the Dandrige house. Off the curb he stepped, and across the blacktop he went. Closer and closer, he made his way to the hulking evil house.

Suddenly, a hand snapped out of the darkness, grabbing him by the shoulder. A startled Charley almost jumped out of his skin.

"Peter Vincent," a voice said, "ready to do battle with the undead."

Charley whirled to find himself staring into Peter's drawn face. He wore the Victorian suit, and had his killing kit slung over his shoulder. His vest and watch fob in place, Peter's whole demeanor was that of his public persona, The Great Vampire Killer.

"Peter, this is serious," Charley said with a gulp, trying to get his heart out of his mouth.

"I am serious," Peter said, pulling himself up to his full height, which still didn't make him quite as tall as Charley. "Here, hold this."

He handed Charley his kit, throwing it open and pulling out an assortment of his old movie props. "Let's see," he said, "flashlights, stakes, hammer, ah yes, cross..."

"What about Billy Cole?" Charley said, hope springing up inside him in spite of his reservations. "How you gonna stop him?"

Peter rose, holding up a small silver pistol with ivory grips. "With this! It is from *Orgy of the Damned*," he said.

"What if he's not human?" Charley said. "Bullets aren't gonna stop him then."

"He walks around in the daylight, now doesn't he? Mmmm?" Peter said with seeming total confidence. Charley nodded, not able to think of anything else to say.

"Yeah," Charley said.

"Well, then, he is human," Peter added, as if that settled it.

He slammed his kit shut and lifted it back on his shoulder. He swung about to face the Dandrige house.

"C'mon," he said, starting bravely toward the house, his head held up, and his eyes flashing with bravado.

The two of them walked across the street, heading toward the house which now seemed to be leaning in their direction to possibly charge and trample them.

"Peter, you don't have to do this. I wanna thank you...," Charley said, cutting a glance at the older man.

"Not now," Peter said, cutting him off.

But Peter wasn't really paying attention to Charley. His gaze was on the malevolent house. It loomed larger and larger above them as they got closer and closer.

Peter began to slow, his nerve draining away as the true evilness of the place began to eat away at him. He finally came to a halt, staring up at the house. Charley, who was in the lead, stopped, looking back.

"What's wrong?" Charley asked.

Peter took a breath, searching for his courage. "Nothing," he said, gritting his teeth, "nothing at all."

He joined Charley, the two of them again walking toward the house. Peter, however, was getting more and more nervous.

Charley took a step onto the front porch, heading for the door. Peter suddenly grabbed him.

"Are you crazy?" he whispered hurriedly. "Not the front door. Let's go around the back and sneak in."

The front door slowly swung open on rusty hinges. *Creakkkkk*, it went, as if it were speaking to them. Peter and Charley looked at the open door, now a dark gaping hole like an open mouth, ready to swallow them.

"Too late," Charley said.

He started moving toward the door. Peter moved with him, his gaze fixed on the gaping open doorway.

"I am Peter Vincent, The Great Vampire Killer," Peter intoned to himself as he went, like it was some sort of mantra that would keep him safe. "I *am* Peter Vincent, The Great Vampire..." They disappeared into the house.

56
BATTLE ON THE STAIRS

J erry Dandrige and Evil Ed suddenly stepped out from the bushes behind Charley and Peter where they had been watching, staring after them.

"We've got them," Evil said with a giggle.

"Shut up," Jerry ordered, afraid the newly made vampire might alert the two now inside the house.

Even as he spoke, Charley and Peter stopped at the bottom of the huge staircase and stared about in the darkness. Nothing moved except all the cuckoo clocks on one wall. Stranger still, they were completely silent even as their pendulums swung wildly back and forth.

Charley pulled at Peter's sleeve, nodding at the clocks. "We can't hear them."

"They probably only make noise to tell Jerry it's time to get up or it's dawn and time to go to bed," Peter said, trying to sound confident, although it was only a guess.

"Right," Charley said, his mind elsewhere. He nodded up the staircase toward the huge oval stained-glass window above. "Let's go." They started up the stairs.

Outside the house, Jerry Dandrige moved out of the shrubbery toward his house, Evil Ed close beside him. They had been out there, hiding the entire time, and waiting for the ham actor and the obnoxious teen to go inside. Now, all Jerry had to do was destroy them, hopefully slowly, for all the trouble they had cost him.

"Let's get them," Evil Ed said with a snarl. He couldn't wait to repay The Great Vampire Killer for branding his forehead with the hated cross. He stepped toward the front door.

"No," said Jerry, grabbing him by the shoulder. He nodded toward the Brewster house. "You wait over there in the mother's bedroom."

"Why?" complained Evil. "What's going to happen there?"

"I'm going to send someone your way. Someone special, just for you," he said with a sinister smile. "Now go."

With that, Jerry pushed him towards the other house. Evil Ed gave him an unhappy glance as he did as he was told, but Jerry ignored it. He glided with surprising speed to the side of his house, lifted his hands, grabbing hold of the clapboard siding and began to pull himself up the side of his house, moving with a terrible silent, effortless grace that would have put Spiderman to shame.

Evil stopped for a moment, watching in awe. Jerry slipped around to the side, reaching the second-floor window to his room. He threw open the window, slipping a foot inside and following with the rest of his body.

Evil shook off his amazement and slipped into Charley's house. The last thing he wanted to do after what he'd just seen was displease his master. The vampire was just too powerful for anyone.

Inside the Dandrige house, halfway up the staircase, Peter suddenly froze, grabbing Charley. "Did you just hear something?"

Charley paused, listening hard. "No," he finally said and they slowly started up the stairway again.

They only took a few steps before Peter grabbed Charley again, digging his fingers into the boy's arm, and his face filled with fear.

"Let's come back at dawn," he said. "You see, he'll be asleep then. And we'll have a better chance of getting Amy."

"Yeah, and Amy will be dead by then, too. Now, come on," Charley said.

He turned to start up the stairs, only to have a voice come out of the darkness on the landing above.

"*Welcome to Fright Night...For real*" a deep baritone voice said, rolling his R's.

Jerry Dandrige stepped into the light, walking along the balcony, a razor-sharp nail peeling back a curling sliver of wood from the railing as he moved. He was a stunning figure looking absolutely gorgeous in a loose gray shirt and dark slacks. One would never suspect he had just climbed the side of the house. Peter almost turned and ran down the stairs when he saw him, but Charley grabbed him, holding him in place even as he looked up at Jerry looming above them.

"Where is Amy?" the teen asked.

"Up here," Jerry said, tweaking his finger, daring them to come up the stairs. "All you have to do is get by me."

He started down the steps. Peter whipped out his cross, thrusting it up at the vampire. "Back, Spawn of Satan," The Great Vampire Killer said.

"Oh, really?" Jerry said with a laugh. He stopped on the step directly above and reached out, ripping the cross out of Peter's hand and holding it up.

He slowly crushed it in his hand, bending it in half and scrunching it down into a ball of ruined metal. Finished, he tossed it over his shoulder.

"You have to have faith for this to work on me, Mr. Vincent."

He started down the stairs again, a terrified Peter backing away, his nerves completely shredded now. Charley, however, didn't retreat. He stepped forward, staring up at Dandrige, his jaw set.

"Stop!" he said, whipping out his cross and thrusting it up at the vampire.

Jerry ground to a halt, staring at the cross. He didn't look happy. Charley took heart and started up the stairs toward him, the cross held out.

"Back!" Charley said.

Jerry slowly backed up the stairs, throwing a hand across his face, the power of the cross too much for him. He finally whirled, disappearing into the darkness at the top of the stairs. Charley glanced back at Peter triumphantly.

"We're gonna make it," he said with a big smile.

Billy Cole suddenly stepped out of the darkness in front of Charley and viciously backhanded him across the face. Charley smashed into the thick stairway railing and flipped over it, plunging to the floor below. He landed with a bone-breaking thud, and lay there groaning.

Jerry stepped up behind Billy and leaned on his shoulder as he grinned down at Peter on the stairway. Then, he slowly stepped around his ghoul and started down the stairs. With a stifled scream, the actor whirled and raced down the steps, slamming out the front door.

57
PETER MAKES A WRONG TURN

Peter smashed through the front door into the Brewster house after having just escaped Jerry and his ghoul, Billy Cole, on the stairway in their house. He'd left Charley behind in his blind panic, and still hadn't thought of him.

He yelled up the stairway. "Mrs. Brewster! Mrs. Brewster!"

No answer. He didn't know she was working the night shift at the winery. He grabbed the phone from the table in the entry-way, dialed 911, and spoke hurriedly into it.

"Operator, get me the —" he began only to stop once he realized there was no dial tone.

He held the phone up only to see the dangling cord. It had been ripped from the wall. His eyes widened in horror as his gaze snapped up the stairs.

"Mrs. Brewster," he said, hoping she was upstairs in her bed and just had been sleeping so deeply she hadn't heard his cries.

He plunged up the steps.

A moment later, he burst through the door to see Judy in bed, her back to him. Her brunette hair was now fiery red, but he was in such a panic he didn't notice. He hurried across the room, relief sweeping his face.

"Mrs. Brewster, thank God. The phone wires have been cut," he said, reaching out to shake her awake.

She turned to face him — only it wasn't Judy Brewster; it was Evil Ed, wearing a red wig ripped from one of the Raggedy Ann dolls that Mrs. Brewster had in the corner.

"I know," Evil giggled in a delighted voice, "*I* did it."

He grinned at Peter as he slowly rose on the bed, the wig slipping from his head. His features were already transformed into those of a vampire with slicked-back hair, elongated face, and white fangs slashing over his lower lip.

Peter staggered back, staring up at him in horror. "Where is the child's mother?" he finally managed.

"Well, apparently, she's working nights, but she left a note," Evil giggled, taking a crumpled piece of paper from his pocket and reading it. "Hmmm-um. His dinner's in the oven," he added hungrily.

He ended with a high-pitched laugh and jumped off the bed toward Peter, landing on the floor with a thump. The Great Vampire Killer screamed and whirled, racing out of the room.

Peter ran down the hall for the stairs, only to hit a side table in the dark, sending him crashing to the floor as the table splintered beneath him. He sat up, groaning, holding his leg, and hoping he could walk on it.

In the bedroom, Evil was wondering in what form he should pursue the ham actor that he now hated and wanted to scare literally to death if he could. He never asked how he knew he could change form now that he was a vampire. He just knew it, and with that knowledge came his choice.

A wolf. Of course, a wolf would terrify Peter Vincent, the "fake" vampire killer.

With that, he began to transform; his back humped over,

forcing him to drop to the floor on all fours. At the same time, hair began to grow on his hands and feet, his legs pushed out, and his feet burst out of his shoes as they turned into paws. The biggest change was to his face; his nose began to push out and his jaws lengthened, as ferocious rows of teeth grew to their length.

He growled deep in his chest as his clothes ripped and dropped to the floor. Hair covered his entire body and turned into a pelt.

In the hall, Peter was struggling to sit up when he froze. He heard a *growling* coming from the bedroom. He looked up, wide-eyed, and stared into the darkness down the hall.

A huge wolf, as ugly as Evil Ed, stepped out of Judy's bedroom, staring back at Peter. Its eyes glowed like red hot coals in the dark and saliva dripped from its huge fangs.

Oh, my goodness, Peter realized, *it's Evil Ed!*

Peter scrambled to his feet, his pain forgotten, and was about to plunge down the stairs when, with a terrible snarl, the huge animal bounded down the hall toward him. With a gasp of desperation, Peter snatched up a splintered leg of the broken table as the wolf launched itself into the air toward his jugular vein.

He slammed the jagged piece of wood into the animal's chest and lifted up, throwing it over his head even as he fell back, the snapping jaws barely missing his throat. The wolf hit the landing railing and plowed through it, plunging over the side.

The wolf spun through the air, smashing the entry chandelier on the way down, hitting the hardwood floor below with a terrible *thud*.

Peter recovered, looking over the shattered railing at the animal below. It was surrounded by the glass shards of the chandelier; the long wooden splinter was buried deep in its chest. Whining and whimpering, it managed to drag itself under the stairs and out of sight.

Steeling himself, Peter started down the stairs, reaching the bottom and peering into the alcove. The wolf sat there, its back against the wall, mostly animal but with a human posture.

Peter watched in fascinated horror as humanity leaked back into the animal's eyes, and his face transformed into that of a normal teenage boy, however, with an angry red cross branded into the center of his forehead.

"I'm sorry," he gasped as he looked up at Peter with suddenly soft brown eyes.

He reached out to him, his back legs turning more human, and the paws becoming feet. The upper half of his body was recognizably human now although both arms remained covered with long hair. There were still claws on his hands where there should have been fingers.

He stretched out a hand to Peter, as though begging for help. Then, he fell forward, turning on his back, staring up at Peter, life leaking out of his eyes.

A hand went up to pull at the stake buried in his chest and the claws gradually turned into fingers, trying to grasp the stake, but he not being strong enough. The hand fell away.

His eyelids flickered closed even as the cross burned into his forehead flared and disappeared, as if God had forgiven him his embrace of The Dark Side.

Peter stared down, overcome with sorrow at the loss of someone so young, someone who obviously wasn't responsible for what had happened to him. It was Jerry Dandrige, the vampire master and his ghoul, Billy Cole, who had done this to Ed Thompson, who was no longer "Evil" at all.

Peter's face hardened. Amy and Charley were still trapped in that house of horrors next door. The only one who could help them was him. He whose courage had failed him again and again. He, The Great Vampire Killer, who had been living a lie his entire life.

Well, no more, he silently swore to himself. He bent down and grabbed the jagged long splinter that protruded from Evil Ed's body and, with a jerk, pulled it free. It was a deadly stake for sure, and would give him a weapon with which to face the monsters next door. Swearing to redeem himself, he turned for the door, leaving the naked body of the beautiful dead boy behind.

58
WHAT'S WRONG WITH AMY?

J erry came through the door into his bedroom with a still stunned Charley over his shoulder. It didn't help when Jerry dumped him unceremoniously on the floor a few feet from where Amy lay, curled up in a fetal ball.

He nodded at Amy as Charley opened his eyes, regaining his senses. "You wanted her," he said. "There she is."

Charley glanced to the side, seeing Amy, and crawled to her. He gently turned her over. "Amy?" he said.

He froze as he saw her clearly for the first time. Her eyes were clenched shut, her face drenched with sweat, and her entire body trembling as if with some terrible fever.

"You see," the vampire said, "you gave me so much trouble, I thought you deserved a special punishment."

"What have you done to her?" Charley asked, looking up at him.

"Nothing much," Jerry answered. "I just bit her a little, and gave her a tad of my blood. But I should think more than enough under the circumstances."

Jerry stared at the boy, waiting for a reaction.

"You bastard!" Charley cried, leaping to his feet and charging him.

Jerry didn't even move, grabbing him by the throat with one hand, stopping him cold, and flinging him through the air with incredible strength. Charley hit the wall and crumpled to the floor. Jerry walked over and threw a wooden stake at his feet with such force, its point stuck into the floor.

"Here," the vampire said. "You're gonna need it just before dawn."

With a bow, he let himself out of the room, closing the door behind him. Charley heard the key turn and stared around the room, gathering his senses. He saw the one window had been boarded up with planks of wood and nailed into the frame. It would be impossible for him to rip it apart, just as it would be impossible for anyone to hear him were he to scream.

Charley turned back to Amy, crawling to her side, and holding her in his arms. Her head fell back. She was worse, with longer fangs, and her eyes partially open, glowing red. Charley threw back his head and yelled as he realized what Jerry meant for him: to be attacked and killed by the girl he loved.

Jerry paused halfway down the stairs, listening to Charley's voice die away. The boy had finally realized what would happen when his one true love awoke. She would be thirsty and he would be the only thing there to satisfy her. He smiled, then continued down the stairs.

59
COURAGE

Peter came out of the Brewster house and faced the Dandrige house, stake and hammer in hand, his face set with determination. Throwing back his shoulders and taking a deep breath, he began to walk slowly toward the front door.

Something was happening to the old Victorian; it was looking more dangerous than ever with fog rolling off the roof and dropping down its sides.

Peter came to a stop, staring at it. He took a breath and hefted his vampire killing kit on his shoulder, as he walked toward the front door, not stopping this time.

Moments later, he slipped through the front door and stepped into the great room, staring up the long wide staircase with the stained-glass window at the top. He peeked down the hall as sounds carried up from the basement. The vampire and his ghoul were down there. He could hear them working. *Good,* he thought and he started up the stairs.

At the top, he worked his way from door to door until he found the one that was locked. He rapped on it lightly, pressing his lips to the crack, and whispered, "Charley?"

Inside the bedroom, Charley lifted his head, still holding Amy as she progressed in her transformation; her hair was now slicked-back and longer with the glistening fangs. She was still trembling, and her body was covered with a sheen of sweat. He put her aside gently and leaped to his feet, hurrying to the door.

"Peter?" he said in a low whisper.

"Charley, I'm going to have to break the door down," Peter said softly. "You make as much noise as you can."

Charley immediately began banging on the wall and yelling at the top of his lungs. "Help! Help! Let me out!"

In the basement, Jerry and Billy were preparing a spare coffin for Amy, dumping dirt into it from the huge ornate coffin that Charley had seen them carrying into the house on that first night, now, so long ago. They paused in their work as they heard Charley's screams.

"I think she just opened her eyes," Jerry said to Billy with a smile.

Upstairs, Peter hit the door from the outside with his shoulder, snapping the lock, letting himself in, and closing it quietly behind him. He looked around, spotting Amy lying in the corner.

"Grab her," he said to Charley. "Let's get out of here."

"We can't," Charley said. "Look."

He fell to his knees beside Amy and rolled her over for Peter to see. She was still covered in sweat, the trembling even more violent now. Her upper lip slipped back, revealing lengthening fangs, and irises flickering red.

Peter's eyes widened in horror. "Oh, my God," he gasped. "He's given her his blood."

In the basement, Jerry paused in his labors to stare up at the ceiling. His ear was cocked. Billy looked at him.

"Something wrong?" he asked.

"Yes," Jerry answered. "We have a visitor."

He put down his shovel, diving for the closest half-window to the outside. As Billy watched, he disappeared through it. The ghoul turned, heading for the stairs and a more traditional approach to the floors above.

In the bedroom, Charley glanced up from Amy's trembling body to look at Peter. "Is it too late to save her?" he asked.

"No, not if we kill Dandrige before dawn," Peter said.

Even as they spoke, Jerry Dandrige in his spider form was skittering up the side of the house, past the living room window and up and up, until the voices in his bedroom became louder and more distinct the closer he got.

"Are you sure?" Charley said to Peter in the room.

"So far, everything's been like it was in the movies," Peter said. "We'll just have to keep hoping."

Outside, Jerry came to a halt, clinging to the shingling of the house, peering through the window, and watching as Charley grabbed the stake he had driven into the floor earlier.

"Let's go," the teen said.

He and Peter hurried out the door, Jerry watching them go. As the door closed behind them, he slipped through the window, hardly giving the transforming Amy a glance as he went to the door to the hall.

60

BILLY'S END

Charley and Peter came out of the bedroom, across the balcony, and started down the stairs only to find themselves facing Billy Cole coming the other way.

They froze as they saw Billy climbing the stairs, only to stop halfway below, a slow smile spreading across his grim features. "Well, what do we have here?" he said.

He started up the steps toward them again. Peter pulled his silver pistol from his pocket. It was one of the movie props from his apartment that was used in the film *Werewolves Howl*. He pointed it at the ghoul.

"Stop or I'll shoot," he said.

Billy stopped, still smiling at him, and their eyes locked for what seemed like an eternity. Then, Billy started up the stairs toward them again, a seemingly unstoppable force. Peter held his pistol tightly with both hands and aimed. Unfortunately, they were trembling, making the barrel shake.

"I mean it," he said. "Don't force me to shoot."

Billy ignored him, getting closer and closer. He raised his huge hands, reaching for Peter's throat. The actor pulled the trigger, punching a neat hole in Billy Cole's forehead. The large man froze, tottering there, and his eyes rolled back into his skull.

He steadied for a heart-stopping moment, with hands still raised, but tumbled backward down the stairs, landing with a *crash* at bottom.

Suddenly, there was a rush of footsteps on the balcony above them. Peter and Charley whirled, staring up as Jerry appeared out of the shadows. With a hungry smile of his own, he started down the stairs toward them. Charley stepped forward, thrusting his cross up at Dandrige.

"Stop!" Charley cried in a strong voice.

"That won't work on me, you fool," he snarled only to grind to a halt.

He stood there, struggling to take another step. No matter how hard he tried, he couldn't do it. Charley had faith, something that had never occurred to him before. Now, he fervently hoped he had it as he silently prayed for the Lord, or anyone else, to help him. The teen took a step toward the vampire, with the cross held out, and his confidence rising.

"Come on," Charley said over his shoulder to Peter. "We have him."

Dandrige stood on the steps, not retreating, but with a face darkening with fury. Charley continued up the stairs, with Peter close behind him.

A furious Jerry Dandrige snapped his gaze past Charley and Peter down at Billy Cole's prostrate form at the bottom of the stairs. His eyes glowed as they burnt into the seeming corpse for a moment before they shifted back to Charley and Peter.

"Do you?" he asked in a sibilant whisper.

With that, he stepped back into the shadows of the balcony, disappearing from view.

Charley looked back at Peter with a frown. "What'd he mean by that?"

"Nothing," Peter said, more confident now than ever before. "He was just bluffing."

Charley slowly began to climb again, with the cross held out, as Peter hugged his back. Behind them, at the foot of the stairs, unseen by either of them, Billy Cole slowly sat up.

Charley and Peter kept climbing, their gazes fixed up the stairs. Behind them, Billy stood and started to climb the stairs toward them. The third step he hit *groaned* under his heavy weight.

Charley and Peter froze, slowly turning to look back. They saw the huge man coming up the stairs toward them, a thin trail of blood leaking from the bullet hole in his head.

Peter whipped his pistol out and unloaded the entire revolver into the man. *Bang, bang, bang!* Bullet after bullet smacked into him. It cast a pale of gun smoke in front of him and Charley, obscuring their view of the stairs below.

They waited, frozen. "What do you think?" Charley asked.

"We got him," Peter said with a definite nod.

Then they heard it. *More creaks of climbing feet*, and slowly Billy Cole appeared through the thick white cloud of gun smoke, his hands stretched out toward them.

They began backing up the stairs again, step by step. Peter stumbled, unable to rise in time as Billy loomed above him. The ghoul grabbed him and jerked him up into the air like a rag doll, about to fling him over the balustrade to the hard floor below.

Charley leaped forward, slamming his stake deep into the creature's heart with a cry, "No!"

Billy Cole froze, his eyes widening. He dropped Peter crashing to the steps and staggered on his feet, grabbing the railing for support. He hung there, a few steps below Peter and Charley for what seemed an eternity as the stake protruded from his heart.

The two watched in horror as Billy's face began to melt and

dissolve, the skin putrefying and slipping away, revealing huge chunks of the grinning skull beneath. Billy raised a hand, staring at it in genuine surprise as it, too, began to melt, turning into green goo, and revealing the bone beneath. The same thing happened to his legs. Green goo ran out of his pants leg, quickly turning to sand, and pouring down the steps in a flood, rushing toward the bottom.

The process of dissolution accelerated as the seconds ticked past, turning his hands into bones, and his head into a skull shorn of flesh until he was no more than a skeleton in clothes. He finally tumbled backward down the stairs with a clatter to land with a crash on the floor below. Bones rolled in every direction. His skull skittered across the floor and banged to a stop against the wall, only a few strands of goo left clinging to it now.

Charley and Peter stared down the stairs at the remains.

"He wasn't human," Charley managed to say.

"No, he certainly wasn't," Peter said. He and Charley backed hurriedly up the stairs, terrified by what they'd just seen.

61

THE ATTIC

A moment later, Charley and Peter rushed into Amy's room. Peter took time to stop and stare at the open window. He figured Dandrige must have entered that way and come up behind them on the balcony. What he didn't know was whether or not Dandrige went back out it or if he was still somewhere on the second floor.

Charley ignored the open window, hurrying to Amy's side. He turned her over, not as gently this time, to see the fangs were even longer, deadlier now. Her open eyes were still glowing red, but she wasn't really moving. She was continuing to make the transition to a creature of the night and there was nothing he could do to stop it — except kill Jerry Dandrige before dawn rose. But where was he?

He sprang to his feet, looking at Peter who had his head stuck out the window. "Do you see him?" he said.

Peter looked down, trying to catch a glimpse of the vampire, totally unaware that Jerry Dandrige clung to the side of the house, flat like a fly, directly above him. The vampire smiled, drawing back one clawed hand to tear Peter's head off when Charley called out to him from inside the bedroom.

"Peter, come quick."

Peter ducked in just as Jerry struck, missing him by an inch. Peter was totally unaware of how close he'd come to being decapitated.

Charley looked up at him from Amy's side on the floor. "She's worse," he said. "C'mon, we're running out of time. We have to find Dandrige."

The two men rushed out of the room, leaving Amy, her body now trembling.

Outside on the wall, Jerry did a hundred and eighty degree turn, staring in through the window and out the open door, watching Peter and Charley on the balcony.

He could hear their voices as Charley asked, "Where is he?"

Jerry smiled and began to climb up the side of the house toward the roof above, moving with astonishing speed that made him seem like a blur.

On the balcony, Charley and Peter looked around, trying to spot Jerry. They suddenly heard footsteps above them.

"He's in the attic," Peter said, hurrying down the hall toward the stairs leading above. Charley followed.

But they were wrong. Jerry Dandrige was not in the attic. He was on the roof above, standing next to the brick chimney. His chin was down in concentration. His face was dark and drawn. His fangs were long and sharp, giving a glimpse of how ancient he must really be. "Edward," he intoned. "Edward, awake!" But he heard nothing back and his temper slipped its leash. "Damn you! Awake!"

62

CALLING EVIL

"Evil" Ed Thompson fell backward from the light. The gaping expanse of darkness unfurled beneath him. Only moments before, he had felt unbridled power coursing through his veins; transformed into a wolf, he'd bounded forward toward that cowardly charlatan, Peter Vincent. He could still hear his pathetic gasps and whimpers as gnashing teeth roared down on the bared throat of the washed-up actor, a make-believe vampire killer. But something had gone wrong.

Ed felt the searing pain near the center of his chest where the table leg had found its mark. Had Peter Vincent lured him into overconfidence, or had he simply scored a lucky shot? As the distant light grew smaller, Ed felt the anger inside him swell. Twice! That ridiculous fraud beat him twice! Ed's head filled with thoughts of vengeance. He seemed to fall faster into the darkness.

"Edward!" the voice of his master, the ancient vampire Jerry Dandrige, erupted from the center of his brain. His descent reversed, and he found himself speeding upward toward the light.

"Awake, Edward!" Jerry's second command was like thunder crashing through the darkness. Ed shot bolt upright, his hand clutching his chest. The stake was gone. All that remained was a slowly healing, jagged tear in his flesh.

"Master?" he murmured through cracked lips. Ed's mind slowly cleared of the maelstrom of hatred for Peter Vincent and drew a sharp focus on the words of Jerry Dandrige calling to him. He'd thought he was dead, destroyed, and now this. His master had come back to save him.

"Fetch my Grimoire," Jerry thundered. Jerry's Grimoire was an ancient text containing dark, powerful magic. Ed understood immediately.

"Arise! Find it in my abode. It is hidden in a secret panel behind the portrait of my beloved. Find it in the wall. There will be a panel that will move with your touch. Use it if need be. I go to finish off Peter Vincent. You must protect it if some mishap occurs, and he vanquishes me."

"Nothing can defeat you," Ed thought.

"No, but accidents do happen, don't they, Edward?" the master's voice replied. Ed knew the master had heard his weakness and doubt. A wave of shame washed over him.

"Now, rise and find my Grimoire. I command you."

"Yes, Master" Ed managed.

"Do not fail me," Jerry's voice said before trailing off. The urgency of the command, however, was not lost on the young vampire.

Where was he? Evil didn't know as he regained consciousness, but he was staring at a shattered chandelier above. Next to it was the splintered railing of the landing. Then he remembered. He was on the floor at the bottom of the stairs in the Brewster house, surrounded by glass shards.

He had crashed through the chandelier above when Peter Vincent had stabbed him in the heart and tossed him over the balustrade. He'd hit the chandelier on the way down and slammed into the floor. The thud echoed in his head even now. He had dragged himself back into the alcove under the stairs where he fought to pull the stake loose, even as he felt his life force ebbing. He couldn't do it.

Ed remembered the shear ferocity and power he felt during the time he transitioned into a wolf and chased that ridiculous old fool, Peter Vincent, down the hallway. But "The Great Vampire Killer" had been faster than he was and sunk the stake deep.

Now, he lay on the floor naked and still reeling from the burning pain in his chest and his return from the darkness. But the pain was lessening. His hand went up to his chest, feeling about. The stake was gone. That fool Peter Vincent had pulled the stake, allowing him to come back to life, but there was more to it than that. He was different now. Very different.

Then he began to realize what had happened. Jerry had bitten him deeply, drinking until Ed had felt cold and weak. For a moment, he thought he'd die in that alleyway. Just as the light inside him began to fade, Jerry had opened a small incision in his own hand and pressed Ed's mouth over it. The sweet, warm blood of the ancient vampire ran down the boy's throat. With every drop, Ed felt his old life fade away. Every cell in his body swam with the powerful gift Jerry had bestowed.

His eyes widened. His master had just called to him. He remembered now. He had heard it inside his head. He must answer. Ed managed to climb unsteadily to his feet, putting out a hand to keep his balance. He was weak and disoriented. He looked down and realized he was totally naked, but it made no difference. There was nobody there to see him. Even if there had been, would he have cared? He doubted it.

Ed staggered down the short hallway, pausing in front of a mirror over the coat rack. He stood for a moment staring at it, but, of course, there was nothing to see. He cast no reflection and now knew what that meant. He had forgotten what had happened in Peter Vincent's apartment and above in Judy Brewster's bedroom where he had shape-shifted for the first time, but it was all coming back now. He was a vampire and happy for it.

The urgency of his command was not lost on the young vampire. He slowly turned and stumbled toward the kitchen and the door to the back yard.

But on the roof of the house next door, Jerry Dandrige was not finished yet. He lifted his head, concentrating on the room where he'd left Amy.

"Awake," he commanded her. "I command you to awake. Kill those who would harm me."

He could feel her trembling slowing and her head rising as she heard him. Yes, she would do as he commanded. "Show me how much you love me, Amy. They are below me in the attic, searching for me. Come out of that room and kill them. Both!"

With that, in a rage, he slammed his elbow back into the chimney behind him. The bricks he hit crumpled and broke apart, the remains clattering onto the roof.

63
YOU HAVE TO HAVE FAITH

Charley and Peter came down the stairs from the attic onto the balcony. There had been nothing up there but junk and they hadn't heard Jerry on the roof above them. He had to be somewhere else.

Peter turned back, locking the door just in case Jerry somehow got off the roof and into the attic while Charley started for the door to Jerry's room. Peter grabbed him.

"You take downstairs. I'll take up here," Peter said.

Charley hurried down the stairs as Peter turned for the door of the room where Charley had been held captive. He opened it, stepping inside to see how Amy was. He was greeted by a female vampire that had once been the young girl, as she rose to her feet, the transformation complete.

The flowing white dress gave her a sexuality she had never possessed before, but it was her attitude that shot a bolt of fear through Peter. She was snarling at him, revealing her fangs, now fully grown. She started toward him, her clawed hands raised, and he quickly pulled back onto the balcony, locking the door behind. A moment later, he could hear her beating at them, making animal sounds that said she wanted to tear his throat out.

Perter stopped at the head of the wide staircase, the huge oval stained-glass window behind him. He didn't see Charley.

"Charley?" he called out, worried as Amy kept beating at the door with a rising frenzy.

The teen came running down the hall below, stopping at the bottom of the stairs, and looking up at Peter.

"What is it?" he said, panicked himself by Peter's cry.

"We're losing Amy, I'm afraid," he said, nodding at the door to Jerry's bedroom. The newly minted female vampire was banging at it from the inside harder than ever, trying to get out.

"We've got to find Jerry before dawn," Charley said, hurrying up the staircase.

Just as he got to the balcony, all the clocks on the wall started to chime as one. Both of them stopped, looking at them.

"He's got to be close," Peter said. "Dawn is breaking right now. Remember, that's why he has the clocks, to warn him."

As he spoke, he backed against a window to the outside when, suddenly, Jerry Dandrige appeared behind him, his hands curled, about to break the glass and grab The Great Vampire Killer.

"Look out," Charley yelled, pointing at the window behind Peter.

The actor whirled to see the vampire snarling at him, even as he clung to the wall outside. The actor fell back in horror. In an instant, the vampire was gone into the night outside.

"We've got to keep searching for him," Peter said to Charley as he recovered his nerve. "He'll head for the basement and his coffin."

Charley nodded and headed back down the stairs as Peter followed him, trying to ignore Amy's pounding to be free. Just as he reached the landing, the huge stained-glass window directly above him suddenly burst apart in an explosion of shattered glass as Jerry Dandrige plunged in from the outside. He swiped a claw at the newel cap to the balustrade above, destroying it, sending a shower of wooden chips flying in Peter's direction.

The actor managed to duck just in time as Jerry landed on the balcony in a crouch. Then, he rose as the older man backed down the stairs.

Charley stood at the bottom of the stairs shouting up, "Peter, draw your cross!"

"Stay back," Peter said to Charley without ever taking his eyes off the vampire.

Charley stopped, staring up the stairs at the actor and the vampire, watching and waiting. Dandrige's gaze bored into Peter.

"So," he said with a smile, his features dark and drawn in his now full vampire mode, nothing in the slightest attractive about him anymore. "Just the two of us at last."

He took a step toward the stairs, about to descend. Peter whipped out his cross, thrusting it up at him. Dandrige stopped, smiling at him.

"Oh, really?" he mocked. "You think you'll have more luck with it now than the last time?"

He started for him again, Peter holding his ground, the cross thrust out in front of him.

"Back!" the actor said.

"You have to have faith for that to work, Mr. Vincent," the vampire said. "Remember?"

He took another step toward the stairs, but the actor didn't fall back. He held the cross up high, defiantly staring back at Dandrige, and refusing to drop his gaze.

Then it happened. The vampire jerked to a halt, staring with slowly dawning fury at Peter, realizing by whatever invisible force was emanating from the cross that Peter had indeed recovered his faith.

He stood there, stymied, snarling at the man.

Peter peered up over his shoulder, out the ruined stained-glass window. On the horizon, the first pink tendrils of dawn were breaking. Now, it was Peter's turn to smile as he shifted his gaze back to Dandrige.

"You're out of time, Mr. Dandrige. Look over your shoulder," he said with a nod.

Dandrige craned his neck to see the rising dawn through the destroyed window behind him, the sun just beginning to glint its golden rays even as he stared at it.

"No!" Jerry said, turning back to Peter with a roar of fury just as a ray of sun slashed through the shattered window and hit him in the shoulder. Flame and smoke burst out and he roared in pain.

He threw himself off the landing, tucking his body into a somersault as he hurled through the air toward the portico floor below, turning into a whirling ball of spinning flesh only to suddenly emerge from it no longer a man, but now an enormous bat.

The bat straightened in midair above the portico and zoomed out and curved right at Peter, hurrying down the last of the stairs. It smashed into him just above the bottom and knocked him back against the steps.

Pulling back its head and opening its huge jaws, the large bat went for the actor's throat. Peter got a wooden stake up just in time, the jaws closing around it and not his throat.

Charley leaped forward, grabbing the bat and trying to pull it off. The bat released the stake and twisted its neck, clamping down on his arm. The teen yelped in pain and fell back as the bat let him go and took flight down the hall, knocking over several statues with its huge wingspan on the way.

They crashed to the floor as Peter helped Charley to his feet. The teen was holding his arm and grimacing in pain.

"Are you all right?" Peter asked, feeling stupid for saying it but unable to think of anything else.

"Yeah. Quick, he's in the basement," Charley said and they both moved down the hall after the bat, careful to avoid the smashed masonry on the floor.

The two of them disappeared down the stairs to the basement as the bedroom door above finally smashed open. Amy stepped out onto the balcony, no longer even vaguely human, but at the same time amazingly sexual, as though she had shucked one identity for another. She was now very definitely a female vampire. A very *hungry* female vampire.

64

HIS MASTER'S VOICE

E d made his way into the kitchen, his master's voice still echoing in his head. He caught a glimpse of the clock above the stove as he passed.

"5:52 a.m."

He had no idea when the sun came up, but he was pretty sure it would be soon, if it hadn't already. He knew that Jerry had pulled him out of the darkness. He would not fail him again.

Ed carefully peered through the kitchen door at the Dandrige house on the other side of the hedge row. The night sky had already given way to a faint orange tint. The first rays of dawn were coloring the sky.

Fear rose inside Ed, but the fealty to his master overshadowed it. Ed swung the kitchen door open wide and leaped from the side porch over the hedge row, landing with a crash on the side lawn of the Dandrige house. The smell of his burning hair filled his nostrils and the skin of his face and hands erupted with pustules.

He realized the first rays of sun were hitting him. Searing pain came from every exposed inch of his skin. Ed staggered forward and dropped into a crouch before the side of the Victorian. He had to reach the bedroom above where the Grimoire was kept.

"Please," he moaned as he launched himself upward to the second story.

An animal howl rose from deep inside him as he propelled his body forward. He knew from his arc that he wouldn't reach the second floor. This was the end. He was going to fall back to the ground and die, screaming in pain in the bright light of the rising sun. He tensed, awaiting his fate, but it never came.

Ed's physical form dispersed, replaced with a cloud of white smoke that rose upward and then poured through a tiny crack in the molding of the second-floor window that opened to Jerry's bedroom. The smoke pooled in the center of the room just above an ermine rug. It coalesced inward, taking form, and Ed Thompson dropped to the floor with a thump.

He was splayed out awkwardly on the rug that lay before the dying embers in an untended fireplace. He pulled back in revulsion as one of the logs popped, and the fire briefly flared. Something primal, something deep, seized him for a moment. Fire. Fire was dangerous for vampires. He knew it instinctively.

Ed stood and pulled the ermine rug around his nakedness. He sniffed and caught the scent of blood. Aroused, but tinged with fear, he picked up something else through the scent. Amy and...Jerry. He inhaled deeper. Mixed in with Amy and his master were the faint scents of Charley and Peter Vincent.

"Mmm-Hmm...delicious," Ed said, giggling as he sniffed the air.

Ed looked up toward the painting of "Amy" above the mantel of the fireplace, the one that had her in clothes from another era. He never questioned it, never wondered how the painting came to be there, or why it seemed to be from another era. Oh, no, his concentration was on following his master's orders and recovering the Grimoire within. He began to fumble with the painting, trying to figure out how to open it.

As his hands traced the edges of the frame, he felt a sharp prick against his finger, and the portrait swung open toward him. He stared at the smooth surface of the wood paneling behind the portrait. Ed reached forward and rubbed his still bleeding fingers across the exposed wood.

Click.

A small panel slid sideways revealing a hidden alcove in the wall. Ed clapped his hands and giggled. The excitement was almost too much. In the alcove lay an almost perfectly preserved black leather tome with orichalcum bindings. Emblazoned on the cover was the crest of the *Societas Draconistarum*, the Order of Dragons.

Ed wasn't sure how he knew this. It felt as though the book had introduced itself to him as he plucked it from its hiding place.

He held the book to his chest for a moment. It seemed to pulse against his bare flesh.

"Hide Edward!" the voice of his master broke his musings. Evil realized his master was in the basement below, already safely ensconced in his coffin.

"Go to the attic!" Jerry's voice commanded.

In his mind's eye, Evil Ed could see the path to the attic, across the intervening balcony and through a hidden panel in the room on the side of the house facing Charley's bedroom. He gripped the Grimoire tightly, mindful to keep the ermine rug around him.

He went through the broken door from Jerry's bedroom, never questioning how it had gotten busted. He realized, dimly, Amy had done it, also on the orders of their master, but he didn't care. He had *his* orders; they were all that mattered.

He sprinted across the balcony and past the kaleidoscope of

sunbeams shooting down from the broken stained-glass window at the top of the stairs. They burned his exposed skin and he left a trail of smoke behind, but he didn't care. Ed sensed the remains of Billy Cole at the bottom of the stairs, but he was already beyond any help Ed could provide, so he pressed forward.

Ed burst into the sparsely furnished room, its contents covered in sheets. A faint hint of blood hit his nostrils. It was slight and not fresh. *Amy's.* Ed giggled.

"Oh Brewster," he said, the truth suddenly dawning on him.

This is where it had all begun. The site of his master's indiscretion with Amy that had sent poor Charley spiraling out of control. Ed headed for the closet. Opening the door, he studied the ceiling. Just above an empty shelf was a seamless panel just like the one that had hidden the Grimoire. He popped his fangs and dragged his thumb across one of the sharpened canines. Once again, his blood was the key. The panel slid open as he brushed it, and Ed leaped into the attic. The panel slid closed behind him.

Ed sat on the floor, surrounded by the clutter of discarded debris from either the house's previous owners or, perhaps, relics from his master's life. He didn't care. What was important was the Grimoire. He crossed his legs, cradling it in his lap and began to study it.

65
SHOWDOWN

Charley and Peter hurried down the stairs into the dark basement; its windows were covered with blackout drapes.

"Why's it so dark?" Peter asked with a frown.

"The windows are draped or painted black," Charley replied, remembering how the basement windows had looked from the outside.

It had happened when the ghoul had threatened him when he was investigating the house. It made perfect sense now. Cole's primary purpose had been to protect Jerry from the sunlight.

Both had their stakes out, Peter with a hammer in his other hand. The floor was a mass of antiques, row after row of them, many covered with dust cloths. Peter dived for the first one, ripping the cloth off only to discover an old chest of drawers. He rushed to the next one.

"Quick," he said, "his coffin; it's gotta be down here somewhere."

They raced down the aisle continuing to rip dust covers away only to discover a line of mirrors, several of them obviously removed from walls in the house above. They stopped, staring at them.

"Well, now we know why there were no mirrors in the house," Charley said.

Creakkkkk went the door to the stairway above them as it opened.

"What was that?" Peter asked, whirling and looking back.

"You keep searching. I'll check it out," Charley said, moving back the way they had just came.

"Charley," Peter said, wanting to warn him to be careful, but it was too late. The teen had already disappeared into the darkness.

Charley appeared down the row of antiques, stopping at the foot of the stairs and staring up at the basement door above. It was partially open, allowing just a sliver of light into the darkness. He called out, clutching his stake nervously.

"Who's there?" he said.

Amy appeared out of the darkness behind him, already having gotten into the basement. She slowly approached, her face deathly white, her hair swept back, and the flowing white dress moving with her. Her lips were blood red and her eyes glowed in the dark with a faint reddish tint. Charley heard her at the last second and whirled to face her with a gasp. She read the fear in his face and smiled sadly, reaching out a hand to him.

"Don't be frightened, Charley," she said, the red disappearing from her eyes, making her seem more human.

She took a step closer and he stepped away. Amy stopped, staring at him. Her voice was a husky, purring whisper.

But he didn't believe her, or not enough, and kept backing away, even as she came closer, slowly loosening the straps that held the dress aloft, exposing more and more of her body, now alabaster white. It made her shockingly desirable.

"What's wrong?" she purred. "Don't you want me anymore?"

He suddenly broke her spell and, coming to his senses, he whipped out his cross and thrusted it in her face. She whirled away with a snarl, burying her face in her hands, softly beginning to weep.

"It's not my fault, Charley," she sobbed, her back to him. "You promised you wouldn't let him get me. You promised!"

He stared at her, guilt boiling up inside of him. He stepped forward, touching her shoulder, letting the cross drop to his side.

"Amy…" he began.

She spun about, exposing a mouth unlike any he'd ever seen. It was horrible; a row of huge fangs distorted her face, all of them ready to clamp down on him! Dripping hungry saliva emanated from her mouth as she dove for his exposed throat.

He whipped the cross up, but not in time. Her forearm smashed into his wrist, sending the cross whirling away into the darkness. Amy straightened, smiling at him as her huge fangs sparkled in the light from the open doorway above.

She began to walk toward him, her sexual interest in Charley gone, replaced by a mad, driving hunger…for blood, *his* blood.

At the other end of the room, Peter desperately weaved his way among the pieces of furniture dotting the floor, looking for the coffin. He stopped before a huge armoire, whipped it open to discover it empty, and was about to move on when he glanced down. There, at the corner, was a small hole with rats scurrying in and out. Realizing something must be behind the huge piece of furniture, he tried to shove it aside, but it would not move. He knew there had to be a way to raise it and began frantically feeling inside for a button or lever or something. His hand hit something and he shoved upward. Silently, the huge armoire rose into the air on its tracks.

A hidden alcove was revealed with a huge window at the back covered with a blackout curtain. Jerry's ornate brass bound coffin sat in the middle on a dais, covered with chattering, crawling rats.

Peter, horrified and fascinated at the same time, called out into the darkness behind him. "Charley, I found it!"

Back at the other end of the room, Charley was backing away from Amy as she stalked him, clicking her huge fangs together, mocking his fear.

"Hurry, Peter! Get it open!" Charley yelled back.

Amy didn't wait any longer. She leaped for him, grabbing a broken down chair and swinging at him. She missed by inches, smashing it into kindling against a trunk. She turned on Charley, empty-handed now, continuing to stalk him.

Before the dais, Peter stifled his revulsion at the rats and rushed to the side of the coffin. He fumbled with the clasps only to discover that they were locked.

"He's locked it from the inside," Peter yelled again.

He grabbed the mallet from his cloak and started pounding at the clasps, trying to free them while Charley continued to back away from Amy.

"Hurry!" Charley called back, his desperation growing. How could he kill the girl he loved? If he didn't, she seemed determined to murder him.

He tried to dodge her as she leaped forward, but she sent a bureau smashing into a wall with her newfound strength, blocking his escape. She smiled at him with those terrible fangs, continuing to push him into a corner.

Back at the coffin, the clasp finally came loose beneath Peter's pounding, and he moved to the next one, smashing at it with the mallet. *Bang, bang, bang!*

Back in the basement, Charley jumped over a pile of refuse to escape, the vampiress diving after him, her long-nailed fingers clawing at his back and shredding his shirt as he twisted out of her grasp.

Back at the dais, Peter broke the last clasp, threw the coffin lid open, and saw Jerry resting beneath him, the king vampire's eyes closed.

He fumbled a spare stake from his belt, pressing it to the creature's heart, about to slam it home with the hammer when suddenly behind him Charley crashed into view on the floor. Amy was fixed to his back, struggling to sink her dripping fangs into his neck.

Peter whirled at the noise, momentarily distracted.

In the coffin, Jerry's eyes snapped open, staring up at Peter. The actor turned back only to find himself looking down at the enraged vampire reaching up for him with his claws. Peter didn't hesitate. He pounded the stake home, blood from the vampire splattering his face.

The actor fell back as the vampire rose with a howl of pain and rage, standing straight up in his coffin like a Jack in the Box. It would be impossible for a human, but not for a vampire, especially one such as Jerry Dandrige.

The stake protruded from his shoulder, leaking blood but not in any way diminishing him. Peter had missed his heart, impaling his shoulder. Amy stopped in her struggle to kill Charley and both she and the teen stared up at the huge vampire standing erect in his coffin, looming over all three of them.

With superhuman deliberation, Dandrige pulled the stake from his chest and hurled it away. It smashed into the far wall, splintering a window painted black, sending a thin ray of sunlight into the room. Dandrige didn't notice as he turned on Peter, and his face convulsed with hatred. He leaped for him, flying the width of the hidden room, carrying him into the basement proper, and smashing him into a wall. He whipped his head back, about to sink his fangs into the actor's neck.

"No!" screamed Charley.

He grabbed the nearest thing he could find, an old vase among the junk scattered everywhere and threw it at the closest blacked-out window. It shattered, sending a wide beam of sunlight into the dark basement.

It touched Jerry just as he was bending Peter back to rip his throat out. It scorched him and smoke rose. He howled in pain, letting the actor go, and stepped back into the darkness. Charley found an old paint can and threw it at another blacked-out window, shattering the glass and letting another beam of light shoot into the basement.

As he went to break a fourth window, Amy grabbed him from behind, trying to haul him back. He found an old wine bottle and slammed it over his shoulder into her head. She dropped to the floor, momentarily stunned.

Across the room, Jerry was trying to find a way through the intersecting beams of light to reach Peter. Using the old bottle, Charley moved from blacked-out window to window, breaking them and letting more beams of the rising dawn stream into the room.

Now, whichever way Jerry moved, he was in sunlight and burning, with smoke rising from his body. Screaming in pain, he dived for his open coffin in the hidden dark alcove. Peter got there a beat before him, slamming the lid with a *loud bang*.

Jerry turned to Peter, safe in the blackness of the alcove. He finally had him in a still dark place. He raised his hands to seize him when Charley raced past, grabbing a large blackout curtain that covered the lone window at the back. Before he could rip it down, a recovered Amy grabbed him from behind. She pulled him to the floor, about to sink her fangs into him as the drape came with him, sending a huge bolt of sunlight streaming into the previously dark room.

It hit Jerry Dandrige squarely in the chest just as he was about to seize Peter, picking him up and throwing him the entire length of the basement as he screamed and fought to be free, leaving a long streaming trail of smoke behind. It slammed him into the far wall, pinning him there several feet above the floor.

He writhed in the golden beam, twisting this way and that, but unable to escape as his body smoldered, a million small fires breaking out all over him as he began to burn.

"Nooooo!" Jerry screamed.

As Peter and Charley watched, unable to tear their eyes away, the vampire's body suddenly exploded in a whooshing ball of flame that incinerated him instantly, leaving nothing behind but cinders floating in the air and the echoing scream of a soul finally going to hell.

Amy stopped writhing on the floor. Charley knelt beside her. She was changing back to a human girl, with her fangs retreating, her hair fluffing out, and her lips becoming more normal.

"Amy," he said, helping her rise and pulling her to him.

She slowly opened her eyes and he saw that she had returned, once more, to the girl he knew. As she stared back at him, he saw that her fangs were, now, totally gone. She embraced him tightly, weeping softly. He held her close, staring across the room at Peter who sat on the coffin's edge, wiping Dandrige's blood from his face with his handkerchief. There was nothing but silence in the room now, the sun shining merrily through the shattered windows, with only a few wisps of charcoal floating lazily through the air to remind them what had just happened.

66

EVIL CASTS A SPELL

E vil Ed sat in the attic as a terrible roar of pain and disbelief erupted from the center of his brain. He felt as if his eyes would burst from their sockets as the realization hit him.

Jerry was dead.

Somehow, Ed had been able to see his master's final moments thorough his eyes. He watched as Charley ripped the black curtain down as his master was about to attack the coward, Peter Vincent. The blast of sunlight hit Dandrige squarely in the chest and hurled him backward across the basement, making him erupt into flames as he flew. He slammed into the back wall where the sunlight pinned him until he was consumed by the roaring flames. He had screamed and fought, but even he had been helpless against the searing power of the sun.

Ed stared down at the pustules still visible on the back of his hands. He ran his fingers over the burnt and blistered skin of his face and head. If the sun had risen higher when he was exposed outside, he would have shared his master's fate.

Ed wanted to weep, but the tears would not come. He looked down at the Grimoire in his lap only to find it was now open. Ed ran his fingers along the edge of the page and noticed that it wasn't made of paper. It was soft, like suede.

Ed's nostrils flared as the faint hint of blood arose from the pages. It was old and powerful blood. He realized it was his master's. Jerry must have used it to create the ink.

Ed stared at the strange words on the page but couldn't make out their meaning. After all, "Evil" Ed Thompson had recently been a teenage misfit just trying to survive high school in the small California town of Rancho Corvallis. Latin had not been part of the curriculum.

As Ed puzzled over the words, a subtle hum rose from the Grimoire, and Ed felt a slight tingle run through the fingertips of the hand that rested on the open page.

They were moving, becoming more and more recognizable as he frowned, doing his best to understand them. The hum rose higher from the Grimoire, and the words rearranged themselves before his startled eyes and suddenly Ed could understand them.

With unerring accuracy, he read the words aloud. "*Voco super te, Dcemone Dominus Bal, ut adveho ut Magister in auxilium, et facere omne quad ex hac clade evanescet, et solum electi possint videre!*"

A pulse of invisible force radiated from the center of his chest, the Grimoire on his lap. The force expanded outward in all directions, passing through the walls, floor, and ceiling. The spell began to reknit the energy of the house, purging it of the residual pain and fear left behind by Jerry's victims and by the destruction of the vampire himself, the energies of whom could act as a beacon to other awakened creatures. The spell would also confound anyone who tried to make sense of the events that had transpired within its walls.

Ed took a moment to marvel at the book. A few years back, he'd played around with the occult by spending his allowance on "authentic" copies of *The Red Book of Appin*, *The Lesser Key of Solomon*, and, of course, *The Necronomicon* by the "Mad Poet", Abdul Alhazred.

All were said to be sources of real magic, but they were all lies. How could they not be? They were sold in stupid occult bookstores open to the public where gullible people could search for some way to rise above the banality of their existence or to have some control of their boring lives.

He knew Jerry's book contained true, unrivaled power. Ed looked down at the book, his hands shaking with expectation, as the page turned on its own accord to a ritual near the front. Ed once again felt the presence of the book in his mind and read the words scrawled upon the page.

"Protegat mi. Absconde mi. Concede mihi protectionem de inimicis meis magnus et sapiens Mercurius. Audiat hoc humilis deprecatio."

Dozens of tiny white-hot balls of light began to dance above Ed's head. One by one, they shot forward, striking the wall in front of him and leaving a faint wisp of smoke behind as they passed through. In his mind, Ed could see the tiny globes burning their way through every surface of the house, maddeningly pinballing through open space into solid objects and out the other side.

Ed became disoriented by the spectacle, but he knew he had to hold on until it was finished, or the spell would fail. Faster and faster, the white-hot orbs zoomed this way and that. Ed gripped the Grimoire tightly and tried to roll with the chaos in his mind.

With fingers clenched, he fought the sensation to pull away. Pain and nausea gripped him, and he started to lose his grip on the book. He stifled a scream as the last of the globes faded out with a hard "pop."

Nearly a thousand miles away, a young girl was violently shaken from her sleep. Her name was Eliza Trace.

67

THE SURVIVORS EMBRACE

The survivors, Amy, Charley, and Peter Vincent slowly rose, meeting in the center of the sunlight filled basement. It looked so different than it had when they had first gone down there, to have their final fight to the death, theirs or his, with Jerry Dandrige. Now he was gone, a scorch mark on the back wall, nothing left of the monster but his naked ribcage with a skull stripped of all flesh sitting atop it.

"We did it," Charley said, looking around with more than a little wonder on his face. "We survived."

"You did it," Amy said to Charley and Peter. She was looking at her hands, the claws gone, and feeling her face to confirm that her fangs, too, had disappeared. She smiled at the other two. "You saved me."

"He saved us," Charley said, nodding at the actor in his houndstooth cloak. "Peter Vincent, The Great Vampire Killer."

Peter smiled. "We all saved one another," he said with a grateful sigh. "Friends till the end. Forever."

All three embraced each other, standing in the sunshine, almost moved to tears.

Whap, something hit them, a shock wave that seemed to

descend from the attic and shook the entire house, no doubt echoing out from there across the entire Dandrige property.

"What was that?" Charley asked, looking up in alarm.

Peter hesitated for a moment, then smiled. "Whatever it was it's gone now, I'm sure never to return."

He went back to embracing the other two, never suspecting how wrong he was.

68

RUDE AWAKENING

Eliza Trace lay sprawled across the twin bed she sometimes shared with her younger sister, Emily. This morning, Emily had gone with Eliza's mother to Pawhuska for another round of intake interviews with the local Osage. Eliza was alone when the first wave hit her.

Her sleep had been fitful, and the warmth of the night air from a delayed autumn had left a slick sheen of sweat on her skin. Her long, black hair was moist and the Siouxsie and the Banshees "Hyaena" T-shirt she'd worn as a night shirt was soaked right through. As the wave of powerful ancient magic washed over her, it was like cold fire.

Frostbite. The dampness on her skin and in her clothes turned to jagged ice crystals. Jolted by the sudden cold, Eliza pulled herself upright into a kneeling position, cracking the frozen back of her shirt in half. She rubbed her hands over her arms to try to generate warmth. Her breath, visible in the warm morning air, came out in jagged painful gasps.

Eliza turned to glare toward the west, the direction the wave had come from. As it had passed through her, it left behind a faint coppery taste in her mouth. Blood. Blood magic. But this was different. It was old and powerful enough to send echoes of its casting ranging far and wide. Eliza reluctantly swung her legs off the bed and reached across for a clove cigarette from her pack of Kretek's on the bed stand.

The rest of her shirt cracked and tumbled off her in stiff shards. Eliza shrugged, put the clove to her lips, and willed the tip to burst into flames. She took a long drag and rose unsteadily to her feet.

Crossing the room, Eliza took her bathrobe from a hook near the closet and draped it over her shoulders. With the extra layer on, she hugged herself and rubbed her arms even harder to restore a little more warmth to her skin. She knew her mother must have felt the magic, too. There were others out there. Her father was out west; surely, he'd be interested in all this.

Eliza headed through the doorway into the bathroom that she shared with Emily. Technically, Emily was Eliza's half-sister; she'd been conceived during some kind of re-enactment of the Roman Festival of Floralia her mother had attended seven years ago. Her mother had been very vague about who Emily's father was. She was told that he was a very awakened and spiritual person. Eliza always took that to mean that her mother wasn't sure or just plain didn't remember.

She wasn't a big fan of the ritual side of magic or group works. Eliza was more like her father in that regard. He was a Thaumaturge, a Magus, or as her mother called him, "a very dark soul." Like him, she had a great deal of personal power to will natural forces to bend so that she could shape them to her purpose. Both her parents were seekers of knowledge and power; that's how they met and why Eliza even existed.

She turned the shower knob, knowing that a warm blast of water was just what she needed to fight this chill. As she stepped into the rising steam, she knew this was the first step toward something or someone important. After her shower, Eliza would cast the runes and ask for their advice.

THE END

ABOUT THE AUTHOR

Tom Holland is an American director and screenwriter of horror and thriller films. His early writing projects include *Class of 1984* (1982) and the Robert Bloch-inspired *Psycho II* (1983), the latter starring Anthony Perkins as the menacing psychopath, Norman Bates.

Tom gained more notoriety, *however, as* a director. His directorial debut was the popular 1980s vampire film, Fright Night (1985) which, at the time, was said to have been responsible for redefining the sub-genre, influencing later films like *The Lost Boys* (1987) and *Near Dark* (1987). The film was a box office hit and garnered three Saturn Awards and one Dario Argento Award.

For his next project, *Child's Play* (1988), Tom again cast Chris Sarandon. The film was a Number One box-office hit in America and a worldwide success, despite controversy over its thematic content. It, like *Fright Night* (1985) has since gathered a cult following amongst horror fans. Tom then went onto direct two films based upon adaptations of Stephen King's novels: *The Langoliers* (1995) and *Thinner* (1996). He also took a cameo role in the Stephen King miniseries *The Stand* (1994).

A. Jack Ulrich is a freelance journalist and screenwriter who has recently turned a page in his writing career and undertaken the daunting task of writing novels.

Made in the USA
Las Vegas, NV
01 November 2022

58543279R00173